Praise for Coydog

"A rough and tumble journey through a landscape as colorful as its inhabitants."

—Steph Post, author of *Lightwood*

"A natural storyteller with an ear tuned for dialogue and an imagination that will keep readers wide-eyed and guessing, slack-jawed, and entertained. A manhunt shouldn't be this fun."

—David Joy, author of *Those We Thought We Knew*

"This is one wild ride. You think it'll go left, and it goes right. You think it'll go up, and it goes sideways. David Tromblay is a force, and so is his madman hero, Moses Kincaid."

—Willy Vlautin, author of *The Horse*

"With a voice and style all his own, Moses Kincaid leads the reader, by the scruff of the shirt, through his rough-and-tumble ride from bounty hunting into the Dantean prison system. He doesn't meet a lot of nice people along the way, but it sure is entertaining to watch fall off the page."

—Paul Tremblay, author of *Horror Movie*

"Quick-witted, fast-paced, unpredictable. *Coydog* is a raucous, wide-open, crime-riddled joy ride."

—Michael Farris Smith, author of *Salvage This World*

"*Coydog* is paced like a small-town stock car race without any rules. And funny as hell to boot."

—Scott Phillips, author of *The Ice Harvest*

"*Coydog* pulsates with intensity. It's scrappy, sharp-edged, wild, and funny. One hell of a memorable ride."

—William Boyle, author of *Saint of the Narrows Street*

"One of the most original voices in crime fiction—wild, wicked, and always surprising. *Coydog* is a barnburner of a novel, a rush of unforgettable characters, rich detail, and unsparing truth."

—Lou Berney, author of *Dark Ride*

"A welcome addition to the burgeoning crime literature of Oklahoma. Moses Kincaid is the toughest guy in Tulsa."

—Chris Offutt, author of *The Killing Hills*

COYDOG

An Anadarko County Novel

David Tromblay

2580 Craig Rd.
Ann Arbor, MI 48103
www.dzancbooks.org

Library of Congress Cataloging-in-Publication Data Available on Request

First edition: November 2025
Jacket design by Steven Seighman
Interior design by Michelle Dotter
ISBN 9781938603389

Printed in the United States of America

10 9 8 7 6 5 4 3 2 1

For Joe, Joey, and Joseph—my only begotten son.

As is every keystroke.

FOREWORD: HO*LAY*, MOSES

I got my driver's license in Oklahoma a long time ago. In a town called Altus. Passed with a 70 and a "hope you don't plan on driving in my town," from an aviator-eyed state trooper in a Smokey the Bear hat. Apparently he didn't think my inability to parallel park and follow up question-which-was-really-more-of-a-comment—"Who the hell has ever parallel parked in this state anyway?"—was as funny as I did. I mean it wasn't all that funny, but thinking about how this trooper looked like an unsmoked bratwurst packed into a hotdog casing was for sure.

At any rate. I'd rather have lunch with that guy than Moses Kincaid. I mean sure, he'd make me tense, but not like Moe would. But that's not the bad part. Because Moses Kincaid will make you calm, too, and that's way worse, because you know shit's gonna work out, but it's gonna be a hell of a journey to get there.

Set in the year of the Great Chicago Heatwave, something I lived through with my wife and infant daughter mostly at the neighborhood fire hydrant controlled by our local youth empowerment club, its mention here is indicative of the ride I just described. Tense memories pepper my reading. I know I'm not going to pass in that heatwave of course, but now I have to worry about one arriving in my future.

The dialogue and descriptions crack but don't clunk. This ain't the easiest kinda shit to write, but Tromblay knocks it out. Chandler,

Hammett, yup. Burke, less so, except for the weather and the plotting underneath—both excellent. Not much Parker here—Moe rarely eats. But when he mentions the writer you've been thinking in the back of your head the whole time—Jim Thompson—you give a little mmmhmm of satisfaction and recognition and dive back into the world he's created.

We could talk about the Nativeness of Coydog, but like the book itself, there's not much to say and that's okay. Things are what and how they are in America, even Oklahoma with its large and distinct Native population. This isn't a "Native Lit" book, but it's definitely one for a college class on that subject. Plenty of folks have been at work writing stories where the characters are incidentally Native, and that's a good thing. Tromblay's in the crew.

Like my man Jacques Derrida, I'm not big on (I)ntroductions, and I'm even less interested in blabbing on when your ass should and could be reading this book. Don't worry. It won't take long, but it's gonna hurt. Shiiiit. You'll be almost done before you realize it.

This is the good stuff.

— Theodore Van Alst, Jr.
Portland, OR
May 2025

"There is only one plot—things are not as they seem."

—Jim Thompson

Or, for those who don't speak Oklahoman:

"Anything can have happened in Oklahoma.

Practically everything has."

—Edna Ferber

I

The Black Lizard bridge that leads folks into Anadarko County feels like it ought not be crossed unless your affairs are in order.

What I hope waits on the other side is a skiptrace who is flirting with a felony vehicular manslaughter charge and ran home to Mommy like OJ, except no one cared enough to send the whirly-birds into the sky and call all cars.

I hope.

I hope the Filthy Thirteen motorcycle gang didn't get too bent out of shape after they heard word two of their brethren died at highway speeds. And I hope they have not decided to track down the guilty party on their own.

What would Doug Llewelyn say?

The pulse of any municipality can be taken with eyes alone. Its degree of destitute can be measured by how pockmarked a place is by payday advance centers, pawnshops, pop-up nondenominational churches in otherwise abandoned strip malls, bottle shops, bail bondsmen, strip clubs, divorce lawyers, DWI schools, and assholes slinging as-is autos with no credit checks.

Never before has a town greeted me with a broke pawnbroker. Its neighbor, the Red Dirt Chop Shop, has a '68 Chevy Custom Camper sans camper for sale parked along the shoulder of Sangre Road. How much they want for it is soaped on the windshield but blocked by a sign that cannot be read so well. It's gone into disrepair—the sign, not the truck, like a family plot with no more relatives above ground. I know this because I wanted to know how much they wanted for the truck, and, since I already sat idling on the shoulder of Sangre Road, I took however much longer to look over the cast-iron historical marker, which reads:

THE LAST "BOOMER" TOWN

ABOUT ¾ MI. EAST

Here 300 armed "boomers" made their last stand for settlement of the Oklahoma country led by Wm. L. Couch; and surrendered to U.S. Cavalry troops commanded by Col. E. Hatch, Jan. 26, 1885. On this site, the "boomers" built log cabins and dugouts for their town, founded on Dec. 12, 1884.

Considering how the town was established and surrendered in the span of six weeks and the site itself is now nothing more than a few acres of decrepit and wrecked cars, it all seems insignificant and extraneous, not warranting the casting of a marker. From what I remember, there wasn't even one of the brown signs telling motorists a historical marker waits up ahead. *Surrendered*, like it wasn't all that bloody of a battle, being there is no mention of a body count. But there is the matter of their naming the road *Sangre*, meaning *blood* en español. Figuring in how the Spanish-speaking population here seems next to nada, I'd wager it's a roundabout way of covering up a bloody past while kinda-sorta acknowledging it without outright saying the boogeyman's name.

Three thousand dollars firm is the price of the Chevy. It comes with a spider-webbed windshield and no bumpers, but every inch of it is primered black, which makes me think it's either dinged to hell or comes with a full rust package.

No, thank you.

This way of thinking is what you get when you spend too much time alone in an automobile. Luckily, I won't have to stay inside my head much longer. Sangre Road becomes a smorgasbord of signs and ads once I creep inside Lawson city limits.

A diner stands on the other side of the fifth church I pass. Its marquee reads: *No one is perfect; Moses was once a basket case.*

Don't I know it.

I order a sweet tea as a show of faith to let the waitstaff know I mean to differentiate myself as a customer—rather than loitering and looking for a pot to piss in—before I make my hurried pilgrimage to the men's room. Said trip to the bathroom does not lead me to believe the meal should come with a complimentary tetanus shot. So I come out in better spirits than I've been in since I realized where this latest paper trail was bringing me.

After I take a swig of their world-famous sweet tea, in walks a man who boasts all the physical attributes of a double-size soft-serve ice cream cone—the extra creamy kind with double the milk fat. Prescription glasses with lenses tinted the color of watered-down rosé cling to the tip of his nose. I say prescription because when he tilts his head back to find an open table, he looks bug-eyed. His dress shirt came with ruffles sewn into the chest, though it is not the bleached white you'd expect to see someone wear with an older tuxedo. I imagine it was sold as ivory, but it looks the color of a midmorning piss following an entire pot of coffee and some multivitamin with 1000% of the recommended daily values.

Both pockets on that shirt are packed with pens sans pocket protectors. Obviously, he's a man who likes to live dangerously. The left side is chock-full of what I'll call Easter or pastel colors, while the right looks like all primary pen ink colors: black, blue, and red, plus one that looks to be stainless steel, and another gold-plated.

Around his neck hangs a shoelace weighed down with no less than two dozen keys. A fist sits plopped atop a cane in which he lends far too much trust. I only say so because the floor lets out a muffled cry, announcing his presence a few short seconds before each footfall while other folks passed through the dining area without the floorboards offering a word of protest. It could be the light playing with the lacquer, but I'd swear the cane bows each time he hobbles this way and that while he negotiates his way to the table.

He swayed in through the side door, too, which makes his entrance all the more notable, seeing as how that door stands a little wider than the one out front to allow for deliveries on dollies that lead straight into the kitchen.

It embarrasses me to admit his pendulum gait hypnotizes me, which is how the waitress surprises me when she announces her presence by setting down a sweating glass of ice water and asking, "Are you ready to order, or are you going to need another minute with the menu?"

"Yes, I am," I say with an embarrassed smile. "I am indeed going to need a few more minutes, please. Everything sounds so mouth-wateringly delicious."

~

I went with a pecan waffle and what they called Huevos Mexicanos. The latter came with biscuits and gravy. I went with that coupling, thinking the gravy would add some sustenance. Without the drink, it came to ten bucks. Not too bad.

The telephone book I acquired from the phone booth outside of the Get-N-Go looks no thicker than a weekly edition of the TV Guide. From that alone, I surmise I'll be on my way in no time, so I rent a motel room at a place that offers hourly rates, where no one wants to be seen or see who is coming and going, where I could shit, shower, shave, and get to work without anyone bothering me about when I'll check out.

I've never visited this town before, but I know the place well enough. The public library operates on banker's hours, there are as many adult bookstores as churches, and you cannot, no way, no how, buy a beer on the Lord's Day. Atop that sits the conundrum of living in a city so small that every citizen shoulders the stress of celebrity. That's to say, when everyone is bored, nobody is boring. There's no minding your own business. Everyone is family. Not necessarily blood, but there's a closeness that causes me claustrophobia.

Being so fresh a face in so small a town, I know I can't set up and surveil someone without more eyes looking my way than will prove beneficial, much like that adage warning away from pointing a finger at someone because of how many others point back at you. That's why I borrow the Bible from the bedside table, the one the Gideons placed in my room, and stand with it out on the corner closest to the Jefferson Lines station, where I preach the Word to passing cars and wait to see who pours out of the bus from Kansas City.

It's the perfect platform to watch the comings and goings without worrying about being an unfamiliar face and drawing too much attention.

I call it tradecraft.

A curbside crazy is easy enough to ignore. And hiding in plain sight is much less nerve-racking when you're a stranger in a strange land and do not know who you need to watch out for other than who you came to find. A panhandler holding a sign and begging for whatever change you can spare may draw the attention of the authorities, depending on local ordinances. But not a sidewalk preacher. Especially in a place where everyone is so afraid of coming off as a piss-poor Christian. I make such a speculation based on seeing so many bumper stickers mentioning Him that you'd swear He is up for reelection.

If I ever take note of someone taking too much stock in what I am saying or doing, I can always cook up a splash of misdirection.

The first instance I feel compelled to do so is with a gentleman who comes out of the hospital in a wheelchair, looking like he's still getting the mechanics of it down. Poor man has no one to give him a push. Though he wheels himself into the package store with enough ease.

When that same gentleman later exits and comes across the intersection toward me, I do not hesitate to seize such an opportune moment and do what I can to divert the attention of every driver toward him. By God, by some miracle, he could stand and walk and navigate that wheelchair up and over the median without dumping the case of beer or any of the bottles of liquor hidden in the brown paper sacks.

I do not want a single soul to miss it, so I holler and proclaim, "It's a miracle right before our very eyes, brothers and sisters! Just hearing the Lord's message has helped this man to walk again.

"Rise and walk! Rise and walk, my son!" I scream above the knocking engines and the nauseating exhaust tightening my chest. "Rise and walk. You don't need no wheelchair. Go on and tell your doctor how he has failed you, but it is the Lord who has healed you!"

If only there were cameras around to capture the moment.

The man puts his head down once he sees he's being followed and judged by every eyeball inside every stopped vehicle. One searing gaze seems cause enough for him to lift his heels a touch higher than walking speeds to get as far from me as fast as his feet can carry him. Fortunately for me, a dozen and a half eyeballs lend me a helping hand.

Amen to that.

As soon as those glances drift back over to me, I juggle around words like *judgment* and *abomination* and *His return* until every last set of eyeballs fixates on the dangling traffic light and waits for it to turn green so we can all get on with our day.

2

The name on the file folder of the bail jumper who brought me here is Eric Drumgoole. He scrambled out of town hours before a scheduled court appearance, which means he skipped out on bond worth more than his house, car, or any other thing he could call collateral. Luckily for him, Kansas did not follow suit when the majority of the country implemented the three-strikes law. Instead, they put an asterisk in their law books for those they call perpetual offenders. While almost every other state sends anyone found guilty of a third felony to the penitentiary for life, Kansas simply doubles the offender's sentence, believing that'd be enough of a deterrent.

As if someone perpetrates a crime thinking they'll get caught.

Mr. Drumgoole is an art collector, so to speak. Both elbows are covered in cobwebs. A spider crawls north up his neck from its perch on his collarbone, though only a single leg shows when he wears a T-shirt. Though a collared button-up conceals it completely and will allow him amongst polite society without notice. A coyote tattooed on his bicep howls at the moon encircling his bowling ball of a shoulder, which only works to make it look all the more rounded. His forearm boasts the black outline of a decapitated Woody Woodpecker, except it's not. It's a peckerwood prison tattoo—a symbol meant to let everyone know, no matter what they alleged and convicted you of, it doesn't matter to him one bit as long as you are purely a white protestant or an honest and true worshipper of Odin.

It's hard to say from the black and white mugshot whether he has teardrops inked beneath either of his eyes, with all the blackheads and as pockmarked as his cheeks look.

The last picture in his file shows both his left and right hands. Between his knuckles and the first joint on his fingers reads *FREE HUGS*.

Me going around with the title of surety agent or bail bonds recovery agent does not garner the same sort of respect as being called a bounty hunter. At least when it comes to laymen. Lawmen will snicker when they're called on the phone or their door is knocked upon to let them know I'm in town, what I'm up to, and who has me playing hide-and-seek.

Some will not care for me because I am not a real cop. Others will not care for me because I am not protecting and serving but collecting a paycheck. Others still will not care for me because I am only poking my head in because they failed to do their job and feel as though I am stepping on their toes.

What they do not understand is how there isn't much else I am made for.

When I was a cop in the Army, I did things thoroughly. When I searched someone's person, they did not come out of it feeling as if their rights had been violated as much as they had been intimately explored, lacking any secrets furthermore—for their safety and mine, as is the mantra taught at the academy.

When evidence showed a handful of food inspectors were bringing in coke and pills along with the produce, CID came to my door, waving a Kevlar helmet and flak vest, saying, "Let's go, Juggernaut."

We hit five houses simultaneously.

At five-foot-eight, two hundred thirty-five pounds, and barely any body fat to speak of, I was something of a human battering ram. Luckily, at twenty-six years old, I did not have much of an investigative mind, so I did not mind being used for my body. Though, that may be because it was never me that gave way when meat met timber. That's not so much bragging as saying construction isn't of the highest quality in government housing. The lowest bidders never bring their A game. They know they'll never meet the future occupants and said family is not apt to complain about a free roof over their heads. Especially if they are guilty of furnishing the place with three times their annual government salary when they've barely fulfilled the first twelve months of their forty-eight-month enlistment contract. Simple math and common sense can go a long way when properly applied.

So can focused violence.

The kick plate on the front door sparked. The explosion punched the inside doorknob into the drywall, which sent husband and wife this way and that. The husband went toward the kitchen and presumably the back door, where a military working dog waited. They love a good game of chase. The wife, however, went for the bedroom.

As did I.

In a stride or two, I got hold of the wife and brought her down to the tile floor. She balled herself up with her arms and legs beneath her. Nothing to cuff, in other words. So I snatched her off the tile by the belt and the back of her hoodie, knowing her legs and arms would fling out to the sides, as if she were freefall skydiving. When I sent her back onto the floor an explosion of black, sticky, tar-like shit shot up her back and down to her knees, like when a newborn baby fills their first diaper.

I cried for the medic, and he professed his hatred for me.

Both mom and dad did their best to bolt and leave their toddler with us, along with a coffee table covered in I-cannot-recall-how-many kilos of uncut coke. Several pounds of a green, leafy substance, stored in bulk-sized coffee cans meant for the post's dining facility, sat along the kitchen counter beside a food scale and enough baggies to keep the Ziploc corporation afloat for the foreseeable future.

Adults from all five households found their way to the United States Disciplinary Barracks at Fort Leavenworth, Kansas. As did I, shortly thereafter. Though they went with criminal sentences to carry out. Before I went, I got sent to Haiti to participate in the peacekeeping efforts following the US-led intervention that undid the coup d'état that installed a military regime three years prior.

The rules of engagement established for that embarrassing little episode did not involve supernatural elements, but I'll say without batting an eye that we did battle zombies on that island paradise. Doing so wasn't so much supernatural as it was extraordinary, much like when a cop comes up against some perp hopped up on PCP, and they won't go down just because they've been shot once or twice or sixty-seven times. Those zombies did the same sort of shoot-from-the-hip, spray-and-pray firing technique as the Iraqis in Desert Storm. Except the Iraqis did not toss down their rifles as soon as they get within range of ours and amble off absently—no longer a threat—so we were no longer able to engage.

Once my time at Leavenworth and in the Army came to an end, I stuck around for no other reason than my apartment lease had not yet expired. I could have hightailed it home, looked for work, dealt with the hit to my credit. I could have used my GI Bill, but there's no way I'd piss that away at some shit-splat school in bumfucked Wisconsin to learn a new trade. That, and my mom downsized to a one-bedroom after my father's funeral.

I'd hate to be a burden.

Because I was no longer technically a member of the United States Military, my landlord argued that the military clause in my lease was no longer applicable. Since I no longer had the JAG office at my disposal to argue otherwise, I took a job with a bail bondsman for no other reason than I liked food in my stomach and I'd grown relatively comfortable around criminal types.

That's making a long story less so.

3

"What can I do you for?" says an Underdog-looking Anadarko County Sheriff's deputy from the other side of the safety glass. I notice a delay between his words leaving his lips and his words exiting the speaker that reminds me of a seventies kung fu flick. Adding to that comedy is how the speaker sounds so tinny the voice seems disembodied. I don't think I laugh aloud. Though I am sure my face gives him a hint of what's percolating in my brain.

"I'm looking for a bail jumper by the last name of Drumgoole. Drum-ghoul, spelled—"

"Yessum," he says and nods his head. "Junior, senior, or—the third?"

"There's more than one?"

"Yessum. Wait a while for a good rain, and another will pop out of the ground. You can bet your ass. Spread across Oklahoma like wild onions, if you don't watch. Which one are you wanting to pluck out of our soil, sir?" he says to me.

"I only have a birthday on him. Sorry. No suffix."

"You have paperwork?"

"I do."

"Hold on now," he says, smiling ear to ear at his own joke. "We just met. I don't even know your name yet. You should at least ask me to dinner first." He laughs. "And my mother will want to meet you, too. My mother, of course, being Sheriff Bonnie McCarty. I'll buzz you back. I'm sure one of our investigators'll help you sort things out."

"Thank you," I mouth, knowing he'll never hear what I have to say.

On the other side of the solid steel door stands a man in a blaze-orange polo shirt who waves me into an office on the far side of the room. It is not an alligator sitting on his chest but an Oklahoma State pistolero wearing a sombrero and a horseshoe mustache and a handkerchief tied around his neck.

I can't stop blinking under all that needling fluorescent light reflecting off those institutional white walls. I can only imagine the impression I make, with all the blinking and my eyes darting here and there.

We shake hands, and he says something. His name, most likely, which I do not catch over the bug-zapper sound of the lights just inches overhead.

I think I offer my name in return.

Either way, he lets go of my hand, and I follow him into his office.

"Which bondsman did you say you work for again?" he says, unsure of why I'd been buzzed back to see him.

"Metro Bail Bonds LLC."

"Ah, you're from the city?" he says, closing his door. The placard mounted alongside the door says the office belongs to CHARLES BOWDRE, DETECTIVE.

"*The* city?" I say.

"OKC," Charles explains.

I shake my head. "Kansas City, Kansas. The one no one ever talks about."

"Kansas City? There's not enough of us to have spare time to serve divorce papers, as much as some guys here would like to make the extra cash. We surely cannot act on a bench warrant from another county. Another state's out of the question. You understand, yeah?"

"Yeah."

"You're free to poke around and see if he's come home, but we cannot assist if he gives you trouble when you attempt to take him into custody. And I'm sure you know, but," Charles says, clearing his throat, "if it gets ugly or out of hand enough for some neighbor to give our dispatchers a holler, we'll treat you like an ordinary civilian. No offense, it's how it is with your profession in our state."

"Yes, thank you—I am aware, and I know you got to cover your ass, too," I say, doing my best to come off like a seasoned veteran.

"Drumgoole's not one to stand and fight. He's a runner."

"Yessir. Best I can tell, he made a beeline straight here," I say and set the case file down on his desk.

"Would you mind if I take a minute to look over his papers and bond agreement?"

"Go right ahead. I prefer to dot all my I's and cross my T's, rather than get shot by some deputy thinking I'm kidnapping a man."

"Smart," he says and tips his head to the side, lifting that same shoulder while scrunching up the corner of his mouth to show he understands where I am coming from. Then I have to sit there while he pulls the file into his lap and reviews every scrap of paper I've brought.

Front and back.

"Kansas City, Kansas?" Detective Bowdre says with a surprised tone while he hoists his left ankle up onto his right knee. "Here I thought he was roughnecking over in Cushing. Explains why he hasn't graced our jailhouse with his presence yet this year," he says, sounding almost disappointed.

"He didn't give his full name. No suffix, at least. I have his birth date, though. Social Security number and so on."

"It sounds like something Junior would do," Detective Bowdre says and clears his throat. "He likes to pretend he's the patriarch."

"Nineteenth of August, sixty-nine," I say, reading the date my employer has on file.

"Junior is in the neighborhood of thirty-five years of age. That's your guy. Senior's serving a life sentence for serial arson southeast of here, as far as I know. Big Mac is what we call it—in case you ask around for directions," he says, looking dead at me to make sure I am taking note. "It's in McAlester, if you want to see if he's gone to visit his daddy since he's come back. Of course, wouldn't be my move if I was looking to avoid a judge."

"If he's come back," I say to minimize my intrusion.

"His boy, the Third," he says while he crushes out a cigarette he'd left to smolder in a nearby ashtray, "isn't old enough to be a guest of anything but our juvenile lockup—which he currently isn't. Unless he's been brought in since you and I began our conversation."

"Do you mind if I talk to him?"

"If you can get him to talk, go for it. You're more than welcome to try." He shrugs. "You've got the mother's information there. If there's money involved, she'd like some. She'll rattle off everything she can if she gets a piece of the pie."

"She's his common-law wife."

"Is that so? Interesting. She sure uses his name like they're wed. If he owes money, child support, or whatever, work that angle with her. Sound good, Mr. Kincaid?" he says, and stands. "If there's nothing else, I need to get back to my own set of problems."

4

The room I let at the Golden Spur Motel isn't what I'd call remarkable. The motel was built in a U-shape, so it's a three-sided affair with a pool smack in the middle of what could have otherwise proved an ample-sized parking lot. Though I'm sure they like to pretend the place was built in the shape of a horseshoe or a boot spur. The one piece of art hanging in the motel's office is a framed postcard of a single thirteenth-century copper rowel spur, on permanent display at the Metropolitan Museum of Art in New York City.

Fancy.

The first box I have to check calls for a sit-down chitchat with Mr. Eric Delvin Drumgoole Junior's blushing common-law bride, Annabelle Lee Lately. The lettering stuck to her mailbox claims her as a Drumgoole. Though there was only so much room. So it reads DRUMGOOL.

Her place sitting on a dead-end dirt road means I can't cruise by and count the cars out front or look for a Kansas license plate bolted onto a back bumper, or spy, with my little eye, if there are any clothes on the line belonging to an adult male weighing in at two hundred and ten pounds.

If I drive through too fast and kick up too much dust, everyone is liable to come to see who the idiot is that took a wrong turn. In that same breath, if I roll down the road slow enough to not draw any attention to myself, I'd also make it obvious I know I'm where I do not belong.

The umpteen bird dogs baying at the breeze make sneaking up on foot out of the question. The one option left is to walk right up, knock on the front door, and hope like hell I don't get myself shot. Oklahoma is and has been an open carry and castle law-abiding state since the cowboys and Indians started playing tug of war with the territory. Had this somehow slipped my mind, the pickup I follow most of the way out to the house has a fresh reminder stuck to the window behind the driver's headrest that reads: *INVEST IN PRECIOUS METALS,* with an outline of a bullet and a brass casing beneath the words *BUY AMMUNITION LOCALLY at…*someplace in too small of a font for me to read.

I pull a U-turn and park on the shoulder behind the far side of a billboard with the car's front end pointed back toward civilization. Once all the way on the shoulder, I pop the hood latch for the international sign of car trouble. In the interest of thoroughness, I pull a single plug wire off the distributor cap and toss it into the truck so no one hopped up on hillbilly heroin can hotwire it in my absence.

I swap out my undershirt for a vest manufactured to stop anything other than a point-blank shot to the chest. Though it can be easily defeated by a small kitchen knife. Over the vest, I throw on a filling station shirt from the Saint Vincent de Paul secondhand store, a hand-me-down from a man named Albert.

Albert hardly seems threatening.

I never met a single Albert while I served. I certainly cannot recall an Albert incarcerated in Leavenworth. Nor can I ever remember a time someone came in to ask the bondsman to post bail for an Albert. That's to say, I cannot say if I look like an Albert, seeing as I have yet to lay eyes on one other than Einstein.

I figure the empty one-gallon gas can I pull from the trunk gives me the look of a sympathetic stranded motorist. Save for the Beretta velcro'd onto the small of my back, hopefully hidden from the rest of the world.

After trudging along a good stretch of red dirt road with a handful of vehicles tearing ass past me, tossing up an unwavering cloud of dust, I look like anything but a law enforcement professional. I'd like to say that was the plan, but that'd be an unfiltered lie. As is everything about to leave my lips meant for Miss Lately's ears.

"Is Eric here?"

"Who?"

"Eric. My car gave out a bit down the way, and I know Eric lives here, so I thought he could help," I say and give the gas can a jiggle.

"The hell you know Eric lives here."

"Eric…Drumgoole. I've been by here before," I say with a shrug.

She latches the storm door, hides her hand and arm behind the door frame. "Where do you know *Eric* from?"

"Hey." I nod at her disappeared hand, "I was just hoping he might have some spare gas to get me back into town."

"Does it look like that bastard has ever mowed this place?"

I don't dare look away, but I make a show of rolling my eyes toward the side yard before I say, "No. No, it does not."

"What do you want with *J.R.*, Albert?"

"Is he home?"

"He might be. I don't know. This ain't home for him, Albert."

"I go by Al."

"You're full of shit too. That shirt's older than you," she says, shaking her head. "What's he done this time?"

"Jumped bail. Missed court. Left the state," I say.

"Who's dumb enough to post for him?"

I respond by raising my eyebrows and letting her fill in the blanks.

"I might be wasting my wind, but I'll still ask whether the two of you are on good terms."

"Nope."

"Why're you going around as his wife then?"

"Two reasons," she says, mashing her nose and forehead into the screen. "I want my son and me to have the same last name. Secondly, it's a whole lot easier to pawn his shit."

Right then I hear footsteps come up behind me. I close my eyes and wait. And I guess I wait so long she thinks I've fallen asleep standing up, because she cracks the silence wide open by saying, "Is there anything else you want to ask me, *Al*?"

I shake my head. "No, but you might see me again." Then she hollers for her son to get inside. It was the Third who'd come up behind me.

"Is my dad back?" he says, hoofing it past where I stand while wearing the same shoes I did at that age.

"Don't know," I say. My father, too, regularly reminded me we are a nomadic people.

Behind me, I hear the screen door latch flick open. Miss Lately lets her son inside the trailer house. Then the deadbolt tumbles closed.

5

I strip down and stand statue in the shower and wait while the water washes the red dirt the Sooner state is so proud of out of the crack of my ass, as well as every other crevice it crept its way into. The dust settled into my eyebrows so heavily I could have passed for a ginger if not for the black feathery mop that'd taken on the look of a drowned crow perched atop my head.

The only promises the Golden Spur Motel's roadside marquee made were clean, cheap, and quiet. I imagine they figure two out of three is enough to keep a guest from taking the time to pitch a bitch. I cannot say with any authority which category my pissing and moaning fell into. When I first sat down to take a dump, I could not find a single square of toilet paper. I shrugged it off and hopped into the shower. There is no sense getting upset over something so silly. It is precisely why one takes care of bathroom business in a particular order. However, upon cutting the water off and searching the restroom for a bath towel, there wasn't as much as a washcloth to be found either.

Butt-ass naked and dripping wet, I go through Mr. Drumgoole's papers once again while the weatherman goes over an overlapping list of tornado watches and warnings, as well as his guesstimate as to how big the hail will be once it hits this part of the state.

"Stay tuned," he says, like a tick.

Every square inch of Anadarko County has proven a pain in my ass. Including the neon orange pleather swivel bucket seat that the back of my thighs, ball sack, and ass cheeks adhered to while I watched the weatherman turn it over to the sportscaster and then some bug-eyed field reporter who brought the news hour to a close with some feel-good fluff piece I forgot before the commercial break came to an end, and my eyelids grow too heavy to hold open any longer.

The national anthem blares to mark the end of the broadcast day, and I spring to my feet to offer old glory all due respect, confused as to where I am. But I cannot quite cling onto my military bearing, thanks to the nausea that floats up to my tonsils before it sinks back to my aching balls. They left the comfort of the pleather chair at a much slower rate than the rest of me when I hopped up to render a crisp salute to Old Glory.

I kill the television set with a slap before the music stops. Then I curl atop the sheets in the fetal position, which is how housekeeping finds me a little after seven the next morning.

6

I dare speculate the unfortunate cleaning lady assigned to my room has laid her eyes on worse sights during her sixty-some-odd years on this earth. I say so simply based upon her going about the business of emptying the trash cans, bookending the bathroom sink with the finest soap and moisturizer sample bottles, as well as making sure there are enough bath towels to last me through the weekend. She does it so quietly it's not her that wakes me, but the warmth of the morning sun on my shins spilling through the door that she'd left ajar while she works around me. She leaves it up to me to decide whether to move and let her know I am awake—let alone alive—and make the whole situation embarrassing and uncomfortable for the two of us. Or I could keep my eyes shut and wait for her to pull the door closed and take herself and her cart of cleaning supplies to the room next door.

I choose the latter.

In an unparalleled show of professionalism, which will guarantee her a healthy gratuity upon my checkout, she drapes a towel over some hard evidence of the X-rated dream I was immersed in when she first turned my doorknob.

While the door stood ajar, my nose caught wind of a bakery and breakfast spot directly south of the motel on the far side of the city park.

More of that insipid Oklahoma State orange awaits inside the

Shortstop Cafe. The Formica countertop, the upholstered seats of the swivel stools, the laminate booth seats, the tables bolted to the wall, the—everything—all boasts that swanky school tangerine or cantaloupe or clay color everyone here holds so holy in their hearts.

The diner seems a proverbial Grand Central Station. Young and old come and go. Traffic cops and transients sit rubbing elbows along the counter. Black, white, and every shade of brown work in or patronize the place. I am certain there is no better spot to be seen in Lawson, Oklahoma, so I seat myself at a far corner table meant for two and put my back to the dead-end hallway that leads to the restrooms.

In the time it takes to blink and turn my head, someone drops off a menu and a cup of coffee without my asking or breaking stride or saying a single thing about it.

The kitchen's offerings look simple and plenteous enough. Though they do not serve dinner. Instead, they serve supper, like the last thing the Lord ever ate. I squint though the glare that the climbing sun and overhead stained-glass chandelier have cast across the laminated menu and turn my wrist until I can read the thing. "Need to borrow my readers?" I hear a server say. I blink and blink and say, "No, thank you. The orange is a bit much this early."

"Oh...I'll give you a minute."

"Thank you," I say and bob my head in appreciation.

She looks Indian. Pretty as anything. Though her green eyes come as a surprise.

Contacts, maybe.

When she heads back toward the register, I wait a fistful of seconds to watch her wiggle through the diner before I turn my eyes back to the menu. As I suspect, there's no rear end on her. From that, I am sure she is native to Indian country. Like my mom, she, too, suffers from noassatall, a common yet sadly incurable affliction widespread among the tribes native to North America.

I keep it simple and order a burrito in case I have to take off quick-like.

Same reason I back into my parking spot.

"More coffee?" she says after she fills my cup back up half the way.

"Please."

"Waiting for someone else? There's plenty of room at the counter if you're alone."

"Oh, I am sorry. I didn't mean to take up a table. I'm waiting for a friend of mine, J.R."

"J.R.?"

"Yah, Drumgoole. Eric. You know him?"

"Yeah—but—if I was his friend, I wouldn't say it so loudly those cops could hear you," she says and lets me chew what I had in my mouth.

"Why, is he in some kind of trouble?" I say.

She scolds me with nothing more than a moment of silence and her eyebrows. "They'll watch you like you're watching everyone else in here," she says, and adds, "Where'd you serve?"

"Hmm?"

"You served," she says, not a question. "State or federal time. You're too comfortable around cops and have a leg out in the aisle like you're ready to run. Or fight. My brothers eat the same way."

"Oh. Is it obvious? Stillwater," I say and wipe my mouth with a fresh paper napkin. "Way up north in Minnesota."

"For why?"

"'Cause I got caught," I say with a flat smile, which I let curl into a flirtatious one once I see she isn't spooked by speaking to someone she thinks is a former convict.

"J.R. isn't joining you for breakfast. I know that much," she says, leaning over my table so only I can hear.

"Oh? Did he call and cancel?" I say, not daring to blink or act too surprised.

"You're a lot of things. From here, you're not. Dumb, you're not.

A friend of J.R.'s, you're not. Not that white boy. He might conduct business with you, but he'd never be seen with you around town."

I sip my coffee while she says her piece. The heavy ceramic cup covers a good bit of my face, which stops me from giving anything away.

This woman is too easy to talk to.

"If you did time. If. You've since spent a good bit of cash covering up your jailhouse ink with some pretty art," she says. "If you're not J.R.'s friend, who're you?"

"Simply a savage who can read and write," I say without meeting her gaze.

"I've heard that line before. Who said it?"

"Sir John A. Macdonald—once upon a time."

"J.R. owe you some money?" she says as softly as she can.

"Something along those lines," I say without offering anything else.

"How much?"

"Enough."

"Enough to hire some help? Must be quite a bit to get you to come all this way."

"All what way?"

"Please. *Yain't from round here, boy,*" she says with her best put-on drawl.

"Okay, fine. You caught me red-handed." I hold my hands up as if under arrest, which makes her let go a laugh. "Are you willing to tell me when he came in here last?"

"Oh, he's not one for fine dining. I'll tell you what—come back at three, and you can ask me whatever," she says and sets the check upside down. "Please pay up front when you're ready, sir," she adds, with a wink and an extra wiggle to her walk when she leaves me by my lonesome once more.

I grow antsy while waiting to get rung up.

One of the cops feels it necessary to say, “Careful, Kaw-Liga. You might want to think twice before messing with her.”

I elect to ignore him, pretending I hadn’t heard. Instead, I pay an older gentleman dressed to match the diner. The old timer walks so quietly and looks so camouflaged that he, too, seems to have appeared in a blink.

I take note of the officer staring at me in my periphery. I look dead at him and correct him by saying, “My name’s Kincaid.”

“Kin-caid, Kaw-Liga, Ke-mo Sah-bee, kind of all roll the same off the tongue,” he says and laughs by himself. “Mess with Elise, and you’ll wish you’d done otherwise, Tonto.”

“Oh, I’ll be all right. She’s sweet.”

“Sweet?” he says. “If you say so.”

“She reminds me of my mom,” I add to shut him up.

7

The morning shade evaporated along with the dew in the time it took me to muscle my way through a breakfast I feel reasonably certain will hold me over until the same time tomorrow—at least. Traffic seems light. Most of the kids from the college probably went wherever they called home or found work for the summertime about a month or so before I followed Mr. Drumgoole to his home of record.

Lawson seems a ghost town.

That said, if I were a peckerwood worried about getting my flight feathers plucked, where would I smuggle myself? The wife was a dead end. So, next on the list is Mamma Drumgoole.

Some mothers cannot conceive of being guilty of aiding and abetting when it comes to her own child—something in the same vein of sacredness as spousal privilege.

"I haven't seen him," she says through the Plexiglas storm door.

"He hasn't called or visited you since he got back?"

"Back?" she says, sounding flabbergasted at the thought. "I told you no already. Let me ask you something now."

"Ma'am?" I say, after I realize we've begun something of a barn dance. And I am not the one leading.

"Did you tailgate him every inch of the way down here like them damn dimwits who chased down O.J.?"

"I did not," I say and shake my head wild enough to be seen

through the dust ingrained in the glass in the door and the film coating her coke bottles.

“Then how do you know he’s made it here? You don’t. You hunting? No, you’re fishing. Why’re you bothering me?”

I don’t answer her questions. I am not about to give her an itemized list of all the shit I shuffled through, deducting and detecting. Or the door knocking and bad acting I’d done.

“I want to see your warrant,” she says, showcasing her impatience with my presence. I can’t help but think there’s a hint in her voice how she’s doing all she can think of to keep me busy while her beloved bouncing baby boy makes it out the back door.

“I’m not a cop.”

“What?” she says and leans forward until the door makes a mushroom cap out of the tip of her nose.

“I am not here because there’s a warrant for his arrest. He got arrested, got a girlfriend to pay a bondsman to post his bail, and ran.”

That gets her to laugh in a way that leads me to believe it’s genuinely the first time she’d heard the punchline. “Well, Mister Not-A-Cop, who might you be?”

“I work for a few bail bondsmen up in Kansas City,” I say. “My name is Moses Kincaid, ma’am.”

“You’re not Officer Kincaid or Deputy Kincaid or Agent Kincaid, or something else with a badge and a commission?”

“We call ourselves bail enforcement agents when we’re testifying in court or working around the jailhouses, but that’s it. I do not hold a license. It’s not required for us or private investigators up in Kansas.”

“What’s all that mean?” she says, staring at my chest as if to let me know she can see the vest beneath my Royals jersey.

“I’m freelance. A bounty hunter.”

“Hell,” she says a split second before she unlatches the door. “You sure quack like a duck.”

“I was a soldier for most of my adult years. An MP.”

"That shoe sure fits you, all right. Have you told his wife that bit about the girlfriend yet?"

"Not yet."

"She'd flush him out if she knew about the girlfriend. I ain't inviting you in, understand? But I'm still going to come on out there onto the porch with you."

"He's not here, then?"

"No, he most certainly isn't. He's not what you would call a momma's boy. Hasn't been since the first time his peter stood on its own. He loves every other woman he comes across, though—according to his own definition of love."

She stops to make sure the door closes behind her. I stay quiet and let her words hang in the air. It seems proper and respectful, and she does not seem done.

"I haven't seen him," she says, waving her hand in front of her face as if swatting a fly or trying to rid the air of the unlikelihood of the idea of her son paying her a visit. "He hasn't had much time for me since he got off the tit. I had to be a father to him, too. Eric hates his daddy. Hates to be named after him. He would love to change it, but it's not allowed. Not with his history. His juvenile record began before puberty ended," she says and adds a smile, pleased with her witticism or perhaps getting off her feet.

"You can grab a seat, too, if you want. Not the wicker one. It's been out in the sun forever—far too brittle to stand your weight. Should use it for firestarter," she says and waits for me to move, which I do not. "Not calling you fat."

"Thank you," I say. "I sat enough on the way here."

"Hmm...you still think you might have to tear off after him. Can't say I blame you." She leans back in her seat and crosses her ankles.

I raise my eyebrows in acknowledgment to let her know I am listening and letting her talk.

Then she prods, "Is it a professional thing? Or more of a your people not having much of a reason to ever trust my people kind of thing?"

"Oh, that can't be helped," I say without letting on to whether it was a or b or both.

"I don't suppose," she says and laughs, knowing what I am doing.

"Mrs. Drumgoole—"

"Oh, no—look it up," she says. "I divorced the sorry firebug *long* ago. It's Forbus again."

"Miss Forbus—"

"Miss Jackie, please."

"I apologize. Miss Jackie—"

"Ask away, Moses."

"I go by Moe," I say, interrupting her this time.

"Moe? As in Curly, Larry, and…you?"

"Yes."

"Ask away, Moe," she says, hiding her smile behind her balled-up fist, pretending to cover a tickle in her throat. "Boy, you got to be a confident SOB to go by that for a name. Or a stooge."

"Or a stooge," I echo back. "Everybody said I was a twin for our terp, Moe, our interpreter, in Desert Storm. Sorry. His name was Mahomed, but Muslim men won't go around by the prophet's name, the same way most Mexican men called Jesús get nicknamed Chuy."

"Well, I guess you do learn something new every day."

"Your son failed to appear at a sentencing hearing after it was deemed he wasn't a flight risk."

"Oh, there are lots of stooges in Kansas, huh?"

"You have to consider how we did not go and adopt the three strikes law like a lot of the country."

"He committed another felony? That's why you're on the hunt. The picture is getting a touch clearer now."

"Yes, ma'am."

"Not his third, though. I can guarantee you that for damn certain."

"It's not as bad as it may seem. Not all felonies are created equal. If I can bring him in, in a timely manner, he may not be so bad off. It was a misdemeanor."

"What'd he do this time?"

"The official charge was leaving the scene of a hit-and-run accident. If he doesn't show up at the courthouse soon, though, they do have enough to twist that into vehicular homicide with criminal intent. He put a pair of motorcycles into the concrete divider on the interstate."

"And they died because of my son crashing into them?"

"Decapitated and twisted up inside their bike frames."

"Not a pleasant way to go."

"No, ma'am. It most certainly was not. The thing is, they were wearing full-face helmets."

"Mmmhmm. And?"

"They weren't riding sportbikes—"

"The hell is that supposed to mean to me?"

"You haven't heard any of this? Usually," I say, and stop to clear my throat, "when one of these bikers—the ones with the three patches on their backs—are wearing full-face helmets, they're trying to protect their identity and in the middle of doing something fairly illegal."

"More illegal than running someone over with a car and taking off?" She scrunches up her face, folding her penciled-on eyebrows into twin mountain peaks.

"Unless they prove him doing so was intentional."

"If he goes back with you, the charge goes back down to a misdemeanor with a fine?"

"I can't promise that a hundred percent. I believe he's facing a month in jail and a fine at a minimum. But you should know, it is highly unlikely the fallen biker's brethren are going to wait for him to be brought in."

“Kansas got the needle or the chair or anything of that sort?”

“You get your boy to come back to Kansas City with me, and the public defender might get a jury to come to the consensus that his shitty driving might be seen as something of an unspoken favor to the public at large.”

“See,” she says and blows a cloud of smoke out of the side of her mouth, “now, I trust you. Honesty goes a hell of a long way out here. The dust kicked off the red dirt roads settles and covers the bullshit and does away with the stink. That’s how come we live out here.”

Without taking her eyes off me, she knocks the cooling ash off the tip of her cigarette and down over the side of the porch railing.

“I am not one to show my hand so early in the game,” I say.

“Who’s asking you to? This ain’t a damnable casino,” she says through another cloud of cigarette smoke.

I make my way down the front porch stairs. “The women around here are a special breed.”

“Grab you one before you head out of town.”

“Unfortunately, I plan to elope with your son.”

She laughs at me, chokes on her cigarette, and wishes me the best of luck, but the conversation is over.

8

"A Sunbird, huh? Turquoise, even. Still, it's a nice war pony," says Elise. She points toward the back hatch and mouths, "Four doors?" while looking playfully unimpressed.

"Thanks," I say. Three o'clock crept up fast on me. Rather than standing her up, I waited in the side parking lot still wearing my Royals jersey, smelling like I'd been doing two-a-days.

"Why not a Thunderbird?"

I smirk. "For the exact reason I am not wearing a Chiefs jersey."

"Oh," she says and raises a clenched fist into the air. "Is there an AIM sticker on the back bumper?"

I shake my head. Open the passenger door and say, "Where can I take you?"

"Nowhere," she says, straight-faced while mine falls. That cop's mockery echoes in my ears. Then she jangles her car keys and says, "I smell like I've been in a diner for ten hours, and you smell like you've been working highway construction, so we're both going to shower, change, and meet up somewhere later."

"That's fair."

Elise walks past me to her car and adds, "Get a Pistoleros jersey. People will ignore you like a stop sign."

"You too?"

"You've already got my attention, cowboy."

That gets me to scrunch my mouth, force a smile, and say, "I'm not a cowboy."

"Indians make the best cowboys," she says.

"Is that so?"

"What? You don't like poetry?"

I don't know what to say back. I squint and cock an eyebrow while her car coughs to life and pulls itself out onto Sangre Road. I stand there wondering, what poem?

That same cop comes out of the diner joking with his partner, who trails behind him, singing about Kaw Liga's red face and wooden head.

"Have you been here all day, Officer?" I say in an attempt to maintain professional courtesies.

"No, not…all day, but LEOs get free coffee during their shift, so…" His stomach and chest jump with another silent chuckle.

"You get what you pay for," I add to stick a pin in the conversation.

9

The light on the phone pulsates beneath the yellowed bulb screwed into the desk lamp. It is not the front desk, but the waitress's voice on the other end telling me I can find her at the casino's steakhouse.

I didn't give her my name or tell her where to find me. Nor did I realize my slip-up until I was back in my room, down to my birthday suit, and lathered up. The ability of a woman to seek and find is nothing if not otherworldly.

I spot her squeegeeing water droplets from the sides of a glass. The hostess seated her in a booth in the far corner of the frosted glass façade of the Cinnamon Steakhouse—purposefully nestled on the far side of the gaming room floor so you have to weave your way through slot machines and gaming tables.

"You weren't so hard to find," I say, taking my last steps toward the table.

She covers her mouth, swallows a sip, and says, "Neither were you."

Elise stands the best she can and we exchange a clumsy half hug before I sit across from her. She interrupts our shared smile to say, "You look…different than I was expecting. I thought you were here to take my drink order when you first walked up."

"Thanks," I say and laugh. "I think. You look nice, too."

"You're welcome."

"Sass so early on."

"Again, you're welcome," she says. "Did you ever find your friend?"

"I went by his mom's place, but he never showed," I say, hoping to dismiss it.

"That's weird," she says. "It's a good thing I didn't stand you up. Twice in one day is more than any man could stand."

"He and I didn't exactly have a date."

"I know." She lowers her voice and bobs her head without letting her eyes leave mine. "You know, I could help you."

"How do you figure?"

"He might only like white boys, but he has a Pocahontas fetish."

"Is that so?"

"Oh yeah," she adds, widening her smile. "He certainly does!"

"Even with the green eyes?" I say, half asking whether they are contacts.

"I'm Osage. There are lots of us mixed up with landgrabbers. Settlers have been teepee-creepin' with us for five hundred years now."

"I was wondering about that."

"Oh?" she says, without a hint of surprise.

"Mine are—"

"Baby shit brown," she says for me.

"Oh, you have kids?" I say, laughing at my joke—along with hers.

"Lots of little brothers and sisters, cousins. Lots of diapers."

"I am so glad my eyes are a reminder of all that."

"Just tells me you're full of crap," she says.

"Oh, yeah?"

"Yup."

"Concerning?"

"C'mon now, you traffic in bullshit," she says, but the conversation gets interrupted by an actual approaching waitstaff member before I can argue.

~

Sometime before the check arrives, I learn the place is called Cimarron, not Cinnamon. Elise has fun with that. I like her smile and her laughter, so I don't protest.

"My dad is Tonkawa," she says.

"Okay," I say.

"That's why we're at the steakhouse," she says with a smirk. "Besides, you look like a meat-eater."

"Okay," I repeat, knowing there is a punchline I've missed.

"You're not from anywhere near here, huh?"

I swing my chin and point a finger up in the air. "North," I say.

"Kansas?"

"Farther."

"You a damn Eskimo?" she says.

"Closer toward Green Bay."

"Hmm, never been."

"North of Chicago and Milwaukee," I add.

"I know where it's at. I just didn't know they had Indians way up there."

"I'm Ho-Chunk."

"A what?"

"Winnebago."

"Like the RV?"

"Oh, okay. More jokes?"

"We should go," she says, and stands. "Do you dance?"

"I cruise sometimes."

"No, I don't mean crow hop. I mean dance," she says and points toward the distant thumping coming from the other side of the mechanical calliope slot machine music.

Of course, I dance. And we dance. How else do five hundred varied Native nations talk when it comes time to powwow. And teepee creep.

10

Elise boots me out of bed before the sun even considers coming up. She's showered and looks like a waitress once again. The air smells of the vanilla-scented scrubs and shampoos she used in the shower. Coffee, too. The latter is especially welcome.

"Thank you," I say and reach to take hold of the steaming cup, which allows the blanket to fall from my shoulder down to my waist and showcase the scars I had not been able to cover with ink.

"Holy..." she says with a gasp she immediately attempts to reel back. "How long did you serve?"

"What? Oh. It's okay," I say. "These are from a clumsy and misspent youth."

"Is that right?"

I say, "I never earned a purple heart," to clarify my point.

Her reaction is one I'd seen from folks in basic training, as well as a sprinkling of times like this one. She turns back toward the bathroom and says, "I have to throw on some makeup."

She does not, but I reply with, "I have to find my clothes," after a mouthful of coffee.

"Top of the hope chest at the foot of the bed," she says and disappears into the glow of the bathroom doorway.

I do not bother with my tie or top button or tucking my shirt into my pants. I wonder whether I should wait for her to finish with her makeup before I make my way to and out her front door.

I stall somewhat by emptying the coffee cup.

"You want me to wait for you?" I say, though I can't tell if my voice carries over the sound of the exhaust fan in the bathroom.

I feel stupid for asking and step toward her bedroom door as softly as possible. Behind me, Elise slaps the light switch off and laughs at the sight of me heel-toeing toward the door. "Why? Are you attached already?"

I shrug, smile, and say through a stifled yawn, "Just asking. Walking you out seems the decent thing."

"C'mon then, Romeo. Walk me out." She wraps her arm around mine, laces our fingers together, and kisses me on the neck right below the ear, which makes my ankle wobble some.

If this was a film, The Big O would sing "Dream Baby" as we drove off in opposite directions, alone with our thoughts. I'd have a smile curling the corners of my mouth, and the last bit of moonlight would sparkle in my eyes.

That's my roundabout way of admitting she was right when she speculated I'd already gotten attached.

II

A knock arrives at my door a little after ten o'clock. The breakfast rush at the diner must have thinned out to a trickle of customers. Back at the diner it would be old men, mostly, slowly sipping coffee, in no hurry to get out into the summer heat. Elise, I figure, must have crept her way over on a break.

A lot can happen on a fifteen-minute break.

An explosion of red blinds me when I open the door to greet her.

~

I come to in the bathtub of my motel room with some leather-clad biker sitting on the toilet, twirling a leather blackjack with his pants around his ankles. I can't breathe through my nose. But when I open my mouth and draw a deep breath into my chest, I can taste the crap he just took and needs to flush.

"You're out of toilet paper," he says, sounding personally disgusted with me, as if I am to blame or it'll explain away the reason for my present situation. He then points the bulbous end of the blackjack at my face. The leather stretched around the outside looks wet with my blood.

Blood takes anywhere from thirty minutes to two hours to dry. That's the window for how long I've been in their company. I say *they* because the Filthy Thirteen Motorcycle Club is a tight-knit group of motorcycle enthusiasts who rarely travel alone and recently lost a brother to the reckless driving habits of Mr. Eric Delvin Drumgoole Junior.

"So, you're not housekeeping?" I point a finger at the asshole perched on the toilet, in the hopes he'll take a swing at me with the blackjack so I can grab it for myself.

Desperation makes you do dumb shit here and there.

"You're a funny fucker."

"I thank you. I'll be here all week. Make certain to tip your waiter."

Over the noise of the television set, I hear someone else ask, "He awake in there?"

"Yup. Hey, bring me something to wipe my ass with. See if he has any clean socks lying around."

"There are some moist towelettes from a chicken joint," the other voice says.

"You are too kind."

"Well, holy moly, you're awake," the second guy says when he steps into the bathroom. "Howdy, Moses," adds the one I'll call the Marlboro Man since he seems more cowboy than Mr. Harley Davidson, squatting on the toilet with knees spread like he's riding a V-twin.

I move my hand to block the overhead light and attempt to identify the third member of our trio. The voice is unfamiliar, but I did recently get a bump on my head. "I'm afraid you have me at a disadvantage," I say, sounding as authentically apologetic as possible. "I do not recognize either of you. I have something of a headache. Sinuses, I think," I add, and I try to force air in and out through my nostrils.

"You're really shitting with him right there?" the Marlboro Man says.

"Why not? He was out cold. Do you mind taking him out of here while I take care of some personal matters?"

"What the hell have you been eating, anyway?"

"Your mom's chili," he says.

The one dressed decently shakes his head and orders me out of the tub.

Two and a half steps later, I faceplant into the carpet. The rugburn stings. I let my mind spin thinking of what else might have spilled onto the carpet before I checked into the room.

"Get up into the bed before you fall again and really hurt yourself but good."

"How considerate," I say, and scan the room for my pistol while I inch my way up the wall from the floor.

I blink a handful of times before I find it in the swivel chair between the AC unit and the bed. That's not where I left it, which means they've already found it. I put my hand on the wall and grope the textured pattern with my fingertips on my way to the bed, doing my best Peter Parker impression, not wanting to crack my head a third time.

I land safely.

"Do we need to tell you who we are, Mr. Kincaid?"

"Matching outfits aside, it's only polite. You already got me in bed."

"I never knew Indians are such comedians."

"That's all right," I say, and prop myself up against the wall with a pillow. "I never found white people all that funny either."

"Fuck you!" Harley Davidson says to butt into our conversation. He marches the length of the room and snatches my pistol off the chair, garnering my undivided attention.

"You might not want to. I am bleeding, after all," I say, certain they have no intention of leaving me for the maid to find cold and stiff. They hadn't thought to hang the do not disturb sign on the door, which I take as a cue they won't be staying too long.

"Does Oklahoma have the death penalty, do you know?" Harley

Davidson asks the Marlboro Man.

"I'm not a hundred percent. But that is his gun, so it would be an easy leap for the cops to call it a plain old case of a drunken Indian committing suicide in a cheap roadside motel."

"Tragically poetic. Barely worth a headline. Wouldn't you say?"

"Indeed."

"The thing is, the whole way here, I was hoping we could get creative with a murder-suicide. Unfortunately, he hasn't tracked down his guy."

"Yet," I say. Interrupting their flirting with one another after hearing too much of them talking about me in the past tense.

"Mr. Kincaid, in case you are unaware, my associate and I are—"

"A gay couple, eloping?" I nod, anticipating getting pistol-whipped.

"You want to get the ever-living fuck beat out of you?"

"The beating's coming whether I whimper, beg, or bust your balls. You're doing me a favor." I laugh. "The cable's out. And I already jerked it."

I bore easily.

"Sit down!" the Marlboro Man says, taking a hopping stride toward his friend. "He wants his gun back. Do you think he's afraid of a few lumps coming along with it?"

I smile at the prospect, and he indulges me. He takes hold of the lamp and demonstrates his rusted high school marching band baton skills.

~

When I come back to consciousness, I deduce he managed to land the base of the lamp about an inch or so above my right eye. Some of the ceramic dust from the shattered base has settled in between my eyeball and eyelid. I try to blink it away, but no dice.

Blinking with that eye, I mean.

That's a roundabout way to say it takes me some time to figure it is swollen shut. When you wake in so much pain, the obvious isn't always so.

The swollen half of my face rests in the pillow. With my good eye, I catch my reflection off the television screen. I can see my l wrists are lashed to the bedpost *way* up over my head with a section of electrical cord. The one from the now busted lamp, I'm willing to bet. I laugh to myself when my vision clears more so and I see my full reflection in the television screen. I look like a ref ready to announce an extra point for their team.

"Look," I say, and rock my head over toward Harley Davidson sitting in the chair, absently fondling my pistol as if no one is watching. "Seeing there are two of you, my safe word will have to be Peanut Butter *and* Jelly, okay? Don't worry, it'll be easy to remember. You look a little soft around the middle, prospect, so you can be Jelly."

The prospect flares his nostrils the way a perturbed gorilla might.

Now it's time to address the elephant in the room, so I look to the Marlboro Man. "Are you okay with being called Peanut Butter? You look like you've had yours packed a few times."

Peanut Butter screams at Jelly, "Goddammit, don't! We've got orders!" So I snap my head back to my left in time to see Jelly headed my way with my pistol held by the barrel.

12

I wake later, still tethered to a bed. But it's oxygen tubing that's lassoed around my head with a loop running around my ears and beneath my nose. My hands are free, but the IVs stuck in me say I should stay put.

"What sort of kinky stuff are you into, cowboy?" Elise says over the beeping monitor and the hiss of the oxygen. I blink and let in the soft light of the darkened hospital room. I laugh, relieved at the change of venue and appreciative of her joke. I try to stop laughing when the stabbing pain starts, but funny is funny, so my "ha-ha-haing" turns to "ow-owing."

"Mr. Kincaid." A woman from the Anadarko County Sheriff's department says. She stands beneath the muted television set in the corner of the room. "Do you know who did this to you?"

"A couple of motorcycle riders."

"White? Male?"

"Yes, on both accounts." I pause to clear the mucus from my throat. "You have them in custody?"

"No, we do not. What else can you tell me about the suspects?" she says, with a pen ready.

"Assailants, ma'am," I say, correcting her. "I do have some compelling evidence of the crime. This wasn't self-inflicted."

"That's fair," she agrees. "What else can you tell me about the assailants?"

"Blue jeans, leather vests. Both were allergic to shirt sleeves. Filthy Thirteen patches."

"Anything about their faces you could tell me, maybe, Mr. Kinc—?"

"Deputy," another voice says from the doorway. "He's going to remain foggy-headed and a little loopy for a while. If you could come back later, please."

She closes her pen, steps out so the doctor can enter the room.

"Mr. Kincaid, do you know where you are?" the doctor says, and leans into what she suspects is my field of vision.

"Not the Golden Spur Motel."

"No," she says, "you're not in your room at the Golden Spur Motel. You are right."

"I'm in the hospital, then. A hospital."

"Yes, you are. Do you have any questions for me? If not, you should try to get some more rest."

I raise my hand as if back in grade school, point at my crotch, and say, "Am I wearing a catheter?"

"Yes, sir. You have been out of it for a while. We can adjust it if need be."

"No. Please. Let it be. I was just wondering. I had a hot date the other night, and I was worried it may have been—too hot," I say with an extraordinarily toothy smile before I roll my face toward Elise in her chair by the window.

"I'll let you be, then," the doctor says. "Can you reach the call button?"

I grab it and wave it in the air, so she can see, and she makes her exit.

"Thought I gave you something, did ya?" Elise says.

"There are lots of new aches and pains over here."

"I'll let it slide, considering," she says, before her forced smile melts into a look underpinned with worry and care. "Did you finally meet up with your friend?"

"No. Some friends of his did pay me a visit, however."

"You party hard, huh?"

"Not really," I say, scrunching up my face. "Some guys can't take a joke."

"You're welcome, by the way," Elise says. "I saw the ambulance go to the motel. I wanted to make sure your chart didn't say John Doe. The deputy told me you're an agent, or a cop, or something?"

"I am?" I say and try to look surprised.

"Shut up, okay."

"Elise—"

"No. Save it." She cuts me off. "You can tell me later. They're keeping you till tomorrow. Then you're shacking up with me."

"I am?"

"Yeah, stupid. Good thing my dogs like you, Moe."

"All dogs like me," I say and smile. Or try to, before I close my eye.

"Maybe," she says and kisses me on the forehead. "I sure do."

13

An alarm clock of Sally Jessy Raphael is not the most pleasant way to wake up, but it did answer why I was sitting in her studio audience in the dream world. At least I wasn't on stage, defending some inexplicable PG-13 kink.

My hands hunt for the button to release a drop or two of morphine while I let go of my morning piss when I hear a voice say, "Did you ever read any detective comics as a kid?"

"Like Dick Tracy and The Shadow? Yeah," I say.

"No, like Batman. You know, the world's *greatest* detective. Because you look like Harvey Dent. Your face is all purple on this side, mister. They sure did a number on you."

I turn my head toward the voice, but she is already on her way around to my good side. Elise's chair is now empty. So there's no one to run interference.

Shit.

"I am wondering if you knew who assaulted you," says the same deputy from earlier. Abby Saunders, according to her engraved nameplate and badge. She looks like a tribal cop, but she's wearing the wrong uniform. Still, I say, "Filthy Thirteen Motorcycle Club. Kansas City Charter. Eric Drumgoole—Junior—killed their sergeant-at-arms and one other on the highway. He skipped town before sentencing," knowing what she'll figure out for herself shortly.

She puts her pen down and tightens her grip on the notepad.

A case such as this will be taken away from her sheriff soon enough. In the course of a single question and answer, her case goes from an assault and a missing firearm at a rundown motel to an investigation involving an out-of-state chapter of a national criminal organization, escalated by two deaths with the potential for more. That, as they say, is the plot thickening.

"Do you, by chance, know or recognize those who assaulted you?"

"No, I did not know either. One did know me, I think."

"Explain, please."

"When I woke in the bathtub, one acknowledged me."

"Was he a bond jumper at some point? One you collected? Or did he post for someone else? Or an inmate at Leavenworth, maybe? Somebody you served with? Lots of vets become bikers. Like the Hell's Angels."

"The guy who started the Filthy Thirteen was Choctaw and an Okie. You never heard of him in school? He was a legend in the Army. The Hell's Angels were disenfranchised airplane mechanics. Nobody really heard about them until they got violent back in the seventies. The Filthy Thirteen have had movies made about their actions during the Second World War. When they were still relatively respectable. *The Dirty Dozen. The Inglorious Bastards.* TCM stuff."

"I guess you know that because you're a vet?"

I shrug. "I've still no idea who they were," I say finally. "My bell got rung before I got a good look at him. They beat me to the point of unconsciousness, repeatedly, so anything I do say, your DA will call inadmissible." That is true. "I'd be happy never to come across those two again." That is a lie. "It's not like I want to go hunting them." Also, an inaccurate statement. And with the skin as swollen and tight on my face as it is, lying comes easily. Whatever is in the IV drip makes me sound as disinterested as could be. Almost apathetic to my own plight.

The deputy excuses herself without further questioning.

~

A doctor comes in around lunch to discuss my discharge, the best methods for at-home care, what over-the-counter anti-inflammatories she recommends, et cetera. My stitches will dissolve on their own, so I will not need to come back for that. The doctor goes on to tell me where the nearest IHS clinic is in case I need further, non-emergency medical care; her nurse will bring my clothes and the discharge paperwork I need to sign.

Elise materializes in the doorway while the doctor finishes her spiel.

~

Afterward, I wait in the wheelchair outside the hospital lobby's automatic doors while Elise opens the passenger door of her car. The cops put my Sunbird in impound so it wouldn't get stolen from the motel parking lot or further pilfered. It's not impounded, per se. Kept for safekeeping as a professional courtesy. For the moment, that's where it'll stay.

I still cannot see much more than shapes in the distance out of my right eye. How far off in the distance? I can't tell, so I can't see the point of asking Elise to help me retrieve my car.

"What kind of cop're you? A detective or investigator, right?" Elise says, subtle as a tornado touches down.

"Not exactly, no." I swish around a mouthful of spit, trying to do what I can to do away with the cottonmouth feeling the pain pills give me. "Have gun, will travel," I add, swiveling my head toward her. "More of a garbage man than anything else."

"Had gun," she says, correcting me, and spins the steering wheel to the right—hand over hand—revealing a field of broom corn grown by the agricultural majors at the college.

"Had a vest, too," I say over the rumble of the engine and the bounce of the tires off the poorly graded gravel road. "And a badge."

"Garbage man?" she says after she straightens the car out.

"I get paid to collect trash off the streets. If they're worth anything."

"It sounds like you're a hobo collecting aluminum cans."

"That's another way to put it."

"But they're people."

"Admittedly," I say, and look over to meet her gaze. "So, not my best pickup line?"

"You pick up the po-po's slack for cash. What Indian girl's gonna get hot for that? You ever watch your dad get cuffed, or behind glass?"

Taken aback, I listen to her. I hear her.

"Do me a favor?"

"Sure," I say back and sit up in my seat.

"Open up my glove compartment."

I do. And there sits my badge, clipped onto its lanyard and leather backing. "Thank you," I say. "These are a bitch to replace."

"It was on the floor by your bed. In your motel room. I don't think they wanted it."

"Have I thanked you yet?" I say.

"Don't worry about it, Moe. I know you were raised right."

I let her think that and sit quietly for the rest of the ride to her place.

14

"What happened to your eye?" Elise's dad, John, says to break the ice before he tucks what's left of the tobacco pouch into his left pants pocket.

"I caught a line drive at a Royals game," I say.

"Mmm, well—oof. I can't imagine how much that must've hurt," he says, showing no signs of sympathy while he shrugs his right shoulder and stump. "If you want my advice—" He waits for me to turn and look at him, so he knows he has my full attention. "Use your hands next time. Haven't you ever heard anybody say, 'Keep your eye on the ball?'" He laughs until he coughs.

Once he finally clears his throat, he adds, "You're telling me you didn't get yourself fucked up by some bikers like my daughter said?"

"Is that a better story?"

"Getting smashed in the face because you couldn't catch a baseball makes you sound like a putz," he says with a shit-eating grin, knowing he'd knocked me down a notch.

I crane my neck to look straight at the empty shirt sleeve dangling from his right shoulder and say, "Who was at bat when you caught that ball, Casey?"

He shakes his head and says, "Charley," without a hint of amusement in his voice.

Fuck.

I stay quiet while he puffs on a loosely rolled cigarette. Together we sit and watch the dogs harass one another in the side yard. I commit to saying nothing.

An eon later, Elise joins us on the porch and asks what the two of us were being so vocal about.

"Vietnam," I say.

Elise looks disheartened.

"Dad?"

He shrugs his stump.

"Do you want to tell him why you can't go around the hay baler anymore, or should I?"

"That damn thing's possessed," he says matter-of-factly before he pauses for a beat to correct course. "I had a whole story cooked up that I meant to tell him. I was acting like he had me stewing. I would have had him kissing my ass, trying to apologize, waiting on me hand and foot. But you came out here and cut me off before I even got going. I swear youth has no respect for our storytelling traditions."

Elise smiles. "Good. You two ought to get along all right, as much as you both like to joke and bullshit people."

"Moe, you Tonkawa?" the old man says.

"No, I—"

"Then I won't like you. Give up now."

"What if he's Osage?" Elise says.

"Only one of them I liked was your ma."

"Whatever, old man. Do you want some tea? It looks ready," she says, motioning to an old giant glass pickle jar warming in the afternoon sun.

"No, thanks," the old man says. "Your dogs pissed on it again."

"Are you sure the lid is on tight? It could have spilled over."

"No, it's sticky on the outside. Tacky."

"Sweet tea gets tacky, too, from all the sugar. If it gets spilled."

"Tastes like dog piss, too."

"You tasted it?" she says.

"I stuck my finger in it and licked my fingertip."

"Inside the jar?" she says. "Are you saying my tea tastes like piss?"

"No, I stuck my finger in the mess on the outside of the jar and then stuck my finger in my mouth," he says. "It was definitely dog piss."

I laugh until I have to excuse myself to go find some relief in pill form.

15

Always on the clock, I tie up the phone line for the better part of that afternoon with Metro Bail Bonds LLC, writing out every detail of Mr. Eric Delvin Drumgoole Junior's file by hand on scratch paper: social security number, date of birth, home address, home of record, next of kin, marital status, all the aforesaid on his supposed spouse as well, vehicle information, bank information from the bond paid for his release prior to trial and sentencing.

Guilt-ridden, he told the court he was prepared to pay restitution and swore to plead no contest if only he could have some time to get his personal affairs in order.

I have to remind my employer I no longer have a recent picture of his mug. The fax they sent to the diner where Elise waits tables came out so dark he looks to be of African American descent, and my artistic abilities are nowhere near where they needed to be to make up for it, so, following some groveling, the Anadarko Sheriff's Office agrees to send out a booking photo they have from a few years back.

With my new notes and yet-to-be-connected dots sprawled out on the coffee table, it dawns on me that if you stare at something long enough—even with one eye—you can still see double somehow. Or maybe it's the codeine the hospital loaded me up with on my way out the door that's made my handwriting look like a 3-D movie when the glasses slide down to the tip of your nose.

"What size are your feet?" Elise's dad says and plops himself on the sofa beside me, which causes me in my relaxed state to slouch toward him some, stopping short of flopping my head on what's left of his stump. He wedges his cane in the cushion between us the way someone might use the little divider at the grocery store checkout. Or perhaps like a caring father.

"Mmmm…ten."

"That a guess?"

"I guess," I say, not so sure anymore. "Depends on the brand?"

"What're you hopped up on?" he says, lifting his lip the way Elvis so famously did, but with a glint of irritation.

"Doctor gave me co…dean." I had to stop and think.

"What, y'ain't been rolled before?" he says.

"Some bones in my face got cracked."

"Hollywood ain't going to give you a call anytime soon. Lucky for you, Elise has a soft spot for strays." He pauses and muses aloud, "I wonder if that stuff would do anything about my arm."

"Why? What's the matter with it?" I say and look over to his left side.

He flops his stump and says, "I feel lightning strikes now and again. It feels like my hand explodes when the electricity leaves my fingertips. I need to numb it."

"Too bad, so sad," I say with a tongue that feels swollen and heavy. I lick the air and do what I can to scrape the cotton off my tongue with my top row of teeth. I try to work up some saliva, but it seems someone turned an entire sleeve of saltines into dust and poured the whole works down my throat.

I cough and cannot stop. I cough so hard I sit up straight without having to try.

My back threatens to lock.

I take shallow breaths to decrease the stabbing pain. I lower my head in the hope that the air will get thinner and cooler between my knees.

"See what happens when you deny an elder something so simple?" John says.

Elise walks into the living room with a glass of water in one hand and a gel mask she's pulled from the freezer in the other. As instructed, I down the water, one small sip at a time, until my cough turns to a lingering tickle. She reclines me back in the chair and works the baby blue gel mask over my head and hair, resting it over my eyes.

"How do you spell relief?" she says, which gets her dad to laugh and say, "Howgh, Quien-No-Sabe. Who is that masked man?"

I pray he works himself into a coughing fit, too. But some prayers go callously unanswered. Just ask Garth. *It's all right. I'll just give him some Pan-Indian grandbabies,* I think and blindly smile.

"Ignore him," Elise says, and takes the glass back. "Put your feet up, Moe. There's nothing on the coffee table that you need to worry about knocking on the floor. Get some rest," she says, and leaves me with the softest kiss on my forehead.

16

The first thing I see with any clarity through my right eye in I-don't-know-how-many days is what I'll call an indigo sky decorated with neon pink clouds. That's to say, Oklahoma does not strike me as all that bad at this particular moment.

Earlier in the a.m., I grabbed a pair of Yoko Ono–looking wraparound sunglasses of the gas station variety while Elise topped off her tank on the way to work. I paid for the petrol, too, on principle.

The purple discoloration has left the right side of my face and since traded places with a dark mustard yellow. Still, it is unsightly. I look at it in the glass until the sun makes the outside brighter than the inside of the Waffle Hut where I sit by my lonesome, perched atop a stool at the counter that runs the width of the front window so folks can people-watch once the town is again populated. I, however, am here to wait for the Lawson impound lot to open.

Bottomless cups of coffee were made for such occasions.

I don't suspect the Waffle Hut loses much cash on the deal. Not with how their coffee runs right through you and cleans each inch of your intestines—better than drinking Drāno.

On my way back from the crapper, my stomach lets go of a muffled yowl in protest of its vacant state, which forces me to pull the menu from behind the napkin holder and hail a waitress so I can partake in the Whole Hog Waffle Taco. I make a show of holding my hand over the top of my coffee cup while I ask the waitress if she has any of the unleaded variety somewhere back behind the counter, for fear of Señor Juan Valdez sending me back to the baño muy pronto.

"As long as you don't mind waiting while I have some brewed," she says. "The road tar from before isn't treating you right?" She laughs. "Ranchers love it."

"Well, meth's illegal," I say. "But your regular coffee's given me the shakes." I mean the shits, but I say the shakes out of politeness. I suspect she understands me either way.

I walk up behind the guy who runs the impound lot while he is still fighting with the gate. Out of courtesy, I drag my feet in the loose gravel to announce my presence and not spook the guy. Do unto others.

"G'morning, Bruce Lee!" spills out of the man's mouth before he enjoys a laugh by himself. He, of course, is poking fun at my throwback sunglasses and my ambiguous ethnicity hidden behind them.

I smile to let him know I get his joke and let him think that's what makes me laugh, too. I peel the glasses off my ears, and say, "Good morning to you, sir," and give him an overexaggerated head nod.

With a face so beaten, broken, and swollen, every movement feels like doing too much.

"Shit, Lord. Who'd you piss off?"

I stare at him through my black, brown, and red bullseye of a right eyeball. "I did not get a good look at their back bumper. But if you got a blue Sunbird in there with Kansas plates," and point inside the gate, "I'll start the hunt. I just need my war pony."

"Oh." I can see the lights flicker to life behind his eyeballs, "Out of the hospital, are ya? Didn't expect you. Those boys usually put a guy in a wheelchair or the cemetery."

"What?" I say. "Have you been borrowing it out for joyrides?" Standing as tall as I can to look over his shoulder and inside the lot.

"No," he says and does all he can to roll his brain around inside his skull while he forces the corners of his mouth into a jackass's smile. "I didn't expect you so soon, is all. The car's fine. Fine as it was when it came in. Cops don't even use 'em for undercover stuff until they've sat for ninety days. It's true, what they told me? You a bounty hunter?"

"That's the short version."

"Might I ask, why aren't you driving something different?" he says with a glance over his shoulder. "Or put a cage in the back of this one you got?"

"I've never chased a bond this far before."

"Well," he says. "Welcome to Indian Country."

"Thanks," I say and smile and look around. "It's nice to be back. When will you all be clearing out?" He can't see the smirk on my face on account of my popping the trunk, but I imagine he can hear it in my voice.

"No time soon. Pretty much anybody who's been here for three generations or more is an enrolled Indian," he says.

I furrow my brow.

"That's not how it works where I'm from," I say.

We count coup and quantum.

My vest got taken. As did my holster. As did anything a cop might want an extra of. Or a biker might take as a souvenir. Or either might want for their next home invasion.

Nothing inside the cab got messed with as far as I could tell. While I wait for the engine to warm, it dawns on me that the impound lot troll had a point. Even if I knocked the guy out, sooner or later the sonofabitch would come to, and there is no way anyone who does not want to stay in my Sunbird for a three-hundred-mile ride could be made to do so.

Window tint would at least help it look less kidnappy. That I can do myself. Unfortunately, I cannot get a police cage from the automotive section at the local Kmart. So I again find myself at the edge of town, outside the Red Dirt Chop Shop, owned and operated by your local, friendly neighborhood peckerwoods.

Peckerwoods keep dogs as lawn ornaments and teach said mongrels to be equally dogmatic when it comes to the supremacy of their blond-haired, blue-eyed Jesus. Which means I stay seated in my vehicle until someone gets curious enough to come see who's idling in their parking lot. *Hank Williams the Roy Orbison Way*, stuck in the stereo's CD player, waits for me to press play, so I do.

17

A knock thunders across the hood of my Pontiac, popping my eyes open. I find an older, ashen man hunched over my hood, peering into my windshield, dressed in bib overalls, no shirt, wearing a well-worn beaver felt top hat like Lincoln. But unlike the Great Emancipator, this fellow looks more like the emancipated. Though, through my confusion, and understanding that anyone in this country can be a mix of anything, I stay quiet and wait for him speak.

"You okay?" he hollers through the glass while he wipes sweat from his face with a canary yellow paisley handkerchief.

"Fuck me running," I say under my breath and kill the engine. I sit a second, and squint through the glass at this elderly gentleman who looks like he'd been carved from knotted mahogany, not sun-bleached pine as expected. I glance back to the woodpeckers painted on the shop window and tow truck door. Then I pop the driver's side door open to plant a foot on the blacktop parking lot. "Do you… were you walking by?"

"Own the place with my son," he says and looks over his shoulder toward the office. "You all right?" he repeats, after he looks back at me.

"Own it?" I again regard the painted cartoon woodpecker on the office building picture window.

"Yeah, for a while now. Awarded the property as part of a

restitution agreement from the crackers who—well, you wouldn't know anything about that," he says and points toward my license plate. "Kansas, I see. Let's talk inside. The heat's killing old fossils like me up in Chicago, so it sure as shit wouldn't think twice about doing it down here."

Inside the shop, he invites me to sit on a cracked leather couch and pulls a pair of pop bottles out of the mini fridge. "Sorry, it's sugar-free, but the doctor tells me I have prediabetes. And I plan to keep my feet."

"Thank you," I say and hoist the icy glass bottle into the air.

"You hear about all that mess up in Chicago last week? Five or six hundred folks died from the heat."

"No, I did not. I've been busy."

"They're saying seven hundred found now," his son, presumably, says from behind another desk, squeezed along the wall on the other side of a row of filing cabinets. "Probably more with no family or people to check in on them."

"Seven hundred," the old-timer says and tumbles the new number around in his head. Then he turns to me. "I can tell you right now there isn't another Sunbird in any of my lots. I won't have much of anything for what you're driving."

Mounted to the wall above his head, I spy an Oklahoma Sales Tax Permit issued to one Severenus Henry DuPree.

"Do I call you Sever—"

"Yep, that's a fun one for most to pronounce. *Saw-vern-e-us.* 'Verne' for short. Or 'Pop' works, too.'"

"All right, Pop. Thanks again for the soda. It's nice and cold."

"Pop," he said, correcting me. "Here we say 'pop' and 'supper.' That's how we can tell a local from a Fauxklahoman."

"Fauxklahoman?"

"It's French-Creole for 'fake Oklahoman.'"

"You're Creole?"

"Grandfolks came up here from Louisiana. Now, what specifically can I help you with today?"

"Have you seen the five-point harnesses they have on helicopters?"

"Sorry to say, we're fresh out of helicopter parts."

"Fortunately, they're the same kind used in race cars. Sport mods, pure stocks, modifieds. I think they are pretty much the standard on dirt track cars."

"I might be able to help you. Might," he reiterates. "Got to understand, most of them we see are folded up pretty bad, burned out, or stripped clean of anything they can reuse before we go get them. We usually crush them and get the cash for the metal."

"I won't get my hopes too awfully high."

"Hate to shit in your grits."

"That may be what's missing from grits."

"I'll stick to my butter, salt, pepper, and cheese, thank you," he says, with a grin. "What we do here is charge forty percent of the new original stock prices for whatever you pull off one of our vehicles. Fifty percent if you use our tools. Seventy-five percent if we pull it for you. We're not out to rob nobody. But we got to keep the lights on."

"Cash work for you?" I say.

Pop doesn't answer. He just lets my words fold into the air-conditioned recycled office air.

When I head out back, I clock two peregrine falcons perched along the power line. They scan the bits of grass and gravel between the rows of automobiles and wait for a mouse to scurry out into the daylight. Seeing those fine feathered friends is a comfort. Not that I am afraid of mice. But mice mean snakes. The problem isn't so much the snakes as having to separate the copperheads, cottonmouths, timber, and pygmy rattlers from the forty or so other kinds of slithering assholes who call Oklahoma home. Whether they can send me to the hospital or the hereafter serves as the deciding factor in whether I will go for the extra point, try to punt them over the fence, or if I'll have to do the high-step freakout that Saturday morning cartoons taught us is the only logical action to take in their presence.

Dirt track race cars are boxy and bigger than most passenger vehicles, with bright paint jobs to ensure they're seen while winding their way around an oval track, no matter their speed or distance from your seat in the stands. Billboards, basically. Not what I'd consider difficult to spot in a field of sedans and minivans and pickup trucks. Especially with hide-and-go-seek being my profession.

Oddly enough, such a vehicle does, indeed, prove hard to spot. But the roof on the one I spot got twisted and collapsed from a rollover or wreck, giving it the profile of a Del Sol stripped of its wheels and tires.

The tell was how it looked like two pickup truck beds sitting butted up against each other: one painted a safety yellow sort of color and the other an unearthly green, giving it the look of an off-brand lemon-lime soda can.

"I'll need to borrow a socket set and a pipe cutter," I say to no one in particular after I waltz once again into the office.

"You found something out there, I take it?" Pop says. "We thought we might have to send a search party for you. A pipe cutter, you say. Whatever for?"

"I can't open the door."

"You can't Bo Duke it?"

"The roof is collapsed a good bit of the way down."

"I see," he says. "I imagine the driver got out of that wreck one way or another. I doubt they left him in there."

"You mean I have to crawl in whichever way he crawled out, but backward?"

"That's me saying I don't remember seeing a pipe cutter. You might be able to jack it up and get in from underneath. I don't know if it's a solid body or not. It might be a tub. It might just be a tube frame. No telling, really. That harness you're after is attached to the frame, not part of the seat, see? You can't yank the seat out, separate the belts from it, and toss the seat. You got to pull the *whole* thing out," he says.

I know lifting it off the ground wouldn't bring me anything but my nightmares to fruition, so I stick the jack in the door between the A and B pillars and widen the gap to where I can get through. The car is built with a solid metal tub that got wrecked and rolled and left looking cavernous. Factor in how it gets warmed by the sun all day and radiates heat after the sun sets, and I have trouble imagining a snake wanting to live anywhere but.

If people think those professional pit crews move lickety-split, it's because no one got to see me work on that race car. It's a safe bet I spent no more than seconds spinning the ratchet and pulling the harness free from the frame, believing myself within striking distance of a clutch of baby rattlers that didn't know any better than to give up all their venom in a single strike. Not that I could have heard their rattles over the blood swishing through my ears as fast as my heart could pump. The thing felt like a convection oven, too, which got me sweating so bad it looked like I pissed myself.

Finally it's mine.

How to get the harness installed into my Pontiac is another conundrum unto itself.

Once I give up trying to figure it out, I feed a guy at a local machine shop a story about how my son is a vulnerable teenager and cannot sit up straight in the car with a regular seatbelt. I make it clear I don't want him slouching in case the car ever crashes—to avoid whiplash and whatnot. So, the harness can't be stuck in the center of the back seat, because he could still slip out of the thing and right through the windshield if we ever crashed at highway speeds.

God forbid.

Since I need to keep one eye on the road, I ask if it couldn't be mounted directly behind the passenger seat. I add that my boy wears a helmet, so I have no concern about him hitting his head on the window.

The shop owner tells me three-fifths of the harness I brought in will match up. But the two additional straps would require him to weld new mounts.

I tell him I don't care how it looks. It's for my son's safety.

He says not to worry. He'll make it look so slick my boy will believe he's a real race car driver. After that, he offers his own story about a cousin with a similar affliction. But his aunt and uncle left him in a group home. So, knowing the personal sacrifice I'm making by caring for my son myself, he doesn't have it in him to charge me too much for the installation.

"Christ," Elise says, when I fill her in. "Lying is like breathing for you, ain't it?"

"No, cop work—investigations—is mostly acting. Call it community theater. I deal with criminals who do not want to be caught. This town is tiny. Sound travels faster here."

"Okay, Columbo," she says, and turns the engine over. "Is there someplace you want to go before we head out to my place?"

"Ah." I search my pockets for a piece of paper I'd torn from a phonebook. "Candy's Toy Box, it's called."

"Excuse me? Come again."

I fish the paper from my wallet and say, "Candy's Toy Box on South Quay Boulevard."

"I know the place you're talking about, Moe, you pervert. You know my dad stays at my place all the time now, right?"

"I need a set of handcuffs."

"I am not into that, Jesus!" she says, way too loud for the windows being rolled up. Her cheeks are flushed, and she does all she can to smooth away her curious smile from the curled corners of her mouth.

“For work. I need some other stuff, too,” I say. “Restraints.”

“Oh, okay,” she says in a tone full of amusement, widening her eyes and arching her eyebrows skyward.

“Do you know of some other place that sells that stuff?”

“I don’t know what kind of stuff that place sells,” she says, blushing again.

“Mmmhmm,” I say and let go a chuckle, as does she while she spins the steering wheel and points her car south.

“I am not going in with you at the toy store.”

“Fine then. Be that way. Sit out in the parking lot. Would you like to borrow my sunglasses, or are you good with hiding your face in your hands?”

“Shut up. I’ll park next door at the liquor store.”

“Oh, that’s a much better place to loiter.”

“All right,” she says, “Fine. Give me your glasses, then. Are you so sure you want to go in there looking all beat up?”

“Something tells me I won’t be the only one in there with bruises. It’s a whatever-floats-your-boat kind of place, right? No judgment and all of that. But you go ahead and stay out in the parking lot. I am sure no one from the diner will recognize your car.”

“Ass,” she says, and smiles, and accelerates to make the yellow light.

18

"Elise tells me you two went shopping," John says, and spears an olive out of a jar he's got squeezed between his knees.

I nod. "We got groceries and stuff. That's where we got the olives."

"And before that?" he says, stabbing at a different olive.

I shake my head, hoping to change the station. "Errands, you know. Odds and ends."

"Odds and ends, huh? Whips and chains is what I heard," he says, with a low growl that grows into a snicker.

"I needed handcuffs and a few other things and figured they'd have the high-end stuff. Town's too small for a tactical supply store."

"If that's your story," he says, and gnaws absently on an olive. Before I can say something back, he lets go of a god-awful "Gawh!" and chokes on what sounds like a mouthful of marbles. The old man spits into the palm of his hand. "Goddammit, they're pitted," he says and slams his fist onto his thigh.

"Mmm—sonofabitch," he moans.

"What's going on?" Elise says, and hangs up the kitchen telephone.

"Broke a tooth," her dad says, sounding garbled.

"What? How? Let me see."

"On a damn olive pit is how," he says, scolding her.

"Shit, Dad. You said you didn't like the ones stuffed with pimento."

"That doesn't mean I like pits. For Chrissake, Elise."

I stand and say, "You got any aspirin in the medicine cabinet, or what's it called, Anbesol?"

"Aspirin, I think. Yeah, yeah," Elise says while making her dad say ahh.

"Moe, can you go and grab a couple for me?"

"How many?" I say.

"A couple," she says with a shrug. "A couple is two, ain't it?"

I bring the bottle.

"Whiskey, please," the old man begs.

"Whiskey will thin your blood, and you'll bleed worse," Elise says.

"Aspirin will thin my blood, too, dingdong."

Elise gives him a trio of aspirin gel capsules, which he washes down with a mouthful of blood and spit while Elise reclines the rocker into something of a daybed.

A while later, he stirs, arches his back, and turns his head to the left and then to the right.

With Elise nowhere in eyesight, he snaps his fingers to get my attention, and whispers, "Hey, what'd they give you for pain at the hospital when you got the facelift?" Pointing to his face in a clockwise motion as if my cracked cheekbones have somehow slipped my mind.

"Codeine," I say. He snaps his fingers two or three times, opens his hand, palm facing up, and stares at me without blinking or speaking. "One," I say loud enough so only he can hear it, before I get up and fish the bottle out of my jacket pocket.

19

Elise has two cattle dogs. They're both Blue Heelers, named Salt and Pepper. Littermates. Both bitches, or dames, I believe, is a better way to say it. Elise let on that I need not worry about which one is Salt and which one is Pepper, seeing as how when you call one, you get the other. Plus, it doesn't roll off the tongue quite right to call Pepper's name before Salt's, even with the latter nowhere in sight. That, she said, was a bit of shortsightedness on her part. But the shoe fits them both, respectively. Salt looks mostly white, with bits of black peppered here and there. Pepper looks mostly black, like a McFlurry that's more Oreos than soft serve.

If anyone wearing a badge ever heard someone holler out for Salt and Pepper, they'd figure it for a poorly veiled code to let everyone know the police were paying a visit—seeing as how they drive black and white vehicles. For figuring this out, cops consider themselves cleverer than the average bear. They'd call you on it, too, to let you know they are aware and unappreciative of your antics. Then, when the girls appear looking every bit of their namesakes, officers tend to deflate and place their dominant hand somewhere else along their utility belts, no longer hovering it over their holsters. This all comes second-hand, of course. I didn't get to see it for myself.

I'm still in the back bedroom, waking from a late afternoon nap with Salt and Pepper and codeine, when a cop lets themselves into the back door of Elise's trailer home and, shortly after that, scrapes the feet of one of Elise's kitchen table chairs along the floor before they plop down hard enough for me to guess their weight like a carnival worker.

I didn't hear them knock or announce themselves the way they're supposed to, so I'm especially curious as to the purpose of this house call, and, as I've been told since childhood: if you're going to eavesdrop, you damn well better pay attention.

Before the cop opened the door and came inside the house—uninvited—I heard another officer come over their radio talking in drawled 10 codes to the emergency dispatcher. His voice sounded slowed for the sake of clarity, combined with the recognizable hangover that follows working outside in the warmest part of the summer all bundled up in a bulletproof vest and drinking cheap coffee doctored with gas station-brand powdered creamer that curdles in the gut.

I knew it to be a police radio in the same way a priest knows when they hear the possessed recite Hellspeak, rather than some poor mentally ill soul talking gibberish. It's a sound that will dry you out and tamp you down in the dirt of the here and now.

Déjà vu is nowhere near the right word for waking from yet another medicated nap to hear the voice of the deputy from the hospital. She asks where Salt and Pepper are, which tells me she's been to the house before.

"The girls are in bed with him. Those pain pills put him down hard," Elise says. She sounds like she is trying to shoo the sheriff's deputy away, the same as the doctor had.

"Good," the deputy says. "The girls taking to him tells me I don't have to worry about him out here with the both of you."

"No, Dad likes him too. Won't let on that he does, though."

"That's something. Your dad don't like himself," the deputy says. "Your bounty hunter boyfriend can take a beating. Wonder if he can hand one out as well."

"Don't know. Don't imagine he'd be chasing after criminals if he couldn't handle himself, though," Elise says. "Coffee'll take another minute."

"Oh, bless you. My ass is dragging, Lise."

She calls her "Lise," which comes out sounding like "Lease" instead of "Elise," so I assume they know one another. So Elise hadn't called the cops, or had the cops called on her. This is something of a social call. I relax a bit.

The need to relieve myself arises, as it does when one first wakes. The problem is, I'm keen to let them believe I'm still knocked out. I don't want to interrupt their conversation, which means I can't flush. Luckily, I don't need to walk with any stealth, though, since the slightest breeze gets the trailer to sway.

I ease myself back onto the mattress between Salt and Pepper and close my eyes to focus on the conversation coming from down the hall.

"Maybe we should become bounty hunters, Lise."

"What now? Like in, what was that show, *Cagney and Lacey*? Can anybody do it?"

"No, they were cops. I mean like *Simon and Simon*."

"Weren't they private detectives and dudes? Yeah, they were. I remember. We could be like Thelma and Louise!"

"Shit, no. You didn't see that movie all the way through, did you?"

"Thought I had."

"No, crazy. Anybody can make a citizen's arrest, you know that, right? Being a bounty hunter is the same thing. Basically, just got to work for a bail bondsman," the deputy says. "I could teach you how to fight and take someone down, cuff and search and all that like they teach at the academy."

"Please, girl," Elise says. "I'll kick your dick in the dirt."

"Your ass'll probably end up in jail, the way you fight."

"What, bounty hunters can't bring someone in dead or alive?"

"Fuck no!" she says, then clicks off her radio. "Hell no."

"Coffee looks about done," Elise says.

"A big cup, please."

"You know where they are," Elise says and slides the pot back onto the burner. "I am not waitressing in my own house. You cops don't tip for shit."

"Sheesh, okay then. Grouchy, aye?"

"Hey, you turned off your radio. You're off duty. You only get free coffee and your ass kissed when I am at work. You're family here."

"Ain't that what they like to tell customers at the diner, too?"

"Please, it's only because the regulars *are* family."

"Fine—but for that, I am *not* getting rid of any more tickets for you."

"You bitch!" Elise laughs into her coffee cup. "That's like abuse of power."

"Join up. Then you won't get any anymore," Abby says. "No, you know what? I remember them talking about how they plan to bring in another dispatcher before fall. Why not apply?"

"What all would I have to do?"

"You know…"

"No, I don't. That's why I asked you, Sherlock."

"Answering phones and talking on the radio and stuff."

"And stuff?"

"You can type, huh?"

"Not like crazy fast, but yeah."

"Okay, then. You'll do fine. Think of it like being a secretary or waitressing: someone places an order, you write it all down, let the cooks know, and then you check in with them until the service is provided. Then you do it all over again the next time your phone rings," the deputy says.

"Sitting on my ass all day?"

"Yeah. In the AC without ever having to walk into a hot kitchen,

Lise. Ain't it better than wearing a skirt and apron that smells like old French fries? Does your hair still smell like fried onions, like my auntie used to say?"

"Maybe."

"That's gross, dude," the deputy says through a growl that comes after she chugged too much and too hot of coffee at once.

"Whatever. Which one of us is getting laid?"

"So what, cousin? You've got a drugged man in your bed. Better watch it. Might have to bring you in if we get any complaints," she says, almost trailing into song.

"Shut up about my love life, aye," Elise says.

"Any good?"

"Shut up!"

"Give me something. Details. C'mon, I canceled my satellite like two months back already. I've got no more Skinemax at the house."

Elise giggles. "Ever think maybe he is only crashing here?"

"Whatever, you're not so stupid. Don't lie to me, little cousin. That's fresh meat," she says, and the kitchen goes quiet. "C'mon, you can't give me that look and then say nothing."

"Change the channel, Deputy."

"Whatever, I have to pee anyway."

"You know where it is. I am going to check on him. He's been out a little longer than usual."

"Okay, yeah. Maybe we should have been whispering, Lise. He should be getting used to those pain pills by now, you'd think."

"I don't know. I'm not a pillhead."

With that, the doorknob twirls and my eyes slam shut. Pepper stirs once Elise steps up to the side of the bed, and I blink my eyes open. "Afternoon," I say.

"Good morning."

"Really?" I say, legitimately confused, and look for a clock. "Time is it?"

She laughs and says, “It’s almost time to eat. I came to see what you are making for dinner.”

“What, am I cooking?”

“Yeah, you. I’ve been working all day, serving food. I’m done with that. Unless you’re paying me,” Elise says and waits to hear my counteroffer. “So, whatcha making us for dinner?”

“My specialty, of course,” I say and scoot myself back toward the headboard. “Chili mac, if you got the stuff.”

“Blah.”

“I’m going to get going, Lise,” bounces down the hall.

Elise puts her chin over her shoulder and says, “All right. See ya.”

“Who’s that?” I say, wanting to see what she’ll say.

“Cousin of mine came over to say hi after work. Wanted to tell me about a job.”

“Oh yeah?”

“Yup,” Elise said. “Yesterday you had me take you to the sex shop, and today I find you in my bed with two girls? Getting a little brave around here, aren’t you?”

I laugh and pet Salt and Pepper.

“G’off the bed, girls,” Elise says. But they don’t budge. They only shift their glances in her direction to see if she means it. “Hey, get down off the bed, I said.”

One hops down onto the carpet while the other stays and stares at Elise.

“Down,” Elise says again. “He’s mine,” she adds and lays next to me.

“Oh, yeah?” I say. “Don’t I get some say?”

“Nope.”

20

The sound of a lone motorcycle wakes me.

It's dark outside and in. The rest of the world is asleep, so I sit in bed and swing my feet to the floor, and into my Doc Martens.

The noise hasn't caused Elise to stir, so I charge into the kitchen, grab the knife block, tuck it beneath my elbow, and fix my eyes on the front door. I pull the cleaver before trading it for a carving knife. I zigzag around the kitchen island, the dinner table, the loveseat, the couch, the ottoman before I take a knee behind the recliner, where I wait in the shadow.

And wait.

I get startled awake by the sound of a Polaroid camera coming to life.

"Are you wearing a pair of my daughter's boots?" John says while he wafts the picture in the air. He darkens the window in the top half of the front door. Daylight has come, but barely. It's that magical time of morning when old folks wake before the birds or the automatic coffeemaker. Though there's no sudden crowing rooster, thanks to the umpteen kept by the neighbor.

"They're my boots," I say and stand, covering myself with the knife block.

"What do you call that color?" he says. "It's…pretty. Purple. Or what's that other one called, mauve?"

"Oxblood," I say, and slide the carving knife back into its self-sharpening slot inside the block. “They’re oxblood.”

“Cute,” he says and sits in the recliner. Without another word, he puts the footrest up in the air. There he sits and sips his coffee while he watches the sun lift off the Cimarron basin.

Had I not crashed where his favorite chair reclined, he might have let me be.

An old man staring out a window with his glasses still stuck in his shirt pocket paints a picture I am not eloquent enough to examine at this particular moment, not with the evening I had. Plus, I can smell myself and need to wash off the sweat and the sex and the carpet fuzz that is now stuck to my scrotum. I leave John and let him enjoy the rising sun—or my full moon—to shower.

I goddamn near die when I step into the tub and fail to notice a bottle of Vagisil tipped and ran down the shower wall and left a puddle of goo the same color as the bathtub.

The top of my head smacks the door.

My back slaps the linoleum.

I spend God-knows-how-long waiting for my lungs to reinflate while staring at a stark-naked lightbulb, which I estimate to be mounted four inches off-center. Eventually I peel myself off the floor and bathe. But not before my vision becomes a blur, and I hear John grumbling about whatever on Earth has the bathroom door blocked.

“Can’t hold it for long at my age,” he says to me, or himself.

“Out in a minute,” I holler.

“Oh,” and “Okay,” and “How about you get out now before I crap my pants,” is what he says back.

The water is tap temp by the time I collect myself. The water heater gave up every drop it had, so I bathe with water pumped straight out of the spring-fed well that comes with the subtle smell of spoiled eggs. As do I, for the remainder of the afternoon.

21

"Daytime is the wrong time to go ferreting out folks like the Drumgooles," John says. He clears his throat to make sure he has my attention. "You've got to go after them nonchalantly. Go with the element of surprise."

"Oh, you mean nocturnally?"

"That too," he adds and places a heavy green canvas zippered bag onto the end table. The stencil on the side reads US. The weight and the oblong triangle shape of it tell me it's a pistol. The box of .45 caliber ammunition he balances on top of the canvas bag assures me we aren't shooting the proverbial shit.

"That's a 1911," he says.

"Yours?"

He nods. "It was my father's. Mine now."

"You giving it to me?" I say, not sure of what is happening, wondering whether Christmas has come early.

He snorts. "Over my dead body. You're a have-gun-will-travel type, aren't you?"

"I am."

"One without a gun. And you're not doing much traveling, from what I can see, either. You need a gun, and you need to get on, don't you?"

"Yessir, that I do," I say.

"All right then."

I don't say or assume a thing. Or reach for the gun. Nor does he.

"My goddamn tooth hurts something fierce," he says. "Warm saltwater don't do jack diddly shit."

"If you want me to drive you to the dentist, all you have to do is ask."

"Is that so?"

"Yessum."

"He'll charge me fifty bucks to open up and say ahh."

"So," I say and point toward the pistol, "do you want me to take you out back and put you out of your misery?"

"That don't sound so bad," he says. "Before we try that. Do you have any more of whatever they gave you for your face?"

"Would you like another?"

"If you would, please. If you're not running low."

I shake a single tablet into his outstretched palm, and John brings his hand to his face so fast it looks like he's about to render a crisp salute.

"Water?" I say and stand to start toward the kitchen.

"No need. Already down the hatch." He sticks his tongue out, showing a chalky white streak trailed toward his tonsils, which reminds me of my time at Leavenworth passing out pills after morning count.

He pulls back on a lever that sends his feet flying almost before I can step out of the way. He lets go of a laugh while I twist the cap onto the bottle and retreat toward the bedroom. "Oh, no. Leave the bottle, barkeep," he says, and places his one hand atop mine.

I don't hand the bottle over, but set it alongside the pistol on the coffee table.

"Where you going now?" the old man says.

"I need a glass of water," I say. "I've got a flavor in the back of my throat. I haven't eaten all day."

"Water ain't going to fix it. Make you some lunch."

"You hungry?" I say and peel open a cabinet door.

"Nope. Thanks. I'm sleepy as all hell, though."

"I can't imagine why," I say to myself and close the cabinet door before I peer inside the refrigerator.

"Slap something between two slices of bread and get back in here so I can show you this government Colt. It ain't dummy-proof like what the Army uses these days."

"Is that so?" I'm still staring into the fridge, wondering whether he is calling me a dummy or merely repeating something he'd heard his father say one time too many.

"Yep. Grab something out of the crisper, too. You'll live longer."

"All right."

"Surprised you haven't died of scurvy, eating the way you do."

"You're not wrong," I say, not specifying what I am referring to.

"Thanks. Now tell me something I do not know," he says.

I contemplate saying something concerning his daughter's bedroom proclivities, but he has the gun in hand. I keep chewing and offer him a smile instead.

"Finish your sandwich and wash your hands before you touch this, understand?"

"Yup," I mutter with a mouthful of Wonder Bread stuck to the roof of my mouth.

Once I join him in the living room again, he drops the magazine and releases all the safeties, goes over all the interlocking plugs and pins until he has it lying in two pieces: the upper and lower.

"I trust you know how to clean a pistol."

"I do, indeed."

"All right. I'm going to sit right here and watch you put it back the way it was, and you're not taking it anywhere until you do it the proper way, got it?"

"Got it."

"All right," he says and lobs another codeine tablet onto his tongue. "Let's see if you were paying attention."

By the time I point the pistol toward the coffee table to perform a functions check, his lights are still on, but nobody's home. He isn't sleeping, from what I can tell, unless he does so with his eyes open. He isn't blinking or reacting to anything I say or do. Not even when I load the magazine to capacity, seat it, send the slide home, and say, "Merry Christmas to me."

22

To make money, you have to spend money. Somehow gas is a buck fifteen a gallon, so I have to break a ten-dollar bill to top off my tank. It should cost me one hell of a lot less, with all the pump jacks people here have for lawn ornaments. I guess not every company passes the savings on to the customer.

Gas stations are the one place where one can loiter with out-of-state plates without anyone taking note, no matter if it's right off the highway or in the middle of historic downtown Lawson. Especially if what you're driving is nothing special. You can grab lunch and one of those fountain drinks that are too big to fit inside any cup holder ever made and sit and watch the cars pass for hours on end with no one becoming suspicious. Most everyone else gets their gas, drains their bladder, fills up on snacks, buys a lotto ticket, and gets out of there as fast as they can.

The only ones who'll notice you are the ones who got there on foot and have no intention of talking to anyone with a badge. They'll ignore you right along with the warning sign that reads NO SOLICITING. You have to look like the sort of person no drunk or dusthead would ever want to ask for spare coinage. But you can't simply toss a pistol onto the dashboard, because someone else will get it in their head how you're there to hold up the place and they'll call the cops. Instead, you have to fix your face in a way that reads "fuck off" and looks incapable of expressing any other human emotion.

The Army calls this *military bearing.*

Prisons use bloodhounds and helicopters and duly commissioned marshals for this sort of work. But here I sit, playing peek-a-boo, hide-and-go-seek, and all I keep wondering is what olly olly oxen free meant when it was first coined. Was it co-opted from something else, or was it something a bunch of mush-mouthed kids came up with while conversing with a puppet sitting on a sixty-year-old man's hand on a black-and white-television show, back when colored was an okay thing to call folks but not to be born as such.

I need to find a book on tape for days like this one.

Two city cops on black and white Harleys pass by a little after two thirty. Then again at the top of the hour. Both of them shift and throttle in a way that is no good for a bike. Not that they put a penny into the purchase or upkeep. It is more of a look-at-me display of horsepower meant to impress a group of college-aged ladies standing on the sidewalk, waiting for the light to change.

The two cops' chin straps are on so tight they couldn't smile if they wanted. They look like they're holding in a log their V-twins and morning coffee want to jiggle out of them. They circle the way sharks do, waiting for their shift to come to an end. Not protecting or serving, but not doing the best job of lying in wait, either. Take away the guns and the badges and about ten years, and it's easy to imagine them patrolling the high school cafeteria for other kids half their size to punch and kick, the same way their dads did to them when they didn't make the football team.

Again.

With those two knuckleheads on the prowl, I know the probability of me seeing Eric is next to nil. Or maybe my resignation stems from how I've done away with 48oz of Jolt and have to piss so badly I can nearly taste it, which makes my attention span equivalent to that of a metal flake paint-huffer.

Staying put in the car and refilling the Styrofoam cup isn't an option, seeing as how the Jolt sits atop more cups of coffee than I can recount. That's to say, I do not wish for my cup to overfloweth. Nor do I want to show my face inside the gas station once again. Instead, I point my car east, into a less populated part of town, until I find another filling station and park beneath the canopy to keep my car cool.

"Bathroom's for paying customers only."

"I'll be topping off my tank. I just need to drain my bladder first," I say to the fucknuckle behind the counter.

"If you say so…sir. You'll need the key," he says.

"All right, where is it hiding?"

"You'll have to prepay for that gas."

"I could always piss in the trash can while I pump gas."

"Wouldn't be the first time," he says.

"Fuck. How much are hot dogs?"

"Free with a full tank of gas."

"Shit, I can't win, can I? Here's a dollar. Can I go piss now?"

He shook his head and said, "Need seven more cents from you."

"Goddamn, you. Here's a five. That enough?"

"That'll do," he says and slides the cartoonish keyring across the counter in slow motion.

I power-walk to the restroom sign and ignore him when he asks whether I'd like chili on my hot dogs. Plural. They're a half dozen for five bucks. The chili sauce comes complimentary.

I piss so long the hot dogs are cold by the time I return the bathroom key to the dickhead behind the counter. Or they could've always been lukewarm.

"You got something against folks like me? Indians?" I say, instead of what I want to—what I practiced while pissing.

"Indian? I hadn't a clue, sir. You could be from anywhere."

"Well, I am from here."

"Oh, you're not in Kansas anymore," he says, and looks out at my

Pontiac parked beside his only pump, adorned with Kansas state tags on both bumpers. “How much do you want to put on the pump?”

“I just wanted to take a piss.”

He smirks and slides a foil-paper sack full of chili dogs toward my side of the counter, where they stay. When I step out the door, I hear him say, “Have a nice day, Tonto,” only the ding that sounds each time a customer crosses the threshold doesn’t quite drown out that last bit like he’d hopped.

“Excuse me?” I say, turning on my heel. “I didn’t catch the last bit.”

Whiter now, and looking like he’s in need of the bathroom key, he says. “Toto. You know—Kansas, Toto, Wizard of Oz, all of that.”

“If you only had a brain,” I say under my breath and let the door slam.

23

The Halfway House Bar & Grill sits smack-dab between Oklahoma City and Tulsa. It's a forty-five-minute drive to the city limits of either place, and Lawson.

How I wound up inside said eating establishment is I followed a vehicle that looked a lot like the one J.R. drove the night he turned two motorcycles into one big pile of twisted metal and charred leather that stunk of undercooked meat and fresh road tar. The two bodies of the riders weren't identifiable as such. The sight was so indelible firefighters killed their lights while cleaning up the mess so rubberneckers wouldn't notice the leaked pools of gasoline and engine oil had a deep red, almost maroon hue to them.

All the aforesaid should be on my mind when I peel open the hamburger bun and splatter ketchup atop the medium-rare-grilled ground beef and the sweating, caramelized onions. Maybe it is, and it's just not enough to turn my stomach the way it might with the sensitive kind. Or maybe I am hungry enough to not have a care concerning off-putting images of roadkill. Or maybe I side somewhat more with J.R. than two dead bikers, after their brothers did what they could to turn my face from convex to concave. Or maybe I've become distracted by a poster advertising the upcoming Oklahoma State Prison Rodeo, held annually in McAlester, Oklahoma, home of the state penitentiary affectionately known as Big Mac. Also home of Mr. Eric Delvin Drumgoole Senior—arsonist extraordinaire.

I put two and two together and scoot back from my plate so fast the bartender asks me if everything wasn't all right.

"Oh, bit my cheek is all. But, while I got your attention," I say and wave a finger at the poster, "I was wondering if that's worth the drive."

"Prison rodeo? It's worth watching. I haven't been in a handful of years."

"Anybody ever make a run for it in the middle of it all?"

"Try to escape, you mean? They've pulled some stunts down there, but I don't think they'd ever do anything to jeopardize a day of fresh air. They're locked down permanently in that place. It's the one prison rodeo that's held *inside* the prison's walls. The audience has a better chance of getting locked up than an inmate going free."

I clear my throat. "Permanently?"

"Twenty-three hours a day. There was a really bad riot a few years back, maybe ten years ago now. And they burned most of the place to the ground while I was in high school. Gutted a good bit of it, at least. Hell, once upon a time, they killed a warden."

"I bet if one of them gets stomped by a bull, the guards don't let go of any tears."

"Hard to imagine. Don't get me wrong, it's a legit rodeo—for the most part. Every event you can conjure. They bring in prisoners from other places around the state. The women's prison sends inmates, too."

"Like a Catholic school mixer, then?"

"Minus the hand job under the bleachers. I'm guessing. You want another?" he says and pulls the pint glass I'd emptied off the bar.

"Nah, I need to get going soon as I kill off these fries," I say. "Water, if you will. And the check, please."

I nod and swallow the last bite of the burger on my plate.

24

When I pull into Elise's place, it is already black outside, but it might as well be the middle of the day. The old man's recliner sits in her driveway, kindling flames tall enough to see as soon as I turned the corner.

Elise sits on the ground, hugging Salt and Pepper with one arm each while she leans back against her cousin Abby, the deputy's, shins. The deputy squeezes Elise's neck with one hand and leans against the front fender of her patrol car.

Elise's eyes are wet. They glisten from the thick smoke coming off the burning Styrofoam cushions.

"What did the chair do?" I say for a hello.

"My dad shit all over it," Elise says.

I ask Elise to repeat herself, but she's bawling.

Quietly, Abby says, "It looked like he took a good bit of your pain pills. The codeine."

I didn't want to ask, but I did. "Where is he now?"

"Funeral home," the cousin says.

"The hell?"

"Lungs and heart gave out, most likely. Some folks slip into a coma, others pass when they take too much," Abby adds. "When someone takes too many like that, it'll make the pulse shallow and hard to find. But they couldn't shock him back. I think he was gone for a while before she found him. We're seeing it happen more and more. Docs hand out those pills to anyone, like aspirin."

"He had a—cracked tooth that was hurting him pretty badly, so I let him have one before I took off," I say. My hands and stomach tingle. My head feels light.

Elise turns to look my way for the first time since I walked up on the two of them. "How many?" she says.

"One."

"There's about six left in the bottle," Elise says, correcting me.

"No, that doesn't sound right. I—I had a lot more than that left. The doctor gave me almost a full month's worth. It ain't been but what, two, two and a half weeks?"

"What time did you leave him?"

"I can't remember off the top of my head."

"Where were you anyway?"

"I went to look for J.R.—Drumgoole, I mean. I thought I found his truck."

"Did you?"

"Wasn't him driving. Maybe the wife? Girlfriend from Kansas City? We hit the tollway, but I lost 'em after the tollbooth."

"Come on, girlie, let's find you some alcohol."

"That sounds magnificent," Elise says.

"Hey, Boba Fett," Abby says. "Will you watch the fire while I bring her inside?"

"Yeah, I got this," I say. "Boba Fett, huh?"

"I don't care much for cowboys. I know Indians. I don't know any other famous bounty hunters. He's goodness for the sake of greed," the cousin says over her shoulder while she walks Elise onto the porch.

"Given that some thought."

"Have you given this any thought?" Abby says, motioning to Elise when she passes through the front door.

I stay quiet.

"Or are you just playing house?" she adds after Elise steps inside. She doesn't wait for me to answer. Instead she twists the doorknob and joins Elise inside for the festivities and mourning.

25

I pick what didn't burn out of the pile of ash. It's warped metal springs and straps, mostly. What did burn, I shovel into the trash once it cools. The rest I sweep into the ditch. Inside, I rearrange the furniture, so Elise won't be greeted by the cavity where her father's recliner once stood.

The diner knows better than to expect her to come to work that morning. The two cousins slept together in the bed, and I did what I could to get comfortable on the loveseat until sunrise.

That weekend, there's a wake for the old man—closed casket, due to lack of embalming. He wanted to become part of the land, not further poison it with all the chemicals they pump the dead people full of. His words.

Just a simple pine box.

It shapes up to be a typical affair: out-of-context scripture followed by finger sandwiches and funny stories. Very little crying. Indians have an incurable habit of laughing in the face of tragedy and trauma and loss.

I've inherited his most prized possession. The pistol. Not his daughter. Indian women aren't something someone possesses. Indians might have a chief running things, of course. Then there's a council, too. But every family, clan, and nation has a matriarchy at its root.

It turns out they don't lower the dead into the dirt anymore with the family still present. The fear is folks might flop themselves on top of the casket. Caskets have flipped open and the deceased have spilled out. I, too, learn that gravediggers are both chatty and cluelessly callous. Who can blame them, though? Those they work with are closemouthed and soulless, as a rule.

Once we leave the cemetery and the number of folks who'd gathered to grieve at the house splits in half, I sit on the loveseat with one of the aunties who looks about the right age to be a sister to the old man. I don't ask her any questions. I sit and listen to her commentary and let go a laugh when there is no more keeping my eavesdropping secret.

I listen to the old woman comment about this person and that one until I begin to relearn the names Elise tried to teach me earlier. Eventually, Elise looks over to see me and the old lady leaning in toward one another, laughing at the room around us, and leaves us to our fuckery.

I don't know how long we sit, but I do remember how our conversation came to an end. One of Elise's cousins interrupted, saying, "You a cop?"

"Huh?" I say, surprised at his voice suddenly over my shoulder. "Ah, hello," I say, and turn to face my accuser. "No. I am not a cop."

"Elise told me you're BIA, like, not even two minutes ago," he says, and points back over his shoulder toward the kitchen.

I shake my head and say, "I work as a bail enforcement agent."

"That's what I said, B—I—"

The old lady cuts him off laughing, as does everyone else who's now listening.

Elise barks at him from the other room, "Stop acting like you finally fricking learned how to spell. Auntie doesn't give money for good grades anymore. You're stupid. It's embarrassing."

"It's okay, Elise," I say.

"No, it's not. He's trying to get all tough with you."

"Look," I say to make sure I have her cousin's attention. "I am a bail enforcement agent. Enforcement starts with an E, not an I.

Okay? I'm not BIA."

He narrows his eyes. I can see the wheels turn inside his noggin, so I elaborate. "A fugitive recovery agent, is that better? Make any more sense to you?"

"What do you do, though?" he says, waving his hands mockingly.

"When somebody misses court and skips out on their bond, I track them down."

"Oh, cool," he says. "So, you're like a real, live Indian tracker."

"You're stupid," Elise yells over the tops of everyone's heads again. "He's a fricking bounty hunter, dumbass."

The cousin's eyes widen. "Badass!" He sits across from the old lady and me, leans in, and stares. His lips don't budge.

Someone says something about him having a crush on me.

Someone else says something else about him wanting to partner up with me and become a bounty hunter himself. He chimes in and says, "Yeah, let me join up, man."

I swat the idea away by saying, "The money isn't great. Splitting it down the middle would make it nowhere near worth it."

"C'mon, I've seen those posters up at the post office: wanted by the FBI, one million dollars and all that."

"That's different," I say. "That's for folks who're successfully evading the FBI."

"Then what do you do?" he says again.

I feel a finger tap on the nape of my neck. I look up to see Elise standing between her cousin and me. "Hey," she says. "Take me somewhere."

"Where do you want to go?"

"I don't know. Anywhere. I am all dressed up. Auntie'll kick everybody out when she's ready to go home, won't you?"

"Sure will," the old lady says. Then she clamps her lips shut and lets out a yawn through her nose, signaling it won't be much longer before she does just that.

26

I turn over the engine and say, "All right, where are we going?"

"I don't know, anywhere," Elise says. "Screw it. Let's go bowling."

I look down toward the floor mat on the passenger side and say, "In those shoes?"

"They give you bowling shoes, ya nerd," Elise says, and I let the car roll back out into the street.

The drive over is quiet, mostly.

"You know, we're going to look entirely out of place at a bowling alley."

"No, not really," she says. "It's dark as crap in there. They have music thumping and black lights everywhere. It's as close to a nightclub as we got until things open back up in the fall."

"Are you sure you're down to bowl?"

"I'm down to not sit in the house, Moe."

No further questions.

"No valet?" I say when I pull beneath the awning. "What kind of nightclub is this?"

"Lawson's finest."

Inside, it's as Elise said: music so loud you have to lean in inches from someone's ear to talk, which adds a whole new level of intimacy to bowling.

Our first game isn't anything special. Both she and I barely break a hundred. That'll change the more I tell this story. We call it a warm-up game, ask our waitress for another round of drinks, and set up another ten frames.

"I'm going to the bathroom," Elise says. "Why don't you bowl first this time?"

I nod, and she bends over and presses her lips to my forehead midstride.

My ball is oily, so it spins this way and that all over the lane. It winds up striking the pins on the far left-hand side, knocks down a little less than half.

Four, according to the monitor overhead.

I dry my hands with the ball return while I wait for a chance to redeem myself. Elise yells my name right as my ball gets birthed back into my waiting hands. I turn my head to catch what she is saying so excitedly but we headbutt one another.

"What?" I say, after making sure she is okay.

Elise places a hand on each of my shoulders. "Eric. Eric… Drumgoole…Junior…just went into the men's room."

I stiffen and look over her shoulder toward the restrooms, and then back to her.

"I shit you not," she says.

I don't ask her to repeat herself over the music and the crashing pins. I take her for serious and make my way to the restrooms without bothering to put my ball down.

Inside the men's room stands one sink, one stall, and one urinal. The stall is occupied by someone wearing jeans and street shoes. He is either coming or going. I say that because he is either yet to change into his bowling shoes or has already changed out of them and decided to take a dump before he hits the road.

A courtesy flush is in order, but I don't let myself get too concerned with how bad the bathroom stinks. Instead, I power-walk toward the stall and tug the handle.

"Somebody's in here, man," a startled voice says. Between the crack in the door and the frame, I catch a sliver of his face, enough to know it is indeed him.

"Sorry," I say. "Are you almost done? I think I am going to crap my pants. Greasy-ass pizza got me, man."

"Yeah, gimme a second."

I rock my feet back and forth, back and forth, to make him think my pants will explode any second.

"Hold on, man, don't shit your britches. I'm wiping…okay?"

I would like to thank the academy.

I step a few feet back and lock the deadbolt while he flushes.

When the latch on the stall door clicks open, I volley the bowling ball into the door with everything I have and race behind it.

I launch myself with my right knee leading the way. My hands cover my face to avoid whiplash—should my plan take a shit.

But that doesn't happen.

Junior doesn't make a sound. Not one that can be heard over the collapse of the door, or the bowling ball wandering over the tile floor toward the sink behind me, or the spreading pool of water that issues from the ceramic tank formerly situated on the back of the toilet.

It looks like the inside of the door slapped him between the eyebrows when I sent the bowling ball into the door. His nose got knocked to the side.

His teeth look loosened, too.

He is, for the time being, what emergency medical technicians refer to as *unresponsive*.

~

Elise loiters outside the restroom. Without too many extra details, I hand her my keys, tell her I need her to go into my trunk and get the bag from Candy's Toy Box.

Meanwhile, I fish the OUT OF ORDER and PISO MOJADO signs

from the janitor's closet and wait inside the men's room for a knock from Elise.

"Holy shit," she says as soon as I let her inside.

"Help me dress him" is my only answer.

When Elise strolls out of the men's room, leading a man by a chain and metal pinch dog collar, everyone who takes their eyes off their bowling lane stares, but no one considers stopping her from leaving. Not when said man is dressed in a leather hood along with a vintage-looking straitjacket, and she's wearing a black pencil dress and a pair of high heels, hair and makeup done in a fashion sure to call to mind one of the simply irresistible women from the Robert Palmer music video.

College towns come with all sorts of curiosities.

Mister Eric Delvin Drumgoole Junior shuffles his feet as far as the ankle chain will allow, almost two-stepping along with the music synced with the laser lights in the bowling alley.

I wish I could have watched the spectacle, but the car needed to be brought around.

Seven coyotes in various states of bloat and decomposition are what I count after I start to keep track. It strikes me there are more lying alongside the highway than I've ever seen upon any stretch of road. They damn near serve as mile markers on the way out of Anadarko County. And with them all splayed out—their population so thinned—I wonder what will become of the rest of the roadkill. Flies can only do so much. Will the other coyotes take care of them? And for that matter, what does it take for a coyote to become a cannibal? How hungry does one have to get before dog-eat-dog becomes literal? I bet the turkey vultures will pick up the slack.

Eagles, too.

Anything can have happened in Oklahoma. Practically everything has. Someone a lot smarter than me said that once. I'll be damned if I can remember who.

27

Overdriving causes one to be as dangerous behind the wheel as a drunk. Things blindside you while you flirt with Mister Sandman, which sends a shot of adrenaline straight to your heart or colon or the medulla oblongata. I cannot say with any real degree of authority how that particular chemical works in the body. But I do know it will cause your last meal flight or fight as well. I also know if you blink too slowly behind the wheel and get nudged awake by the rumble strips along the shoulder of the road, it'll do a better job of waking you than any alarm ever devised.

Elise shoots up in her seat, too, and looks down into the looming ditch, then over at me in the driver's seat. "You want me to drive?"

The gimp is gone from the backseat, settled into a cell, where he'll loiter until the judge is ready to deal with him Monday morning. If the incarcerated members of the Filthy Thirteen don't turn him into their newest biker bitch and personal pincushion before then.

"Find someplace to pull off," she says through a yawn.

So I do.

The city sidewalks seem long since rolled up, but there is one building that looks like it still supports life at this hour. The wall facing the freeway reads BIKER FRIENDLY. But the parking lot has cars aplenty.

The one light in said parking lot lights the last few spots closest to the building. Behind that, a cornfield, which gives the whole place an if-you-build-it-they-will-come kind of charm.

"Moe, why're we at...The Outhouse?" Elise snickers.

"I need to pee. Where better?" I say and crack open my door along with a smile.

A few steps later, I pry open the steel door on The Outhouse, and we step out of the buggy early autumn evening.

"I have a feeling we're not in Kansas anymore," Elise says blinking rapid-fire.

The smoke is thick, but I think we are both trying to process the scene around us—a strip club without any live nude girls in sight.

"Nope," I say, and angle an arm over her left shoulder to draw her attention toward a vinyl sign over the bar that explains why we paid five bucks each at the door. We slogged into the middle of an apparent *extreme dwarf wrestling show*. "We're in the land of the little people now," I say.

Then I head to the men's room. I leave Elise with my wallet—so it won't get picked while I piss—and in charge of finding us a table as close to ringside as feasible.

The first bout is extraordinary to watch, as is often the case with things first witnessed. The first fighter to appear is dressed as a farmer in overalls. Over his shoulder he hoists a two-by-four piece of timber. Instead of Hacksaw, he goes by Hackblade. It's cute. Elise and I share a laugh and a smile. Then his opponent appears.

King Midget is a man who I'll call frighteningly athletic. If I ever had to apprehend him, I'd just shoot the little bastard, the same as I was trained, as an MP, to simply shoot a Green Beret whenever one got drunk and belligerent on base.

28

Any asshole who thinks they can step into a ring with a professional Thai fighter or boxer, or onto the field with any other trained athlete, and do what they do successfully is just that: an asshole. That includes exotic dancers, cheerleaders, rodeo clowns, bull and bronc riders, as well as luchadores and *wrasslers*—sumo and dwarf, too. And when some asshole wants to spread their cheeks and expose themselves to the world, there's not much better to be found on cable TV for those sitting ringside.

Take Exhibit A, for example, who I'll call the Ric Flair of asinine spectators amongst what's grown into a standing-room-only audience. I don't remember his mouth staying closed for more than a fistful of seconds all evening long. So when the announcer quiets the crowd to let us know the challenger for the evening's main event has taken ill, and, since the night is still young, they are wondering whether someone from the crowd might take on their champion, the dipshit presents himself ringside without hesitation. Ole fucknoggin even grabs a feather boa from one of the ring card girls and drapes it over his shoulders before he slithers between the ropes and into the ring.

He peacocks his way around inside, struts beneath the beauty lights, and takes a victory lap before the match ever begins.

Another ring card girl enters with a clipboard in hand. The announcer asks the enthusiastic gentleman if he wouldn't sign a form.

His only question is a simple one, "What for?"

"In case of bodily injury," the announcer says.

Ric answers back with a crooked smile and a shake of his head. He puts pen to paper without examining to see exactly what the glowing white form entails. When he lifts his hand away from the clipboard, a man known professionally as Lil Hank shoots beneath the bottom rope and forces Ric's head and feet to trade places.

John Lee Hooker's "Boom Boom" rings out from the speakers, and Lil Hank screams, "You're in my house!" almost echoing John Lee as he finishes the first verse.

Ric rolls onto his back and looks up from the faceplant he'd made on the mat, stupefied.

Lil Hank wears a horseshoe mustache and toddler-sized cowboy boots, Wranglers, leather vest, and a blood-red do-rag to keep the sweat out of his eyes. Beneath that, a freshly bic'd head. Nothing for anyone taller than him to grab onto, in other words.

Pain fills Ric's eyes. They glisten. He snarls, humiliated. Lil Hank sees this and beams—as do I—along with everyone else sober enough to give their undivided attention.

Before Ric can get back to his feet, Lil Hank explodes into his gut like a cannonball shot close range at a strongman in a freakshow back.

Except Ric folds in two. Seconds later, after air returns to his lungs, and Ric can focus, Lil Hank towers over him. Ric tries to sit up but makes that face everyone makes when they are not entirely certain if they've let go of a fart or are about to shit themselves. But Ric's broken ribs. When that sort of paralyzing pain first washes over a person, there's nausea, of course, but things move in slow motion. Vision can blur or go completely white while pain like that shoots through you, like Batman disappearing behind a smoke bomb.

Meanwhile, unbeknownst to Ric, Lil Hank sails from the top rope through the smoky air of The Outhouse, parting the clouds while he flies. Midair, he clutches a folding chair like a makeshift parachute to break his fall, but it seems this man was born with the gift of flight and instead uses it to knock Ric senseless. Again, Lil Hank towers over him, taunts him, before he pins Ric to the mat with the greatest ease. The whole crowd takes part in the ten count. Fun for the whole family.

He'll be goddamned, so Ric kicks his legs at the last second and wriggles his shoulders off the mat before the ref can slap his hand a tenth time. So it looks like we will get our money's worth after all.

29

Not a single instance of anything good in the history of the spoken word ever came from someone beginning a sentence with a hushed, "Don't look now, but…" Yet that is what Elise leans in and hollers into my ear: "Don't look now, but this place is crawling with those filthy fuckers."

"Yeah," I answer, annunciating at my very finest for the sake of clarity, so I will not have to repeat what comes next: "This is what happens when the circus comes to town. The freakshow makes an appearance too."

"No," she says. "There's a giant-ass Filthy Thirteen patch painted on the back wall in the ladies' room."

I give her my full attention.

She rolls her eyes toward the front door, takes hold of my wrist to lead the way out. I do not resist her charms.

"You want to drive?" I say.

"Yeah, sure," she says, taking the keys and trotting toward my Pontiac, more panicked than I. I have a bad idea slowing me down.

Broiling exhaust bogs down the darkened, damp night air on my way to where Elise waits in the car. I sit in the passenger seat and toss a handful of plug wires onto the rear floorboards.

"What…did you do?" she wants to know.

"The same thing I used to do when my mom was too drunk to drive but wouldn't give up her keys," I say. "Drive, please."

Elise puts it in gear, crawls across the parking lot, and eases us out onto the highway. Only then does she turn on the headlights and assume her role as the getaway driver.

"There wasn't anybody watching the bikes?" she says, swiveling her head to check the trio of mirrors after merging off the on-ramp and into the slow lane.

"Nope. Who would monkey with their bikes outside of their clubhouse?" I smile. "They're pack animals. Their bikes were huddled together, so I didn't have to go hunting."

"You're an idiot, Moe."

"I love you, too," I say.

Elise doesn't say anything back, but I can hear her smile. Or maybe I imagine her face radiating heat like when she blushes. Or maybe I mistake that for the defroster warming up the windshield to battle the plummeting temps outside. "Cruise control will save on gas," I say with closed eyes, settling into my headrest and smiling at the windshield.

"What's on the stereo?" Elise says.

"On one station, there's a beleaguered preacher. A singsong priest on another, followed by a joyous pastor after that. Or the one before. I remember an angry preacher somewhere on the dial too. Oh, and the farm report. The station from the college is playing techno. Listen to that for too long, and it'll hypnotize you—we'll wake in either the ditch or the next world."

"Any CDs?"

"There's one stuck in there. Hit play," I say.

She does, and Roy Orbison sings Hank William Senior's "There'll Be No Teardrops Tonight."

30

An American bison's eyeballs do reflect light. If they're looking in the direction of oncoming traffic, that is. It's the same for a deer or a dog caught in a set of headlights. It's a good thing, too, since a mature bull can tip the scales at a little over a ton. A moose is the only thing I have ever heard has eyes that do not reflect light. Maybe because their eyeballs hover around ten feet off the ground, and most headlights are mounted around two feet off the road. Generally speaking, bison, or buffalo, have two speeds: stampede or stroll. They are also capable of standing still. Dead stop, as some call it. But they do not stand while they sleep. They don't always roam the prairie, either. It turns out paved highways have much to be desired over a potter's field following a respectable rainfall with so much weight on such tiny hoofs.

With bison or buffalo on every populated continent, you'd think there'd be one in the constellations.

It takes me a while to realize I am staring at the stars. I didn't think stars flickered the way these do—are. Before they come into focus, everything looks as black as I imagine the inside of a coffin once the lid is closed, six friends lift it, and six feet of soil gets shoveled on top. To be honest, it feels like I fainted. Like I can't see, can hear, but have not yet passed out. And all I can hear is ringing.

The ringing lessens, my vision sharpens, and I blink to get the blood and diced-up cubes of auto glass away from my eyes. My arms feel pinned. Too heavy to move. The moonlight sparkles through what is left of the windshield and lets me know I was not ejected from the vehicle. The dash and glove box came so close I could almost use it for a chin rest, had my seatbelt not locked up and lashed me to my seat.

Then I hear the radiator gurgle and hiss.

The hood's been peeled off toward the driver's side, so I have an unobstructed view of the radiator. It's been shoved into the fan and tamped onto the front of the engine block. Beyond all that mashed engine mess, I see the wild-eyed expression of a buffalo staring back at me.

It's him I hear gurgle and hiss.

I've only seen them on postcards and TV till now. The bumper looks embedded in its side, which is split. The wound heaves and hisses when it tries to take a breath, like the buffalo grew gills courtesy of its loitering along a quiet and curvy stretch of Oklahoma State Highway 99 during the early morning hours. And then the world stops revolving around me.

Elise.

I force my stiffened neck to turn left. My vision blurs, doubles from the spike in pain. Two objects occupy the same place. I blink, not believing my eyes.

"Elise—Lise!" I bark. But she doesn't blink. Shock leaves folks unresponsive. Unable to respond. That's basic first aid. A spinal injury does the same. As does the fear of one.

I growl at the pain and undo my seatbelt with my left hand to reach her, and look for a pulse. When the belt slides off my right shoulder, gravity pulls my right arm down between the seat and door. That's to say, I have no control over it. It's dislocated. It doesn't hurt. Nothing does.

My whole self feels like a sleeping foot finally waking.

I put my left hand on the side of her neck to support her head while I put two fingers alongside her windpipe. When my fingers slide lower on her neck, her head flops onto her right shoulder, pinching my palm in between in doing so.

There's a thick foggy area between touching someone to check for signs of life and the dead moving and touching you. It's not something you can prepare yourself for. Knee-jerk is the only honest way to categorize what happens.

To say I shot out of my seat and onto the blacktop might be a sloppy way of describing the scene. But when the realization kicked me in the gut, I couldn't figure out if I was going to throw up or soil myself. And doing either—on or near her—horrified me beyond any emotion I can articulate.

So, while doing figure eights, fighting gravity, I stood on the centerline and bled.

Elise marrying the steering wheel marked the end of our love story.

I reach through the shattered window, close her eyes, and turn, so she won't see my tears.

31

"Are you trying to tell me if I send a deputy ten miles up the road, he's going to radio back that there's a turquoise Pontiac with a dead buffalo for a hood ornament and your girlfriend, also deceased, behind the steering wheel?"

I cast my eyes down to my lap and interlace my fingers, pantomime, flap them as best I can. "More like mushed into than behind," I say back to the Pawhuska Police lieutenant with the dust from my last two codeine tabs still on my lips. "I counted ten mileposts. Maybe a few more. My head doesn't feel the best."

"When's the last time you got a good look at yourself, son? The folks who called us said they thought a zombie had crawled up out of the grave and come to town to wreak who knows what sort of hell," he says. "You really should thank them if you get the chance. I think pain has you on autopilot. You might have merged back onto the highway headed to Tulsa." He turns to look south. "Do you mind telling me where you were walking on such a beautiful Sunday morning?"

"Toward some church bells."

"You need a doctor. Talk to Jesus some other time."

"Don't doctors go to church?" I say, still convinced it was a good idea.

"Let the boys in the ambulance take you to get patched up. That shoulder looks mangled. Out of the socket, separated, something.

You should see it."

I roll my eyes down and to the right and say, "Neck's too stiff for that at the moment."

"Yeah." He closes his notebook and tucks it into his breast pocket, behind his badge. "I could not wager why," he adds, and gives the EMT a head nod.

I squint my best to read his badge number. 521. I like those odds—the odds of remembering those three digits versus his rank and name, given my fuzzy demeanor. "Nighty night, Deputy Vegas," I say, and let the paramedic ease me back onto the gurney.

"Vegas?" he says, confused, and looks down at his nameplate and back at me, which makes me chuckle, then cough. Rinse, lather, repeat.

Cops don't like getting laughed at, but it's hard to get too mad at the freshly concussed.

The IHS staff treats me for said concussion after a trip to the radiology department. They treat me for a separated shoulder, too, both of which I am told will heal on their own with enough rest, relaxation, and fentanyl—an analgesic—which I pronounced *anal-geese-sick* when the doctor first hands me the vat of a bottle. It looks big enough to kill a buffalo.

"It's for around-the-clock pain management," the doctor says.

"Hell of a lot of them in here." I shake the bottle, which does not rattle as much as one might expect. "And two refills," I say after I scan the label again. "Are they even worth a shit? How strong're these?"

"Flush them if you don't need them. Or sell them. Whatever you do with them after you leave here is beyond my control."

"That's all right. I have a job," I say to the condescending prick. "Fugitive recovery agent," I add, and pocket the pills.

"With one good arm and no vehicle? Good luck."

"I wasn't aware pain pills are the new wampum in Indian country."

"Yeah, well, hey, don't drink with those either. Nurse'll walk you out in a minute or so," the doctor says before he disappears, and pulls my curtain closed so I can change back into the clothes I'd worn the night before, blood and salt-stained from being sweat-soaked.

I smell like a farm animal. Or a farmhand. Or a slaughterhouse, maybe, with a hint of dead buffalo.

I find Osage Laundry less than a block away from the Indian Health Center. But I am not about to drop my pants and leisurely loiter around the laundromat like it is my living room. Indians have been killed for far less in this city.

The proprietor stenciled NO SMOKING onto all four canary-yellow walls with fire-engine red spray paint and saturated the place in shadowless fluorescent lights. It turns out the town is so tiny that it's one of those places where no one bothers to lock either their front doors or their car doors. It's the kind of place where a woman will leave her family's wash unattended while they attend Sunday services—and brunch. God bless them.

Two signs hang inside the laundromat. One sways over the rumbling washing machines and reads WASH OILY CLOTHES HERE. I can't imagine someone washing their Sunday best in such a fine facility. Not with the foam ceiling tiles smelling of roughneck and ranch hands. The other sign says, SMILE! YOU ARE ON CAMERA. Above that, attached to the wall with double-stick tape, is a fake surveillance camera, otherwise known as a psychological deterrent. The manufacturer of this one doesn't even bother with a battery-operated red light to look like the real deal. There isn't even a cable to tuck into the ceiling. But I'm no thief. Indians trade. So I pull off my shirt and toss it into a basket of dirty clothes before I go about browsing through a dryer full of clothing that has ended its cycle and already cooled off somewhat. The pants I have to cuff. And I'll need a belt, too, if I don't want to walk around with my hands stuffed into my pockets so they can serve as suspenders. Fresh warm socks are nice to slide on. But I keep my own underwear. There's no way I'll ever slip into someone else's skivvies—clean, starched, pressed, or otherwise.

Osage Laundry is the first building after the first streetlight on the north end of town. Or it sits right before the last streetlight on the north edge of town, depending on your direction of travel.

I walk south a handful of blocks to Main Street.

Some things are easily missed when driving versus walking. The smell of a restaurant kitchen tucked down a side street with no real signage to speak of, for instance. But life and a handwritten sign next to the hostess stand that reads LOCAL CHECKS ONLY tells me to take my appetite elsewhere. Far friendlier waitstaff exist at national chains. Especially when they are teenagers and twenty-somethings who would never notice you wearing their dad's shirt. Or pants.

Unfortunately, I find only local charm is on the menu in downtown Pawhuska. Luckily, life has also taught me that just because you are hungry doesn't mean you get to eat.

It's also taken the time to teach me to not gaze down any darkened or dead-end alleyways. But my granddad once told me the second half of the bit about the cat getting killed by curiosity. And who can't help but be a bit catty on occasion?

Alleyways can house any number of boogeymen. But when hymns are trickling out onto Main Street rather than used oil or a drunken hobo's morning piss stream, it's worthy of further investigation.

This particular alley dead-ends at a monstrosity of a stage built out of past-their-prime railroad ties. As are the two dozen mirrored rows of backless pews. The preacher speaks no louder than one would if they sat across the table at a diner between the breakfast and lunch rush. Yet his voice creeps along the entire length of brick walls, loud enough for all who have congregated to hear the message, giving the alleyway a Sermon-on-the-Mount kind of feel, which compels me to plop my ass cheeks down in the second to the last row.

~

The line to take communion is slow going. Hurry up and wait enters my life again. I'm not an active Christian by any means, but I know how to take orders, camouflage myself, and act uniformly with those around me. It's called soldiering in the Army. It's the same as being one of the Lord's sheep come Sunday morn.

The little square of bread they offer for communion is the first thing to enter my stomach since the previous afternoon. Pills aside. It does little more than make my gut growl. The gentleman who has the job of splashing the wine across every communer's tongue must have been a fixture at his fraternity keggers. He knows the precise angle to tilt that chalice so parishioners don't choke or even need to swallow. In fact, he pours it right down my throat so smoothly I swear I commit the involuntary sinful act of gluttony while receiving communion. I, too, will testify that the Savior's blood was clotted. Chunky, maybe. Perhaps even pulpy.

After I receive the sacrament, I don't bother to wager whether the sin of my picking out a new outfit from the laundromat has been forgiven courtesy of my one act of congregation and communal prayer. But I do still take a minute to meditate.

I sit and ponder my life choices on the pew along with a peppering of elderly women once the service comes to an end. They are waiting for their husbands to bring their cars around. My legs will not do as asked. Usually, the only time God punishes on the spot is when you're thumbing through the Old Testament.

Luckily, loitering in an outdoor church isn't against any enforceable laws.

32

"G'afternoon, Moses," I hear a vaguely familiar voice say over the hum of all-terrain tires lunging along a neglected stretch of highway. "I got to worrying. You breathe all kinds of shallow when you're out of it."

To speak proves difficult simply because the right side of my face is stuck to the rear passenger-side window of a patrol vehicle. It feels as though someone licked my cheek and shoved my head into the window in the hopes it would stick, like some toy from the bottom of a cereal box.

My neck is at what I will call an unnatural angle.

I try to put my left palm on the seat to sit back, but my left wrist is handcuffed to my right. I yank my arm out of the sling, which forces me to shoot up straight in the hard molded plastic seat, so I slide and slip and mash my face against the cage.

Seconds later, seconds before the pains leaves and gets replaced by nausea, I manage, "How-ow-ow-ow!"

"How?" the cop says. "I thought you people didn't say that except in the movies."

"Let my people go," I say, and do my best to blink away the tears welling in my eyes. "Deputy Vegas?" I say without moving anything other than my lower jaw, not wanting to invite any more pain or agony.

"How do you like them apples? Or was it *odds* you said earlier, in the ambulance? I figured we'd cross paths again. You got the look of a repeat customer."

"521 odds."

"And it's Lieutenant Wair, not Deputy Vegas."

"Wire?"

"No, stomp on the *W* when you say it. It's like *liar* but with a *W* starting off."

"Liar, huh?"

"Yep, and now it's time for some truth-telling, Moses. I have some questions." He hoists an evidence bag up for me to see. "Got your wallet here, a shitload of cash—we'll circle back to that—and enough pills to sedate a few dozen folks for a holiday weekend. I dare say it's not worth charging you with attempting to distribute, since I found you outside your mind, putting every preacher in town to shame after every other churchgoer had resigned to enjoy a quiet brunch downtown. We can call that disorderly conduct easily enough. It's a far lesser charge and considerably easier for me to prove. I'd lock you up, but you need to dry out. I don't want to listen to your clamoring while I'm at my desk," he says, and peers at me through the rearview mirror. "I can understand you being distraught with your girlfriend and the wreck, et cetera. But the cash. Let's chitchat about the cash, shall we? We'll be on the road for a while. Let's come clean about that little mystery, at least."

"The cash is mine. It's my twenty percent. What's left."

"What sort of job did you do to garner that sort of cash? For that matter, what makes you so brave as to walk around with that in your wallet?"

"Where're we headed? Fewer houses are zipping by now," I say and do my best to swallow another surge of nausea.

"County detox center in Bartlesville. We don't have one, and the Osage says you're not theirs."

"I'm not," I mumble. I lick away the white frothy crap from the corners of my mouth. "I'm Ho-Chunk."

"Don't you go getting sick back there…goddammit!"

"What?"

"Blow chunks? Are you about to blow chunks in my cruiser?" the lieutenant says, rapidly slowing the car and undoing his seatbelt. "Tell me, damn it, so I can pull off onto the shoulder. I do not want to clean up my car again."

"No." I slap my back against the seat behind me. "I am Ho-Chunk. Wisconsin, you know?"

"No. No, I don't. What the hell are you doing down here?"

"Playing chicken with buffalo," I say.

"Speak up."

I clear my throat with such force I feel a pinch. The pain makes my throat frothy, so I swallow that down, too. I know better than to spit on a cop's floor. "I'm a bail bonds recovery agent."

"Shit. You one of Ephrem's guys?"

"Never heard of her," I say and bat my eyes.

"Shit. I'm going to turn around up here. You like barbeque?"

"Are you paying?"

"Absolutely," he says, and lifts the evidence bag into the air again. "I've already seen you're wad."

"It's feast or famine with my profession," I say.

"I vote we feast," he says, and smiles into the rearview mirror the way a dog will when it sneaks a mouthful of fresh cat shit from the litter box.

33

The Pig Shack sits caddy-corner from Osage Laundry. We're within eyeshot of the scene of the crime I remember. Lieutenant Wair sits with his back to the laundromat, and I do all I can to not glance at it over his shoulder. I didn't want to allude to any degree of guilt.

"Eat," he says. "That'll fix a few of your problems."

I keep chewing and keep listening. Oklahoma barbeque is different from the Kansas City style. Not better or worse. Different. Dry, but that's why there's sweet tea.

"The pain doc set you up with a ninety-day supply of fentanyl atop whatever he pumped you full of for all the swelling. And then you went to that alley church with that goof-ass preacher. That's your day thus far?"

"Since I saw you last, yes. I woke up in the back of a cop car."

"You were blacked out but never unconscious, really."

"Oh."

"You know, that preacher, he makes his own communion wine."

"Oh?"

The lieutenant laughs at a joke he didn't share and says, "Ever heard of sour mash?"

"Whiskey?"

"Yeah, you need to make sour mash to make whiskey. That's what they boil and distill. If you ever make it to Tennessee, take a tour of Lynchburg. It's pretty impressive. Worth the price of admission. Anyway. For wine, there's something similar called must or mustum. They take that and do whatever to it to make wine. If they don't turn the must into wine, it keeps right on fermenting. It tastes like rotten fruit. But that preacher says communion shouldn't be a pleasurable experience in the first place. Should commemorate Christ's suffering with something that puts a sour taste in your mouth. Anywho, the stuff ends up being somewhere between twenty-three and twenty-five percent alcohol. Mix that with the party pack of pain meds you got, and you're setting off into orbit."

"And I become a walking, talking *Sunday Morning Coming Down,*" I say.

"And Bingo was his name-o," the lieutenant says in a singsong voice. "Pass me a paper towel, if you would please. When we finish up here, I'll ride you out to the Cavalcade Inn. It's not a big draw for tourists, but if you're a soldier, you've slept in worse accommodations."

"I appreciate that."

"What else?" he says to himself, but for my benefit. "Your car is in the salvage yard on the north end of town. I'd clean it out before someone else does that for you. The wreck yard will probably buy it off you for scrap, part out what they can."

I nod.

"Your girlfriend's mother's family has been contacted. A few of them still live around here," he adds while spinning a finger overhead, meaning inside the three square miles of the town.

I shake my head at all of that, keep chewing through some burnt ends, and give up my right to remain silent by saying, "We were coming to visit. Her family."

"Yeah, I know her family. They're known. They've been working to revive the buffalo herd. Look, the best advice I can offer right now is to clean out your car once you're feeling more like yourself. But don't let them talk you into buying anything off that lemon lot they got out there. Mourn your girlfriend and that automobile of yours in your own way."

I chew and listen.

"Do me a favor, please, and deadbolt yourself into your hotel room if you're thinking about drinking while on those pills. I'd also advise that you not open the door at that place unless someone has dropped you a line letting you know they are coming to visit beforehand."

"I can scrap."

"No, you can't. You couldn't even wipe your ass and blow your nose at the same time right now."

"My mind wanders too much while I'm sitting to give that a try."

"I'll let your girlfriend's family know where you are staying."

"We didn't ever get—never got—the chance to meet—before."

"Hell of a circumstance. The funeral should be in a few days. I can pick you up or tell whatever deputy is going to lead the procession to grab you on the way. County usually does those escorts."

I nod again and swallow more than I can chew.

34

Pawhuska Pull-A-Part & Salvage sits three blocks west of the Osage Indian Baptist Church. After we pass the salvage yard, there's another four blocks to drive until we pass beneath the archway marking the entrance to the city cemetery.

I sit in front of the patrol car this time.

I decide to not make myself known or go out of my way to call attention to my presence at the visitation, or the wake. I can't say why. It seemed moot. I let myself imagine it would feel like hi and goodbye in one breath. So I hold my tongue, hold my breath, and do not part my lips one time.

Still, I feel like the mystery woman in the long black veil. Though I know I am just another boyfriend whose name they'll never remember.

No one comes over to me to shake my hand, slap my shoulder, say sorry.

What do you say to the guy who damn near died alongside her?

I said goodbye to Elise when I closed her eyes, and again when they forklifted my Sunbird into the crusher so they could pay me by the pound for the aluminum and steel.

Elise's aunties and uncles and cousins laughed and spoke amongst each other, telling stories of her life, as storytellers do. All stories, if continued far enough, end in death. That's Hemingway, the king of cutting stories short.

35

When we first met, Lieutenant Wair mentioned he was worried I would merge back onto Oklahoma 99 and walk my way down to Tulsa, where traffic isn't so thin. That highway only goes so far south before it sends you back toward the middle of nowhere. But my thumb, as it turns out, can take me in any conceivable direction.

El Gordo Auto Sales sits between the Tulsa Greyhound bus station and a Cuban cuisine lunch counter that boasts the best Cuban sandwich in town. El Gordo should have had the tagline "As-Is." That said, there is a 1982 Dodge Mirada for $5k, tax, title, and a topped-off tank. The 360 V8 is why he's asking so much for such an aging and obscure automobile.

"Most are 225 slant sixes," El Gordo says while he pops the hood.

"So what?" I lob back. "It's still an automatic."

"Petty drove one," El Gordo says through the toothiest smile he can manage.

"Did he drive this one?"

"No, he did not."

"Good. 'Cause you're barking up the wrong tree. I was raised a David Pearson fan."

"No shit?" El Gordo lets the hood slam down and latch itself closed, defeated. I can almost see the hamster behind his sparkling eyes stumble and try its best to regain some traction.

What I said to him was absolute, unfiltered shit. I find auto racing about as engaging as watching tennis on a ten-inch black and white TV with a busted antenna and a blizzard already in progress. It's like white noise in every sense.

Which means, I still watch.

"How long," I say, "has this automotive relic squatted on your lot?"

He seals his lips and doesn't offer an answer.

"How many miles has it been test-driven in that time?" I add.

"I'd have to check in my office."

"Thirty-five hundred sounds fair, doesn't it?"

"Fair? Four sounds more like it to me—if we are negotiating."

"Nope."

"No?"

"I mean, I'll need a set of new tires, right? Which I'll buy elsewhere. I couldn't even get up to speed with the mismatched socks you slapped on her. Everything is used on this lot, right? Cars, tires. I bet the oil, too. If I buy this car at all."

"The car tops out at 185."

"Not with dry-rotted sidewalls. Thirty miles an hour, max. And what color paint is that, Granny Smith green?"

"My mechanic said it's called Sour Apple. Said it would help it sell—make it look like the race car it is."

"Race car," I echo. "Thirty-five hundred. That's all you'll get out of me. You can pull someone's pants down tomorrow over the price of that Plymouth Arrow pickup."

"Hell, I'm tired of us two standing around and tickling each other's ass. I'm ready to head home. My pens and paperwork are inside. How do you want to finance this?"

"I'll pay you cash in full today."

"Fuck me. Cash?"

"You are not my type. Besides, I just got out of a relationship."

"Breakups can be a real bitch. So can women. Sounds like yours took your car and left."

"I'd rather root for Petty than talk about her with you," I say.

He gets the hint.

I let him lead the way into his malt-shop-turned-used-car-dealership, where I sit in the cracked-pleather chair facing his desk and marvel at the goldfish bowl of a place.

"Moses, while we are sitting, shuffling through these papers, I hope you don't mind, but I have to ask about the sling and the limp." He casts his eyes over my other shoulder to examine the clock on the wall. "Call me nosy. I just want to have something to tell my wife when I get home late."

"Please, call me Moe," I say and look down at the sling. I unfurl my fingers and coil them back into a fist while I consider how much to give him.

"Okay, Moe. Moses on the title, though, right?" he says and plunges his pointer finger down on top of the papers.

"That's right," I say. "Moses on the title." I run my tongue between the outside of my teeth and the inside of my lips, wanting to rid my mouth of the cotton feel. "My girlfriend ran a buffalo down with my car."

"Christ all Friday! Some ladies shouldn't drive, now, should they?" He laughs. "And that's how you screwed up your shoulder there? Boy, I'll tell you, seatbelts cause more injuries than metal dashboards ever did, as far as I am concerned. What about that limp you got, same same?"

"I kicked the buffalo in the face until it died, too."

"You kicked a buffalo to death? Like punted it? Went for the extra point? On a one-ton American bison?"

I don't offer any clarification on the matter. I let El Gordo fill in the blanks in my story along with the tax, title, and registration.

"Well, hell, what did that innocent little buffalo ever do to you?" he says, fishing for more conversation.

"Killed my girlfriend."

"Hell, man. Sorry. You said 'too,' and I didn't catch she died *too* until now. I apologize." After that he adjusts himself in his seat and gets as businesslike as possible. "I'll need you to sign this top one in triplicate, if you could, please," he says and mashes his teeth together to not let anything else slip out of his soundhole. I say soundhole simply because everything else about El Gordo's physicality matches that of a Mariachi guitarrón.

The next morning, I have wheels, but I missed the checkout window by the time the fentanyl fog lifts. A burning question arises as to what I'm still doing in Oklahoma. I ponder the pros and cons of staying for however long, and somehow become convinced that, given enough time, I can find the answer amidst the smoke rising from the toaster. But a violent sneeze snaps me back into here and now.

36

It's weird—for lack of a better word—the number of fledgling couches and recliners that take flight from truck beds moving at expressway speeds. The downside is how, unlike Hippie Christmas, none of them are any good for the taking. There's no nursing them back to health, no matter how many popsicle sticks you have on hand.

I've seen crews pick crows off the shoulder of the highway with pitchforks, along with the rest of the roadkill, and return them to Mother Nature. But I can't help but wonder how many state agencies play hot potato with the responsibility of collecting the furniture left for dead on the interstate, until it becomes part of the landscape and grows grass and other flora thanks to all the bird shit splattered on it by passing flocks.

That's my roundabout way of saying my extended-stay room has a freeway-facing catwalk that dead-ends at my door, which I claimed as my front porch once I took note of the motel tan I'd gained since I lost Elise.

My overnight poolside tanning sessions beneath the neon saguaro cactus have left me with what I'll call an olive hue. The pool looks green, too, whether reflecting the neon light off its rippling surface between the hours of dusk and dawn or while the water warms in the high-noon sun. I wouldn't bother with a NO LIFEGUARD ON DUTY sign if I ran things around here. I'd post a

DUCKS UNLIMITED sign along the fence and save a nice chunk of change on chlorine, which I dare speculate the motel's proprietors were happy to have cut with tricycle motor piss.

My olivey hue made me unrecognizable to myself in the silver-flecked bathroom mirror. Though the look grew on me once it hit me how somebody might mistake me for an Italian or some other sort of Mediterranean-looking gentleman, rather than a coydog that wandered off the reservation.

"Checking out today, Mr. Kink—aid?" the housekeeper says, stuttering over a Freudian slip once her eyes catch the handcuffs and other bondage restraints piled atop the chest of drawers next to the leaning tower of pizza boxes from the Pie Hole.

"Not that I am aware," I say, knocking the bottle of fentanyl and a box of .45 ACP ammunition into the top drawer of the bedside table, along with the good word gifted to the motel from the Gideons, and the 1911—all of which I hope to hide from housekeeping's prying eyes. "Towels, though, please," I add, pointing toward the pile of damp towels outside the bathroom door.

"I hope you're not leaving us," she says—not so much looking at me as absently trailing her eyes up the bedspread toward my hand that holds the nightstand drawer closed. She distractedly sets a stack of clean linen at the foot of the bed. "You're so quiet of a man."

I can see the B-rated horror movie flicker behind her eyeballs when her expression goes blank and her face falls. She has it in her head she'll find me after I've emptied the bottle and the contents of my intestinal tract onto the bedspread. I'll soil everything down to and including the mattress, staining it so badly maintenance will have to drag it out to the dumpster—maybe light it on fire for good measure to exorcise all of its demons. That, or she figures she'll have to sponge my blood, brains, and bile off the grooved wallpaper so they can rent the room in time for the weekend crowd. She'll tip herself from whatever cash waits in my wallet. She'd shit herself if she saw how much that was. She wouldn't have to take the bus back and forth to work from the wild west side of Tulsa. If she were smart, she'd sign the title of the Mirada over to herself and take a little vacation until she could shake the image of my bloated corpus.

Her theory makes sense, minus one glaring plot hole: I've fallen for Oklahoma. Elise has been committed to the earth here, so I, too, have a connection with the land. And then there's a hangover of some sort. Survivor's guilt. And grief, a demon I cannot send back to hell until I learn its true name.

~

Four months have passed since another former soldier came to Oklahoma from Kansas. That motherfucker loaded a box truck down with forty bags of fertilizer, almost three hundred sticks of stolen water gel explosives, and used enough detonation cord to strangle the life out of one hundred and sixty-eight unsuspecting souls—nineteen of which were children.

It seems like the news has been running around the clock since that van exploded. The breaking news updates of entered evidence and findings of the grand jury reported from outside the county courthouse proves more than I can take. So I take myself for a long romantic walk out into the arid August afternoon.

After walking for I-don't-know-how-long, I spy with my little eye a business front advertising notary, process services, and state-certified bail bonding services. Proof I am nearing the low-rent district on the south side of downtown, nearing the Tulsa County Jail. Some folks go their entire lives without as much as slowing their vehicle when they pass such an establishment. Yet to me, the state-certified bail bond agent's office looks a lot like an employment agency.

I pull open the door, which strikes a cowbell dangling overhead. Next to the horseshoes for hat racks, they've mounted spurs along the wall for coat hooks. There's a mirror framed with what looks like a wanted poster from the old west. All that's missing is you. Beneath my feet, I see a cowhide rug carpeting the sitting area.

At least there's a theme.

The place seems empty, so I take a seat on a bench upholstered with a knockoff Pendleton blanket. The bench is bookended with two matching Ma and Pa cedar post rocking chairs. Centered above where I sit is an electric-blue Mexican sombrero, a beaver felt ten-gallon hat, and a hastily spot-welded aluminum trail's end silhouette. All HECHO EN MEXICO. Across the way, on the bond agent's desk, sits a pair of horns that look like they were stolen from the hood of Boss Hogg's Cadillac.

"Howdy! Take a number. I'll be one minute," comes booming from behind a door with a hand-painted crescent moon and northern star, followed by a flush.

Scattered over the coffee table looks to be about two to three years' worth of *Cowboys & Indians Magazine,* plus a coffee can for an ashtray.

"I'm guessing you're next," he says after he exits the bathroom but before he flops his back up against the door to get it to latch all the way and give the tiny exhaust fan a fighting chance. He being the bail bondsman, who could best be described for a casting agent as a Black Garth Brooks. But not a Chris Gaines type. "Coffee's still hot," he says, and looks off toward the back corner of the building. "I wouldn't say no to a cup, too, if you're pouring one for yourself," he adds before he heads back toward his desk.

I pour him a cup and bring it over to his desk before I go back for a cup of my own. From the far corner of the office, I can see how the buffalo shoulder mount on the wall above where he sits has a cavalry Stetson plopped atop its head. The theme did indeed come together nicely. Though the comedy behind the autographed headshot of Leon "The Boogie Man" Coffee poised between the creamer and the percolator did not dawn on me until after the fact. Short of getting caught up on his nickname, beneath that cowboy hat and all the clown makeup, it was hard to tell a Black man stood reared and ready to go inside that bull-fighting barrel.

"God gave you two hands. Why don't you use them?" he says, and points a hand at mine stuffed into the front pocket of my jeans.

"I was hoping to find a 'help wanted' sign in your window," I say.

At that, he scoots his chair back, slides open the center desk drawer, and disappears his hand inside. "You're about as subtle as an auctioneer with a case of the hiccups, aren't you?" While I am still busy translating his analogy, he elaborates in plainer language. "I'll be equally coy. What are you hiding in that hand you got stuck inside your pants pocket there?"

I look down at my right elbow and flap it like a chicken wing for him, hoping he'll get the hint he has nothing to fear. "I got into a car wreck a while back. The doc gave me a goofy-looking sling that got me questions I didn't care to answer. But I'm babying it now for the most part."

"I'll buy that and tell you to keep the receipt. People are too nosy nowadays," he says. "Pull up a chair."

I do.

"Work?" he muses, sounding skeptical. "I don't need any help around the office. There's always work that needs doing, but you can't be any geek off the street," he says, loosely quoting a pal of Billy Bonney. I stay quiet, let him talk, and chew on my coffee, which somehow thickened while it cooled. "I don't have applications handy for people to fill out," he says. "This work boils down to a person's resume."

"I am fresh out," I say.

"So, start with your name."

"Moses Kincaid."

"Fuck no. That sounds too starched," the bondsman says, way

too friendly for how long we've known one another. "If I keep you around, I'll call you 'Kinky.'"

"Okay," I say, unamused and equally unconcerned, considering how nicknames and call signs get given out indiscriminately. "And what do I call you, sir?"

"Sir? Shit. My name. Arlo Bice."

"Bah-ice?"

"Yeah, Bice. Like *Miami Vice*—just with more bass," he says.

"Okay, Mr. Bice."

"Arlo."

"Arlo, then."

"No, that's not what I am meaning," he says and clears his throat. "Mister Arlo."

Mister Arlo stands a whole head taller than me, at least. About six and a half feet tall, by my best guess. The buffalo mount wearing an official US Army Stetson gleans a bit more meaning once I let it marinate. He also has a framed rodeo advert boasting a special guest appearance by Bill Pickett, the bull-dogger, along with the movie poster for *Buck and the Preacher* on either side of the buffalo. But truly, the rack of Gatemouth Brown and Charley Pride LPs alongside the stereo alone told me who I was dealing with.

"We're about the same age, I'm guessing," he says, "I'm messing with you about the Mister Arlo thing. Don't disrespect me, and I'll do the same."

I scoot back into my seat and nod in agreement.

"You can view now as the appropriate time to dazzle me with your resume."

"Former Army—"

"Cavalry?" he says, cutting me off, stretching his pointer finger toward the taxidermized mount above his head.

"Nope," I say. "Custer had enough scouts."

"Indian, huh? Wasn't all that sure."

"I was an MP, last deployed to Haiti. Spent some time at Leavenworth, Kans—"

"Which side of the bars?" he says, not wanting to waste another minute on me if I give him a wrong answer.

"I got to go home at night."

"Mmm, okay. I am not interested in hiring a thief to catch thieves, is all. Putting insurance on you folks is bitch enough already. Don't bring any inherent vice in under my roof. What else you got?" Arlo says, looking bored and bound to find something eluding him in one of his desk drawers.

"Worked around Kansas City, collecting bail jumpers and other strays after that."

"Finally," he says, looking up from his drawer. "Relevant work experience."

I don't want him to know that is it, so I stay quiet like I am being polite and waiting for him to add something else to his appraisal of my resume.

"Haiti was last year, wasn't it?" he says, searching the desk calendar.

"It was," I say. "I got out a little before last Halloween."

"It's only August, so you've been at this for less than a year?"

"A little over six months," I say, already seeing where things are headed.

"So, you're not green, but you are not yellow either." He squints at me. "You're not going to pad your CV and tell me how you were a Ranger or Special Forces or any other kind of Billy Badass? Airborne, bomb squad?"

"Nope," I say. "I am what I am."

He smiles at that, wets his lips. "You're a broke dick Popeye wanting to work as a bounty hunter. For me? Is that the whole ball of wax?

"Time heals all wounds," I say, not wanting the interview to be over because of a bum shoulder. "And freelance is fine," I add before it's too late. "Private contractor, or however you want to phrase it. I don't need medical or dental. I got IHS and the VA for that."

"No, that won't be an allowable condition of your employment with me, Kinky. See, as an employer, I am a lot like a jealous girlfriend—I won't share my men with anyone."

"That's fair."

"A good man is hard to find."

"Steady work is hard to find."

"That it is. Now, if we're done feeling each other up, I think we know who is pitching and who is catching," Arlo says, and pauses to clear his throat and close his desk drawer. "Some guy put his Viper up as collateral against his bond. I did not think that dingaling would let his trial date come and go without showing his face, but that is why business is a-booming."

"Okay."

"I'm going to give you an address now," he says, and peels a Post-It away from the pad before handing it across the desk to me. I scan the address, see it doesn't say "Go to hell" or something in the neighborhood. I pocket the paper and look up in time to see him toss a key at the left side of my head.

"What's this for?" I say, running my thumb over the snake's hissing mouth.

"Fetch."

37

Hiding in a bathroom might look dumb or cowardly on TV, but it works. No one heads to the bathroom ready to fight. There's always a degree of vulnerability lurking in there that you can't ignore. So even if they fling the door open when you least expect, it's still your ambush.

Admittedly, I've become something of a fainter since Elise wrecked my Sunbird. Stakeouts and lying in wait don't mix well with muscle relaxers and pain pills. So I sit here and let them have this moment. I sit; they stare: the mullet, the bonded pair of Muscovies, the black bear, the boar or javelina or peccary, an almost albino mule deer staring over its shoulder, an antelope, a mountain goat of some sort, and a tom turkey splayed out for all to envy. But if I have to point to something about this trigger-happy cheesedick who spaced his court date that provokes me to the point I give fewer than two shits about what I have to do next, it's the mounted silver and white malamute head this fuckface mistook for a wolf.

First, we have to finish the five-dollar trip to the cardiologist I grabbed from Lil Squealers. We being myself and whoever's matching set of black-mouth curs woke me on the toilet in the shitter attached to the trophy room and study where the Viper lives. Elise once took note that dogs loved me without exception. Dogs like pizza too, without exception, fortunately.

I woke with them trying to thieve the pizza as stealthily as they could. Well, one tried while the other stared me in the face and drooled on my knee. Poor guy was so excited for a piece of pizza that his red rocket rubbed against my Docs each time his tongue wagged because he was too polite to steal.

After I divvy up the pizza bones, I set out to find the garage.

A car wreck is hypnotic in that it forces a person to pause what they're doing and watch, stare, gawk, give their undivided attention. A car wreck at interstate speeds can be magical, too, in that motorists are here one second and gone the next. Poof. So, you rubberneck and try to figure out the magician's trick. It's the same when one stumbles upon two gentlemen sport-fucking—playing hide the hotdog—in what was thought to be an empty house and on a red velvety slate billiard table erected between where I was and where I needed to be.

The one with the bowed head and rounded shoulders with his back to me gets consumed in the task at hand. The fellow lying in the kitchen with his head where the billiard balls would've been—had they been using the table for the manufacturer's purpose—I believe got blinded by the stained-glass Meyda Tiffany chandelier overhead, which sways ever so slightly with each thrust. Or maybe he cannot help but be held by the captivating eyes of his lover amidst their afternoon delight.

Either way, I've been told not to disturb men when they're working for as long as I can remember.

Either way, I avoid detection.

Upon further investigation, to my surprise and delight, someone installed carriage doors in the garage. Those two barn door rollers would have made the Tin Man envious. All I have to do is slide the latch to the left and give the doors the slightest nudge with the back bumper of the Viper and off I go.

Suppose someone could somehow manage to sputter their lips and clear their throat at the same time, loud enough to feel a pinch in the back of their throat. If they could manage that then you, too, could hear the sound a Dodge Viper makes when its room-temperature tires skip from a cool-to-the-touch painted and polished concrete floor out onto a blacktop driveway warmed by the early August late afternoon sun.

Curled up alongside where the Viper was coiled waited a pretty pink car the Boss had even the manliest man wanting to drive, back in the day. Had grand theft auto not been such an undesirable resume bullet for someone in my line of work, I might have taken the Mary Kay Caddy for a test drive. I could keep it and open Pink Panther Private Investigations.

But I am no thief.

When fleeing the scene of a supposed crime during daylight hours, it's best to stay with the flow of traffic, observe all posted traffic laws. Don't drive like an asshole, in general. Use blinkers, too. Most folks don't know that a cop can jail you overnight for everyday traffic violations just as easily as they can write you a ticket but with slightly less paperwork. The reckless operation of a motorized vehicle can get turned into manslaughter quicker than a wheelman can shift into a higher gear and vanish. That's to say that I did not expect the Viper's owner to give chase. Not on a day when he's been deemed absent from court.

But I've applied logic where there was none before.

I now know Mary Kay cars aren't pink. The color is called Mountain Laurel, according to all reports. When a Mountain Laurel boat floats up behind you with a shirtless and seemingly naked man at the helm, it doesn't draw one's attention as immediately as a reasonable person might suspect. Neither will a Dandelion Yellow Viper mildly exceeding the posted speed limit and missing a yellow light—coincidently rolling through a red, according to a traffic camera. However, a pastel-pink Mary Kay car barreling down the road, gunning its engine in an affluent residential area, might as well be a clown car with its every move tracked by spotlight for all to see while it races toward the center ring.

Somewhere north of Twenty-First and Lewis, the gentleman behind the wheel in Mary Kay Caddy illegally changes lanes while navigating an intersection without signaling and begins following me at what I'll be so bold as to call an unsafe distance, since I can hardly see his hood in my rearview mirror, let alone his headlights and blinkers. That's when he takes to gunning his engine and shaking his fist at me, as if I were the asshole who put the car up for collateral.

Conduct unbecoming a golf pro, if you ask me.

While behind the steering wheel, he shows no regard for his fellow motorists or oncoming traffic. Nor does he pay any mind to any obstructions in the road ahead—or pedestrians. So I do my best to drive assertively. I figure he'll attract the attention of the cops once we near where they live, lurk, and loathe.

Through my rearview mirror, I can see he has a car phone pinched against his ear with his shoulder. He has to take his eyes off the road to shift, which results in erratic driving, which should get him stopped by the police, though I can't recall passing any gas stations or donut houses in the Pearl District of downtown Tulsa offering free coffee and carbs to cops. Whomever the driver of the Mary Kay Cadillac has on the other end of the line has him responding sharply. His lawyer, maybe.

Or Arlo.

Luckily, there are still more gears at my disposal to help me get away from the accident waiting to happen. He should have called 911 if he thought he was the victim of auto theft. In my professional opinion, he is far too emotional to be operating a motorized vehicle on a public roadway, which is why I am about to create a safe distance between the Viper and the Mary Kay Cadillac.

That's not an excuse for piss-poor driving on my part; it's the reason for goosing it the way I did with the lights flashing and stop arm out. Short buses are hard to differentiate from delivery trucks when moving at highway speeds through a business district on narrow one-way streets lined with skyscrapers dosing the place in shadow.

38

Before the cowbell goes quiet, the bail bondsman, Mister Arlo Bice, says, “Key, please.”

I hook my thumb over my shoulder and say, “I left it with the grease monk—”

“Huh?” Arlo says, sounding a touch angered along with a splash of confused.

“I hid it at—” I try to say, but he cuts me off again by leaving his chair and coming around his desk straight at me.

“Tell me how you hide something that looks like a fire truck fucked the Batmobile?”

We both freeze, OK Corral-style, and let our shadows simmer for a second.

“Every one of those things runs hot,” I say and pull his part of the triplicate paperwork out of my shirtsleeve and sometimes sling. “This is where I left it when it boiled over. The shop’s name is at the top of the paper there, along with their phone and fax. It’s an exotics shop up and over a few streets. And it is painted bright yellow, so Bumblebee, from the Transformers, works better than a fire truck.”

“Bumblebee,” he echoes. He stalls a second or so before the right side of his mouth curls into a smile, and his knife hand turns into an open palm and a handshake. “Saw that shit on TV—live at five,” he says. “Sit if you like money.”

And I do.

"I'm sorry for scooting around the school bus when it was all lit up, but I had to shake the guy. At least he stopped for the kids."

"Nah. He welded the front end of his wife's Mary Kay Cadillac to the rear end of a short bus full of handicapped kids from a group home on—"

"Say what now?"

"Yeah, and you left the scene of the accident," Arlo says. "Cops couldn't figure out what the hell he was talking about his other car for. They ran his name and added public nudity to his list of charges. Those charges stick like taffy with vulnerable children in such close proximity. He might even get added to the sex offender roll, after serving his time." Arlo adds after he heaves himself back down into his chair. "The airbag saved his neck. My man's been arraigned and awaiting sentencing," he adds. "They had to move that busload of kids after he ate the ass end—"

"Sorry for that. I figured he'd see it in front of me, being so much taller than the Viper."

"Yeah, well, we see how well that turned out. They were screaming their heads off for the news crew. Happier than—you know."

I swallow to hide a smirk. "The car's in for an inspection and estimate. You're not out of any cash that I'm aware of."

"Then you won't be either. First time driving a car with guts and all those extra gears?"

"Oh, no. Not at all," I say, doing my best to save some face in front of my new employer. "But the tranny in that Dodge runs a lot smoother than an old Honda-type spring clutch."

"Well, whatever," he says with a hint of disappointment in his voice. "I would have liked to have been able to at least test drive the damn thing when I brought it to the auction house. But I am not out any cash, so fuck it. How'd you get the car?"

"Don't ask, don't tell," I say, and wait for him to cut me a check for services rendered.

He gives me a measuring look, then scrawls his pen across his checkbook. "What do you carry?" He leans over his desk and lets his eyes loiter in the neighborhood of my crotch a touch too long for my liking.

"Discover," I say, to his confusion. "It's not as widely accepted as Visa or Mastercard, but it's gotten me out of a jam or two."

"No, for a sidearm, I mean," Arlo says. "What do you wear on your hip when you collect a bounty? Or repo a vehicle put up for collateral?"

"I got a Chekhov."

"No shit," he says. "I don't dick with Russian-made hardware myself. Most of that stuff is disposable. I buy American or Italian, if at all possible."

"I'm joshing you. I got a hand-me-down 1911. But a Chekhov is dependable," I say. "It'll fire every time."

"How long until you're a hundred percent?" Arlo points at my slumped right shoulder.

"Any day now," I say as coolly as I can. For show, I roll both shoulders forward and back and wait as long as I can to clear my throat and let go of the growl unnecessarily moving my shoulder garners. "I'm babying it, mostly, now," I say, swallowing the pain as best as I can in such cramped quarters.

Somersault into the next week, and I find myself playing I-spy at the courthouse for Arlo. The job is to ensure he knows who amongst his clientele failed to appear on their reported court date before a bench warrant can be issued in their name. Once one does, I get to play hide-and-seek for cash.

But I do not.

After another week of that, I am finally back in the saddle, behind the steering wheel of my prized—paid in full—'82 Dodge Mirada, headed south out of Westwood mobile home and RV park while, over the speakers, Roy Orbison serenades some pretty woman, doing all he can to convince her she's not alone anymore.

"Why do—" Arlo asks.

"Huh?"

"Why do you drive a pistachio-colored stock car with an automatic transmission and vibe out to elevator music?" Arlo says.

I don't answer straight off. First, I swat the directional signals with my middle finger. "It's called Sour Apple, the color. And that's the Roy Orbison on the radio. Stereo. In the CD player. I had to track down a new one. My last one got left in the car when I had it scrapped," I say, giving up as little as possible.

"What's wrong with Elvis? Besides, fuck, I figured you for—speed metal."

"Pistachio?"

"Yeah," Arlo says. "Like the nuts, you know? Them little green expensive shitting things. Or the pudding, the same color as your ca—" he says but laughs at his own joke before he can get it all out.

"The color is Sour Apple green," I say again. "You need to stop buying generic pudding and get checked for colorblindness."

"Fuck Doctor Huxtable. Key lime–looking then," Arlo says. "Wait," he adds and chokes on another chuckle before he clears his throat, "Was that a selling point for you? Did you pay extra for a pistachio paint job?"

I kept him in my peripheral while I watched the road and add, "Salesman said Richard Petty drove one."

"That so?" Arlo says. "What'd you say to that?"

"I told the guy I didn't give a shit," I say. "I don't care about the Moonshiner Olympics."

"Now you're hanging shingles," Arlo says and cackles. "You watched the Duke boys as a kid as surely as you watch NASCAR straight after church on Sundays now. That show was about where race car drivers came from. And you fantasized about driving the General Lee as surely as you fantasized about parking in Daisy's Jeep.

NASCAR is a natural fandom for you."

He has my number.

"Saturday, too. I was a David Pearson fan when Mister Petty drove *this* model," I say, and knock my thumb against the steering wheel.

"See?" he says and punctuates his point with a smug smile.

"So, is that it then?" I say to grab his attention. "Has the mystery already gone from our budding relationship?"

"You don't have me figured out. I can guarantee that."

"Okay," I say.

"Go on then, take a stab at what makes me tick."

"You're from Oklahoma," I say and give it gas to get off the on-ramp as quickly as I can before he can confirm, deny, or elaborate. We both slink into our seatbacks and keep any thoughts to ourselves once the tranny catches third while the engine clears its throat.

After two lanes squeeze into one and the speed limit gets cut in half, the RPMs calm down enough for the engine to allow conversation in the cab again, so Arlo says, "You must like to think you're harder to read than Chinese braille. But you're far from it, m'man."

I ignore the thing he said—mostly—and do my damnedest to change the station by addressing what'd been weighing on my mind for the last half of a mile or so, "Draping an American flag over a load in the back of a pickemup truck to keep something hidden isn't the brightest decision someone could ever make. Not one of those funeral-sized ones they drape over coffins. Not when they are not supposed to touch the dirt and that motherfucker said, fuck it, it's a tarp now. Now it looks like there's a damn dead soldier in your truck bed," I say at the person putzing the Luv truck down the road in front of me.

"Huh?" Arlo looks at me the way you do with the drunk at the bar who stumbles into the stereo and scratches the record, makes it hop, and the place go quiet.

"Farmer fucking John," I say, leveling my pointer finger at the vehicle directly in front of us, which slows to a stop no sooner than the words leave my mouth, thanks to the construction worker dutifully operating the SLOW/STOP sign.

The truck shivers to a halt, which shakes a shoe loose from beneath the flag-turned-tarp, forcing me to snap the volume knob on the radio to the off position.

"Did you see—?"

"Still do," Arlo says back to me without needing to hear the whole question. "The fuck should we do?"

"Ain't that a cop running their lights up there, at the end of the detour?"

"Somebody, sheriff, probably. Could be a trooper," Arlo says when he feels the car roll forward. Only a few seconds after the sign got spun for us to go SLOW does the guy spin it back for us to STOP again.

The human speed bump lets traffic go one at a time, so Arlo and I watch while the pickup gains speed and the shoe disappears from sight. I shift my weight from the heel of my foot to my toes to set the brakes and say, "Does that dude have a radio?"

"Nah, Mex-cans use ESP to communicate with each other. That's why it's called Español," Arlo says through what sounds like a clenched jaw. "Tell that motherfucker there's a body in the back of that truck. Goddamn, Kinky!"

"How'd you know expec—"

"Tell 'em," Arlo says.

"All right," I say, and quiet Arlo by rolling my window all the way down as fast as my left arm can crank. I crane my neck and holler out my driver's side window. "Hey! Stop that truck you just let go!"

"Sir, no-no," he says. "You stop—stop," he pleads and steps in front of my car, holding out his other hand palm up. "One minute. Soon you go," he adds as if I haven't gotten the hint.

"Listen to what I said," I shout out the window, but he isn't hearing it. So we sit and listen to the engine mumble under its breath in solidarity. As soon as we're through, I give it gas to close the distance between where we are and where the parked police cruiser sits; as quickly as I can without completely pissing off the highway construction crew.

Arlo unbuckles his lap belt and leans out the window, arms and all, and goes about doing all he can to grab the undivided attention of the officer behind the wheel, hollering how he thinks he saw a body in the back of the farm truck and the officer ought to think about checking it out, barking the guy's tag number at him. But the cop turns out to be a mouth breather, dead asleep in the driver's seat.

"Fuck me running," Arlo says and slams both cheeks down onto his seat. His back and shoulders heave from him waving his arms and screaming. "A damn Rescue Annie doll." Arlo turns to look at me to see what I make of the situation.

When I come off more amused than shocked, Arlo adds, "Tulsa's finest," for good measure.

"Work or play, boss man?" I say and stick my two pointer fingers toward the shrinking farm truck.

"Work," Arlo says and looks for his seatbelt.

39

Following their early Wednesday evening private practice sessions at Skateland, across the way from where Wonderbread once baked white bread night and day, the vast majority of the Green Country Derby Dolls flock to the White Crow Bar the moment bucket night gets underway. I gather ladies' night would prove bad for business, seeing as how it's all women, besides Arlo and myself and whoever's kid is playing pinball, jamming the flippers the way a lab rat will when wanting another taste of heroin. That's to say, an Indian and a Black guy walked into this lesbian bar and handed a ten-dollar bill to the lovely Native lady posted at the door named Ursula, according to the bluish prison ink scrawled across her throat. I figured it for serendipity, how we strolled up in time to see her stroke out.

Divine intervention, almost.

Knowing the signs of a stroke can save a life. But her speech didn't sound slurred. Though all she said was, "Ten each, gentlemen," while perched upon a barstool and without slouching this way, that, or the other. Thankfully, before I open my mouth to ask if she's okay, Arlo takes the time to tell me, "Her left eye is glass," which she makes worse by winking at me when I pass her and follow Arlo inside.

Staring is sometimes caring.

Inside, a pack of blockers waits along with an indecency of jammers, and if one of them was a bail jumper, missed court, or caused Arlo to lose his ass on a posted bond, there isn't shit I am going to do about it. Bodyguard work isn't part of my job description. I've never been rich enough to gamble with anything but my life. And the odds aren't in our favor.

I've watched enough roller derby to know I am not shit when put in the same room. I won't even get smart with a carhop on roller skates at a drive-in diner, no matter how skewed my order gets between the time it is given and received. I can guarantee there is a kind of coordination and athleticism at work in these ladies that'll garner an ass-whooping with the same degree of handicap as going against Sugar Ray Robinson while wearing a sumo suit.

Something new I learn, though, is how at a lesbian bar, when a guy approaches a group of ladies with the intent of cutting one from the herd to have a word on a private matter, they all eavesdrop. Even the jukebox takes a second to see whether the next quarter came from Canada or the good ole US of A before it seeks out the next ten-inch single to play.

I expect Alanis Morissette or Natalie Merchant, but Johnny Paycheck is the voice that rings out of the speakers, crooning over his friend, lover, and wife while the Green Country Derby Dolls close ranks around Arlo.

I lower my ass onto the barstool in closest proximity before clearing my throat loud enough for Arlo to know I left him by his lonesome and have resolved to do little but stare a hole in my reflection behind the bar once my sweaty pint of whatever comes coldest off the tap arrives.

Something else I learn is that there's a roller dame nicknamed Bashin Shred-Her who looks like a better-looking and slightly more athletic Wonder Woman, had she hailed from the actual Amazon. The good Lord gave her a head full of that black silky, wavy hair that'll lower a man's IQ when it spills down her shoulders and bounces in that Rita Hayworth way. Unfortunately, her name is Charinda Bice.

Or Mrs. Arlo Bice, for the punch-drunk.

Arlo smiles at me with pity once I catch onto how he's seen me staring. I smile back by way of the mirrored glass and turn my eyeballs elsewhere in the interest of self-preservation. I stare into my beverage and do all I can to read the maker's mark at the bottom of my pint glass, rather than look at the glistening midriff and lower back of his spandex-laden wife.

I near the bottom of my second glass of Colorado Cool-Aid and hear someone say, "Why's he call you Kinky?" before she lets the air out of the foam seat cushion on the stool beside mine.

An admittedly innocent enough question.

I answer by saying, "I got blessed with one of those names so formal no kid should ever get branded with it." Out of curiosity, I lift my head and scan the mirror behind the bar to see who's come to keep me company.

Charinda.

I must look spooked, because she says, "Relax. I'm not going to sneak up on you and smash you in the head when you least expect it. I am *not* vodka," she adds, all but deafening me when she annunciates "vodka" over the jukebox and chockablock crowd, but she drops the "d," so it comes out sounding like "va-ka," as in Cuernavaca. The barmaid gets the hint and brings the bottle over, along with a lowball glass for her.

Arlo interrupts whatever is about to spill off her tongue by saying, "You two naming your children yet?"

"No," I say again, this time into the glass. Hoping the conversation will turn to work.

And it does. "Kinky here is an accident-prone Indian tracker—retired MP, US Army," Arlo says to Charinda, while massaging my shoulders as if needing to soften me up for something extra special. "But gets shit done."

"I didn't retire from the Army," I say to correct him. "I only gave them six years—Desert Storm and the intervention in Haiti. I suppose an officer could retire after six, but I was enlisted."

"Kinky is a meat-and-potatoes kind of guy. But Charinda here, Kinky," Arlo says to make sure he has my attention, "Charinda is a gravy kind of gal. She walked onto the Wranglers arena football team over in Okie City as a linebacker, so she works for me less until the season ends. She'll be lending us a hand on this next one. She's a derby girl, too, in case you didn't figure that out for yourself."

"Linebacker?" I say to her.

"I ran hurdles and threw shot put for OU and didn't want to get off the field just yet," she says. "Do you still play the field?"

"I just got out of a relationship," I say, and that's all.

"Well," Arlo says. "Kinky, today is the day you start looking for a new man. And let me tell you this right now, Charinda is a hell of a wingman. She loves chasing after dudes. Ladies sometimes, too." Which I assume is why we don't get to stick around for the dykes-do-drag show.

40

In 1988, after a domestic dispute went wrong and sparked a lengthy manslaughter-turned-murder trial, one Charles Denver McDaniel got sentenced to life without the possibility of parole in Oklahoma's only supermax penitentiary. Why anyone still gave two hoots in August of 1995 has to do with how he found his way out through a rec yard fence one afternoon in the latter part of April in 1994, walking away from a life of solitude and servitude and even worse foodstuff.

"Feeling felon," Arlo says and adds a tickled grin that gets frozen on his face for a good long while.

Chucky slipped some months later when he gave an employer his particulars in exchange for a paycheck. His bossman had to have him on their insurance, and he figured he'd be all right with it being such a shit splat production. And he was, until his employer filed tax forms. That's when the Social Security Administration did their due diligence, flagged the file, and let state and federal authorities know.

That aside, Arlo is the type of businessman who knows how to hold a grudge against individuals who've caused him a second mortgage. And now, as Arlo sings, "He's *wanted!* Dead or alive," loud enough for some treble to bleed into his voice.

He displays a genuine happiness I've never before seen with someone who wasn't a paid professional actor. It's bred by begrudgement. It's the kind of glee that causes others in the room equal parts unease and moral discomfort, bordering on guilt by association, and premeditation, while he spins the tall tale that is Charles Denver McDaniel's looming demise.

As luck would have it, state and federal authorities discovered Chucky's place of employment to be little more than a traveling circus and decided to devote their limited resources to something other than a such a low-profile case. They figured some local LEO would eventually pull him over for a moving violation, and they'd get a phone call to come to fetch.

"Somersault into today," I say to hurry things along, "and he is where?" The dashboard lights and oncoming traffic silhouette Charinda and Arlo, so I get to see them share a silent look across the center console. "You're going to have to clue me in here. I didn't wear my court clothes today. For a good reason, am I right?" I add, from the rear bench seat of their Crew Cab opposite the booster seat on the rear passenger side. I didn't know they had kids. Nor do I remember seeing any pictures at Arlo's office. Of course, who would want jailbirds to get a good look at their offspring?

~

Every inch of the outside of the truck is coated in at least an eighth of an inch of that matte black spray-on bedliner bullshit—including the camper shell and the brush and grille guard—that'll exfoliate the exposed flesh of anyone who brushes up against it, no matter how gingerly. Bug juice or bird crap could never eat its way down to the metal no matter how long it goes unwashed, is the reason for the aesthetic choice, Arlo told me, when asked. He later added it could be parked in any neighborhood and look like a shadow recognizable to everyone who lives there. It even got backed into once by a guy who didn't see it parked behind him. The truck could pass for an armored van headed from this bank to the next one in the middle of Nowhere, Oklahoma. It also looks a lot like a storm chaser, minus the stickers from the financial backers who bankroll the necessary monstrosities often seen racing down the roads throughout tornado alley.

"He's held up at the state club house with a couple of other bikers. An ex old man of mine let on a few days back," Charinda says while Arlo chews his way into the next gear.

Charles Denver McDaniel had been on the run since the April before last and wasn't spotted until—or since—the Memorial Day Blowout hosted by the Nowhere, Oklahoma, chapter of the Filthy Thirteen Motorcycle Club. For those just now tuning in, that's the same bike club that tried to beat me to death once upon a time at a cozy roadside inn not too far from where we were headed now.

Legend has it the Filthy Thirteen Motorcycle Club began when veteran demolition saboteurs of the 506th Infantry Regiment of American Armed Forces folklore returned stateside and didn't feel an overwhelming urge to partake of Uncle Sam's offer to pay for a college education.

Once their numbers grew enough to necessitate a few franchises, chapters and charters sprang up along I-35 all the way north to Duluth, Minnesota, and south to Laredo, Texas. Though their headquarters still sits near the hometown of the original acting sergeant, Jake McNiece, born and raised in Maysville, Oklahoma.

Most folks fear the Filthy Thirteen of the here and now purely on principle. Perhaps that spawns from how they've kept on with the time-honored tradition of McNiece scalping folks in WW2 once communication became a stalemate. He, too, cut his hair in a mohawk and wore warpaint. As did his men. Which scared the shit out of the Nazis enough to issue bounties for the lot of them.

"Sound good?" Arlo says.

"Yep," I say, not mentioning I hadn't heard a word said by either of them since they mentioned the Filthy Thirteen. Nor did I let on how we were on our way to pop in on close cousins of some old business associates of mine. Nor did I bother to interrupt Arlo and mention how I thwarted the Filthy Thirteen interstate plan to exact revenge upon the man who murdered the Kansas City chapter's sergeant-at-arms and his pet prospect by mowing them down with his pickemup truck. I kept quiet on the matter mainly because I didn't want to get into how they ambushed me, beat me onto the sidelines, and relieved me of my earthly wares, resulting in liberally applied prescription pain meds and me digging into the hide of Oklahoma like a tick.

Rural Oklahoma is a way to say any place other than Tulsa or OKC. Nowhere sits some seventy-five or so miles southwest from the outskirts of the latter. Bandana Rick's sits east of Fort Cobb Lake and serves as sort of a trailhead for an RV park and campsite leading to said lake.

"Why the fuck are we camping? Did I miss something?" I say.

"Obvio, Tonto," Charinda says.

"You know that means *dummy* in Spanish," I say.

"I am sorry, that wasn't in the form of a question," Charinda says, and giggles at me before she opens her front passenger door to top off the tanks. Arlo finds it funny, too, but I feel like the third wheel on a date with a couple clawing their way through the seven-year itch.

We drive another twenty minutes to the other side of the lake and get a room at the motel. The roadside sign where we stop next just says MOTEL, which I take to mean four-diamond service and too many amenities to mention.

Once Arlo hands me the key and we get settled—which prosecutors might try to later label as lying in wait—I see the sign for Ester's Lakeside Motel on the inside of the fire door of our cinderblock room. Their cinderblock room.

Everything that follows flirts with premeditation.

41

Had I gone the hero's path and opted to become an infantryman, I could have, as a veteran, displayed all the same skills of someone able to properly wear a uniform and show up on time. Had I lived to receive a set of discharge papers, my name would have been on my shirt until it got etched into my free footstone, courtesy of a grateful nation. Instead, my time as an MP got me primed for an illustrious career as a professional witness. So here I sit.

Arlo tells me I got asked along more for surveillance than anything else. "Keep an eye out" is all the direction I get. He means for me to keep track of who comes and goes, what they're driving, occupied how many times, when the lights finally get cut off in the clubhouse for the night, et cetera. Cop shit.

Across the gravel parking lot from Ester's Lakeside Motel stands a foreclosed-bar-turned-clubhouse for the Nowhere chapter of the Filthy Thirteen. They've since bolstered the property value with a splash of curb appeal by installing a ten-foot privacy fence around the entire lot.

Smart.

Arlo and Charinda watch *Cybill* and *America's Funniest Home Videos*, followed by the local evening news. Meanwhile, I put a foot on the brake long enough for one of them to notice and darken the room's one window anytime anyone comes or goes from the clubhouse. Of course, we aren't watching for anyone special. We are only waiting until everyone with someplace better to go does so. Arlo wants to wait until everyone staying behind has a chance to get tucked in or blackout drunk or spun out enough to be vulnerable as a dog taking a dump. Much like how a slasher waits for campers to start to fuck before he brings their campfire stories to fruition.

Five commercial breaks without the red glow of the brake light drawing Arlo or Charinda to the window summon both to my driver's side door.

"Time to get moving," Arlo says.

"Why? You paying hourly? I thought there'd be pizza, if not s'mores." I sit up in the seat before I shoot them a smirk to let them know I know they soiled the sheets with their lustful ways.

"What's parked inside the gate?" Arlo says.

"A baby blue Astro Van. There's a golden or pea soup green Ranchero. Only two bikes, though. One was a trike, the other had—"

"A sidecar?" Arlo says.

"Yeah," I say and turn to look at him again. "With a big-ass Hound of the Baskervilles looking thing riding shotgun."

"I ain't worried about any dogs, chihuahua or Cujo," Arlo says and disappears behind the truck. "Suit up."

"That makes one of us," Charinda interjects, loud enough for me to hear over the slamming driver's side door while she snaps the front flap on her flak jacket. Arlo looks like a ninja turtle in his. He holds a twelve-gauge Benelli shotgun with a pistol grip receiver, adjustable buttstock, and breacher barrel, which looks more menacing than any sawed-off could ever hope to. The barrel of the damn thing looks like it has teeth. But we are here to take a bite out of crime.

It looks that way so it can chew into a wooden door like a termite, but breach it without a ricocheting shot injuring anyone once it turns to toothpicks.

Thousands of sex-deprived cicadas serenade long-lost loves, covering the crunch of our footfalls on the gravel while we approach the clubhouse, so we don't have to get into character until after we're inside the gate.

Arlo carries that monster of a shotgun in one hand, the way a ballplayer would when headed from the batter's box to home plate. Reminding me more of Casey Jones than any of Splinter's pet projects. He then twists the doorknob with his left hand, and we all hold our breath. Together, we listen for the tumbling blocks and compressing springs, along with the satisfying click, which lets the three of us pour into what would have once been the barroom as gently as a puff of baby powder to the balls. The hinges haven't a thing to say on the matter either. Not even sleighbells chime to let the barkeep know we've come to wet our whistles. We hear no weight shifting on bedsprings from any back rooms. No one even crashed out on any of the umpteen couches and loveseats strewn around the former barroom.

The place reminds me of a VIP lounge for an underground Goth nightclub, only with nondescript, muted colors and furnishings. Who knew Odin-worshipping white supremacist bikers would also harbor a love for Scandinavian DIY furniture? The cluster of end tables and coffee tables turns this place into Pac-Man's maze. A dynamic entry would have resulted in nothing more than a couple of knocked knees, some searing shinbones, and the elephant of surprise tiptoeing off into a neutral corner. That said, someone could have fallen ass over tea kettle for certain, and all the tripping and stumbling and accompanying cussing would have alerted x amount of Filthy Thirteen members as to our presence. Instead, Arlo walks in as if he'd forgotten to close out his tab, and we follow on his heels like lemmings.

Some art school dropout painted the motorcycle club's colors on the green felt of their one pool table, which probably screws up every shot ever taken. Dart machines set the place aglow, along with the Best Little Whorehouse in Texas pinball game featuring Burt and Dolly and the twins on the scoreboard. Down the hall, a hinge snitches on someone. Arlo spots him before the guy sees us. He says something to Arlo along the lines of "Who? Shit, no! Fuck, Ne—" but that's all he gets out before Arlo raises the Benelli and shoots him in the face from no more than an arm's length away, cracking his jaw with a bean bag round that shoves the guy's entire self into the wall behind him with the excess energy. That's when and how we announce ourselves. From there on in, there aren't any skid marks.

It is all crash and no brakes.

"Shit, sweetie, shit. Shit! Go hide, like I said. Go on. Now—ah," a woman says from somewhere farther down the hallway—where the pool room used to be, I believe—in a desperate-sounding whisper from behind bared teeth. Answered by the pitter-patter of little feet, followed by the sound of a reeling spring, punctuated by the hiss of a hydraulic piston.

The commotion draws Arlo and Charinda toward the ass end of the building. Before they can figure out which door exactly, a woman bursts out of her bedroom and takes a bean bag to the bridge of the nose, which sends her tumbling back to bed.

The tavern hallway isn't well lit. It is dark, as are the clothes they wear. So Arlo aims center mass of the target that presents itself, I am assuming.

He isn't headhunting, I assume.

A V-twin grumbles to life out back of the building, and we give chase.

The first door I come to swings into the kitchen. Out of instinct, I slam it open hard enough to crack the tile wall behind it and bust the doorstop free from the baseboard. The Army taught me to do that with a door, so in case anyone is standing behind the door—lying in wait—they won't be once their teeth and jaw get loosened.

After I find no one hiding or arming themselves in the kitchen, I lock the door from the inside and Duke boy my way out into the barroom through the serving hatch.

I can't tell where the other two have disappeared. The place grew quiet while I was otherwise occupied. The jukebox hums how they do, but that is about it.

The big guy with the broken jaw stirs when I turn his direction. Muscle memory manages to roll both my shoulders forward and the rest of my body into a fighting position. He freezes and goes limp except for the two hands he holds out in front of his face in case I swing.

But I don't.

He exhales in relief the best he can, given how fucked his jaw looks. His eyes tell me where the others went, so that's why I head the direction I do. But first, I take hold of him by the knees, ragdoll him onto his stomach and check for weapons of any flavor. Which he doesn't appreciate but understands to be just business.

I think he figures we aren't law, but we aren't bad guys, either.

A second bike kicks to life around the time I step outside, into where the outdoor smoking lounge would have been if it had not been turned into a dog run. I turn left in time to watch Charinda Heisman whoever off the motorcycle and onto the gravel. The bike would have probably gone over, too, had it not been the one with the sidecar.

The guy falls in a way that's usually followed by a referee's whistle and the peddling of popcorn, peanuts, and cold beer while the medics make their way onto the field to check for a pulse or to ask how many fingers. Almost as if he got blindsided by a linebacker.

Enter the woman with the broken nose, now with a crossbow in hand.

Like a deer will, I duck the second I hear that arrow let loose. Then I run like my life depends on it. I stop, drop, and roll like my ass is on fire. Hear echoes of my bootcamp drill sergeants say, "I'm up—He sees me—I'm down."

Gravel goes this way and that when I slap the ground and spin onto my back. I hit the gravel so hard I go numb. I can't draw a breath. I think, maybe, I've been got by an arrow. Bulletproof does not mean arrow-proof. Or knife-proof, if Oklahoma trafficked in normal circumstances.

I don't feel the foot-asleep kind of numb, but the sort that comes over you when you're still trying to figure out if that thing you grabbed onto is burning hot or freezing cold. Either way, you're struck with the same calming confusion as a Judas cow, but you can't get yourself to let go until your nerves are done playing catch-up.

With my wind elsewhere, I let my mind wander as well and resolve to listen to the motorcycle idle and let the world around me percolate. I feel I should mention the arrow from the crossbow missed one and all. It flew out into the blackness and didn't clang loud enough for us to hear when it came back down to earth.

The gravel grows warm.

I've sweated so much that my shirt is saturated and stuck to me here and there, to where I can't tell whether I am bleeding. Bleeding isn't always painful. Shock takes care of that, mostly. The lesson that follows is always painful, however.

I later learn the Filthy Thirteen like to keep crossbows handy, so the weekenders renting cabins within earshot of their clubhouse don't hear a gunshot and try to get the Anadarko County Sheriff's Department out there before anyone can hide a body and cannibalize the horse they rode in on.

Charinda absently flips the engine switch on the handle bars of the Panhead to off, sits sidesaddle on the bike to catch her breath while it coughs itself quiet. She stares off into the darkness like a seasick sailor in search of a horizon and says, "Fuck me," through a frothy-sounding growl which grabs all of our attention.

An even more concerning fact I learned a smidge too late is that there are more tigers in Texas and Oklahoma than in the wilds of Siberia and Asia combined. Someone in their right mind might ask who would want a pet that could kill them and eat them or eat them out of house and home. And I'd answer that it is outside of my comprehension. It seems the most likely reason the statutes concerning the ownership of big cats got penned so loosely and worded so vaguely and regulated even more sporadically is because the imbeciles in office thought buying one would be rarer than a Bigfoot sighting. Sadly, any idiot with an extra two grand can get a hold of one just like any other prized, pampered purse pooch. However, I hear tigers are great companions that love to lazily lounge around the yard during the day and lie in the lower limbs of a shade tree at night, where they'll wait to ambush any low-hanging fruit who might walk beneath for a midnight snack. Which is one way to say, we discovered a tiger loitering in the tree out back of the Nowhere, Oklahoma, Filthy Thirteen clubhouse, which could not stop staring at Charinda with what I can best describe as playful curiosity.

I don't move a muscle, aside from my quivering sphincter.

Meanwhile, a tiny red dot the size of my pinky nail appears on Arlo's chest, doing figure-eights courtesy of someone's heavy breathing and shitty shooting stance.

Even piss-poor marksmen have a signature all their own.

I cannot see one on me, but those damn things are like bad breath or body odor. Once you smell your own, it's too late.

I find laser sights on a crossbow a bit too much, but it got the Filthy Thirteen's barn cat's undivided attention. With their night vision in the neighborhood of six times stronger than ours, tigers prefer to hunt at night, crushing the neck and skull of their prey first before gorging themselves on nearly ninety pounds of meat in one go.

A fully grown tiger can jump ten feet into the air from a standstill and over twice that if they take to the air at an all-out run. But a cat is a cat. So the cat follows the red dot into the Milky Way where it disappears when Arlo shoots the woman with the busted nose and laser-sighted crossbow in the face, again.

She falls the same way one will following a sucker punch that flicks off the lights and joins me on the gravel lot. My nose leads me to believe she might have wet herself.

Cats are opportunistic eaters. It can't help itself. A house cat will not wait any measure of time after its owner expires. A fresh kill is a fresh kill. And everybody knows a meal tastes that much better when you're not the one who prepared it.

Just ask any lion; not the lioness.

The sound is as indescribable as indelible and ushers in my second wind, which gets me off the ground in time to put some distance between myself, the still-settling puddle of piss, and the famished kitty making a meal of her backstrap.

~

The woman with the crossbow has—had—a kid about two or three years old, judging by the clothes piled up in the laundry bin. Somehow, he's already fully patched into the Filthy Thirteen Motorcycle Club.

A Prospect patch would have been cuter.

Back inside, the three of us work to extricate the whereabouts of one escaped and very much wanted Charles Denver McDaniel.

The big guy with the broken jaw manages to say, "Chucky?" then whimpers a little, then growls, then cusses when Arlo asks where the guy is in plain language. It turns out it smarts to talk after your bottom jaw receives blunt force trauma and enough time passes for shock to take a leave of absence.

Charinda drags the dude she Heisman'd off the motorcycle in by the belt loops and sits him on the loveseat, alongside the still whimpering broken jaw.

"See," Arlo says, "she's a *real* Wrangler. Walked on with no one giving her a problem."

"No doubt," I say and cast a glance toward the front door of the clubhouse.

"I've got eight more of them bean bags to get what I need out of you," Arlo says to the two gentlemen on the loveseat. "If we got to play twenty questions with you—"

The guy Charinda sacked says, "Man, suck my cock. See what you get out of me that way—"

But a shot gets fired into his chest that shakes all but Arlo.

"Seven," Arlo says, correcting himself before he clears his throat and swallows to try to stop his ringing ears. Or so I'm guessing since I'm doing the same. "Now you know what it feels like, too," he says to the guy Charinda sacked.

The guy needs a minute. He bows his head, rests his chin on his chest, regards the floor beyond his feet. By all accounts, he'd elected to open his ears and keep quiet. Of course, later, we caught on that one bean bag round to the chest at point blank range is enough to defibrillate a person's heart. That's why no one thought to render aid. That's not an excuse. That is the reason why what happened happened.

Arlo ejects the spent shell and says to him, "Lost your train of thought?" then racks another round. "Choo-choo, asshole. Don't interrupt me while I am conducting an investigation." Then he looks to the big guy with the broken jaw. "The sooner you give us your undivided attention, the sooner we can stop imposing on your hospitality."

Maybe what he says sounds rehearsed, but that's what happens when ninety percent of your workday fits the dictionary definition of tedium. See also: Arlo is a funny fucker when he's not playing the part of the big, scary Black man.

I imagine he says it because he figures the guy is paying no attention to anything but the spent plastic shell casing rolling to its final resting place beneath a couch. He seems fixated on it, so we let him be. We figure him for the strong silent type who prefers to suffer in silence. Someone who figures us for the proper authorities. So, we did not mean to leave him for dead.

Here's hoping that's enough to absolve some sins.

"Charles Denver McDaniel is where?" Arlo says to the big guy with the broken jaw. "Tell me which nook or point us toward the cranny where he can be found—por favor. I am not leaving without the little bastard. Sorry. Munchkin?" he says and cranks his neck toward my direction, making sure no one new has entered from stage left. "Kinky?" he calls out to make sure I know he is talking to me rather than about me. "Ain't that what you call them up there in Kansas?"

"I'm from Wisconsin," I say.

Arlo chuckles. "I hope I didn't get ahead of myself when we made each other's introduction earlier this evening. To clarify, we are searching for an escaped inmate. Usually, the US Marshalls handle these things, but only for so long. Manhunts cost cash, and Uncle Sam has a short attention span. Unfortunately, Chucky's bondsman might take the forfeiture of his full bail amount personally. That'd be me. That house was spared when Greenwood burned. My granddad owned it. Now the bank rents it to tweakers on Section 8."

"This is like a vendetta?" the bloody, but breathing, biker says.

"Where might I find him?" Arlo says again. But before he can answer, the jukebox comes to life and spoils the defiant atmosphere.

The breathing biker takes his time but eventually offers, "Treehouse. Chucky's hiding out in the treehouse. I don't like that shotgun-riding motherfucker."

"Kinky!" Arlo belts out.

"Yeah?" I say.

"You remember a treehouse?"

"A tiger I fucking do."

"Thanks for reminding me. I almost forgot the man-eating kitty cat," Arlo says.

"No problem, quién-no-sabe," I say back to Arlo's sardonic ass. "There any Orbison on their jukebox?" I jut my chin toward where the Wurlitzer stands.

"Why?" Arlo says.

"Last request," I say before I disappear down the back hallway.

"Don't be so damn dramatic," Arlo says. "Y'ain't going alone."

"Excellent," I say. "I'm sure the tiger will appreciate a bean bag to bat around after it eats us. Bound to get bored eventually."

"Kinky, shut up and grab the bow and arrow," Arlo says.

"That's just fucking racist, ain't it?"

"The crossbow, I mean, Kinky, goddammit—" Arlo interrupts himself with what I'll call a stupefied sort of laughter. "I'm Cherokee Freedmen, dumbfuck. Y'ain't looked at the plates on my truck, Tonto?"

"I don't what the fuck that means."

"Still, you'll look like Rambo if you wrap your shirt around your head an—"

"Yeah, take it off!" Charinda barks out before Arlo can finish his thought.

"I was an MP, not SF."

"And now you're a pussy?" Arlo says.

Charinda hisses at that, and the big guy with the broken jaw laughs until he cries, which draws all of our attention. Since he has the floor, he does his best impression of a ventriloquist and whispers, "There's three of you. Maybe a fourth waiting. Do you know how many we got? I don't. Can't count that high." He unfurls his fingers until he runs out, shrugs.

"If you don't stop your talking," Charinda says, "you're going to get your ass beat to the tune of—"

"Buck Owens," he says through the froth and spittle. He chuckles until Arlo jams the breaching barrel of the shotgun into his cheek, gifting him a new hole to bleed and breathe from, along with a few busted teeth.

"Who stuck their hand up your ass and got you talking?" Arlo says before he draws his arm back. Arlo looks like he hopes the guy will give him reason to unwind, but the poor feller has nothing else to add to the conversation. I doubt he can see through the tears or breathe through the pain, much less talk with that mess of a mouth.

I slap my back against the push bar and open the rear door.

With crossbow in hand, I train it on where I last saw the kitty, using my foot to hold the door open while the other two pour out behind me. Arlo brings bean bags, and Charinda takes hold of the crossbow by the foregrip and says, "You'll need both hands. But I'll be watching your ass the whole time."

Charinda blushes for me, and from off in the distance, Arlo hollers out, "Kinky!" again. "If you would please join me front and center?"

So I do.

Arlo stands bowlegged, arms crossed high on his chest, staring at the tree directly behind the clubhouse. "You see the little girl with bleach blonde hair wearing the princess nightie playing peekaboo up in the deer stand?" he says.

"Yeppers," I say. "And?"

"She's got a goddamned goatee, you see that, too?"

"Now, yeah. It's the hormones they put in the milk, I think," I say.

"Fetch," he says, echoing when he tossed me the keys to the Viper and left me to my devices. That is when Lil Hank, the pro-dwarf wrestler of The Outhouse infamy, comes off the top ropes wearing a pretty pink nightie and a Goldilocks wig.

I will need both hands.

Charles Denver McDaniel, aka Lil Hank, latches onto me midair and wiggles himself around until he gets to where he can pinch my windpipe with the ditch of one arm and smash me in the ear with the other fist more times than anyone other than a medical examiner could count. Arlo later tells me I slowly yelled, "O-u-c-h," before taking a knee.

I don't recall.

However longer later, I scream, "Somebody shoot this motherfucker, how about it?"

They can't stop laughing.

Arlo and Charinda wait for him to tire. But the little shit is powered by angel dust. So I do things I am not proud of.

42

"I'm not riding in that truck. Forget it right now," Chucky says to one and all along with some other stuff underlining his perturbment.

"State law requires you ride in a booster seat, sir," Arlo says to Chucky before I hoist him into the cab of the truck. He cusses and kicks, but I hold him at arm's length until I buckle him into his big boy seat and settle onto the other end of the bench, behind Arlo, who already has the truck in gear.

I catch our passenger glaring in my peripheral, looking a lot like Grumpy, so I say, "Friends to the end?"

"Fuck you. Fuck that movie."

"Lil Hank?" I say, wanting to make sure, since I hadn't seen him since the night I last saw Elise alive.

Charles Denver McDaniel says, "No autographs," and exercises his right to remain silent.

On the way to the interstate, we stop to get gas at the Love's north of the Sugar Creek Casino. I pump. I shift this way and that to catalog my new bumps and bruises while wondering what I'll feel like in the morning. As a countermeasure, I fish a few tabs of fentanyl from a pocket and send them downstream. They taste like shit on a dry tongue, but some pains must be endured to dodge others.

At some point, I holler out to Arlo, saying, "How big is this—*damn*—tank?" but whisper the *damn* for some reason, which is when I first notice someone milling in my periphery too close for comfort and for no good reason I can come up with. So I turn to let them know I see them. Which is when another joins us and breaks the awkward silence by saying, "Can't let you take him," which gets punctuated by at least two more Filthy Thirteen members crowding me on my other side.

I turn to face the spokesman of the group and see the second gentleman brandishing a handgun of some sort in my direction.

Fuck.

I don't think I say anything argumentative. I keep my cool as best I can. I continue fueling and wait for the pump to click to a stop. Once it does, I free the nozzle from the truck and swing it toward the pistol-packing bikers with the trigger pulled and the pump set to full auto.

I manage to drench the whole Hee-Haw gang in eighty-seven octane before they know what to do. Don't-make-any-sudden-moves tops the list of good decisions.

Arlo fires the engine and truck lunges forward fast enough and far enough away to where he can watch what happens next in the blind spot mirror, where he can be sure he won't get sent to the upper room. Though they take it as a sign I've been left, so they all take a collective step in my direction.

I get tunnel visioned.

Charinda issues out of the ether with a glowing cigarette lighter freshly plucked from the truck's dash. The cherry coils stop everyone dead. This subtle act lets the gentlemen who've congregated know she should not be confused with some meager biker bitch. Meanwhile, Chris LeDoux's cowboyed-up cover of Aerosmith's "Fever" rains down on my shoulders from the truck stop speakers, fucking up the atmosphere. But the security footage still shows a clear case of self-defense.

The scene has all the drama of an action film flashback, minus the lit car lighter tumbling toward the pooled gasoline in slow motion, simply because the thing isn't anywhere near as big as the grain on the gas station's camera footage. *Instantaneous* is the word the reporter uses later.

Luckily, most Filthy Thirteen members are wanted men already, atop being members of a national criminal organization. Sadly they do not supply medical insurance for their members, so a poker run will have to follow the funerals, for those who survived. That said, law enforcement aren't willing to put as much time, effort, and cash into investigating who did what and why as one might expect following the torching of a gas station, considering the victims. Fortunately, the ass end of the truck got caked in the beloved red dirt of Oklahoma legend when we hightailed it out of the tiny town of Nowhere. Coincidently, Arlo drove the most popular vehicle on the road that year, too. We didn't even drive off without paying.

No harm, no foul.

43

I didn't work the next day. That weekend, though, I realized going to watch the Green Country Derby Dolls in all their glory proved a better time than sitting mourning Elise by my lonesome. Except for the empty seat where she would have sat.

Maybe she always will.

Accept that an elbow leaves a better bruise than any punch, no matter how expertly thrown and landed. An elbow turned blunt instrument almost always gets missed at roller-skating speeds in the midst of a wriggling sea of blockers and jammers. That's not to mention how a blocker's elbow to the ribcage, right below the armpit of a passing jammer, makes the same sound as a tree falling in a forbidden forest.

The sound of that crunching bone gets lost among the crowd that could make most golf enthusiasts piss their pants. It passes by the lips barely a whisper above the sound of a hundred or so hard rubber wheels rolling on the hardwood rink floor, the huffing and puffing and blowing of hot breath from the ten women circling the oval track, along with the three uniformed officials and the twenty teammates screaming constructive criticisms from the sidelines, foaming at the mouth until their turn comes.

That's not to forget the sound of a handful of comically pubescent teenage boys doing their damnedest to empty their shoulder-slung coolers before the end of the first period, but all get drowned out by a college-aged kid who spends his days sweating at the carwash for minimum wage and a sliver of the tip jar before coming to the community center to sell 3-2-1 beer on commission—unless my nose is telling lies.

What the Green Country Derby Dolls' jammer thought got screamed to the entire arena had to get whispered to a ref after tapping out of the jam. Then a blocker named Elbow Smacaroni gets ejected from the game for not fully grasping irony or the rules of roller derby. Whispered, as that's all anyone can get out through cracked bones and swelling that'll take three to six weeks to heal. But first, there's this bout to win.

Bashin Shred-Her rolls toward the cafeteria window, where the EMTs lie in wait. Roller girls get hurt all the time, but injured is something else. It's bitchy, to begin with, but to hit someone that hard in the middle of a match sanctioned by the Women's Flat Track Derby Association, which people had to purchase tickets to come witness, seems unbecoming, especially when you are the center of attention.

Unsporting contact can be dealt with by either a thirty-second timeout while standing along the outside of the track or planting your ass in the penalty box. If a skater does that seven times, they're fouled out of the game. Then it's see you next Tuesday, and they get officially expelled, the way an elementary school principal does with cunty little kids who can't keep their hands to themselves on the playground.

An attack like that only comes when the challenger knows they've lost, so instead of playing by the rules, they make it personal.

Charinda's ribs are cracked, not broken.

I'll never understand why derby girls and dwarf wrestling troupes share a love for Limp Bizkit. Or maybe that speaks more to the state of my generation. I can't figure it for the life of me. Freddy's not exactly someone I'd categorize as a badass, considering he couldn't cut it in the Navy—or spell biscuit. The Green Country Derby Dolls are, even sans Bashin Shred-Her, who'll sit out the rest of the season if she knows what's good for her.

Ursula, the bouncer from the White Crow Bar, slips the star onto her helmet and becomes the lead jammer with the same ferocity as a Jenny Craig dropout retaking the field at the neighborhood Golden Corral after dropping the kids off at the pool.

I don't remember the day of the week of the roller derby match—Friday, Saturday, or Sunday, maybe—but I do remember that night being one that'd make any soul regret renting a single-wide trailer house on the banks of eastern Oklahoma's Arkansas River. Me, mostly.

Especially.

The evening air got so damp my place took on a funk. The orange marmalade-colored sky proved enough to make me feel ill—nauseated—what with tornado alley in my backyard and me quickly realizing how it was all part of the literal calm before the storm.

At least I had a tab or three—or how-many-ever it took to knock me out back then—to slip under my tongue and distract me from the wind flinging dirt and debris from dumped garbage cans and sending lawn ornaments this way and that, raging to a point I got convinced I just might wake on the set of *The Wizard of Oz*.

The storm ushers in the kind of windy that flips dumpsters and turns dirty diapers into missile hazards, busts windows, and dents aluminum siding. But I have the Big O, who sings to me about the candy-colored clown they call the Sandman, tiptoeing his way into my room to sprinkle stardust and whisper, "Go to sleep. Everything is all right."

I inch my way to my bed at the end of the hall, kitty-corner from the two-person Jacuzzi tub that comes standard in such lavish accommodations. Inch because the trailer twists and flexes—breathes—the way a cargo ship will while navigating the gales of November on the Great Lakes.

Lightheaded is one way to explain how I feel when I leave the bathroom and go for the bedroom. When I open the door and step through, depth perception goes out the window. I waltz into the room before my eyes can adjust and I knock my head on something and dusk goes dark.

44

I wake in a mysterious, far-off land to the sound of an idling V-twin that sporadically snarls the way a lion will when wanting the world to know he wants nothing more than to fuck and gorge himself on some water buffalo and nap, but he's willing to settle for a fight. Or to eat one of his young. V-twins are easy to recognize by ear, defined by the popping echoes that come off the straight pipes. The blasts bounce off the barren steel walls, ceiling, and concrete floor, begging to be let outside along with the exhaust forming a halo around my head.

I'm awake enough now to notice the fog thickens with each purposeful breath I draw. Or maybe that's the result of whoever twisting the throttle. My neck is rubber. Along with the rest of me. I slept with my chin on my chest and it stays put after I wake.

The first thing I see is blood. The second thing the needling fluorescent lights bring to my attention is a pair of shiny silver steel fishing hooks meant for musky or, maybe, sharks, which suspend me nearer the ceiling than the concrete floor. That's to say, the flesh and meat of my upper pecs—north of the nipple; south of the collar bone—got pierced sometime after I got forced to take a power nap.

I catch sight of an individual in the corner of my periphery quietly busy in the shop below, seemingly ignoring me. It takes all the strength I have to raise my head enough for my eyes to follow the steel cables that run from the hooks up to the chain fed into the hoist above my head. The ceiling looks nondescript: steel-framed with corrugated metal sheeting. Gray in color, to be exact. Gathering that piece of circumstantial evidence leaves my rubbery neck stuck in the full upright position, leaving me looking like a Pez dispenser ready to give up the goods. But it gives me time to fixate on the nuances of the ten-foot-tall tripod, complete with the manual engine hoist they used to hang me up to dry the way a slaughterhouse does with kosher-killed cattle.

Since assumption is the leading cause of divorce between men and authenticity, I should mention how my hands and feet fell asleep but failed to wake when I did. They made me a marionette without bothering to animate my limbs, which I take to mean they want me to play dead until I get it right. The pain searing from my chest grows to a point I can't muster enough air in my lungs to express it. Instead, I tremble while pink piss drenches my crotch and pantlegs and drips down to the floor from the toes of my boots.

"Motherfucker," I hear through an old speaker from somewhere outside my periphery. Then I hear someone dump floor-dry on the slab beneath me. Then I smell kitty litter. Fresh Step with flavor crystals.

Fuck this hurts.

The chain jingles and unfurls, giving me a sinking sensation. He lowers me like old folks fuck, slow and jerky, wounding my chest even more so.

I sink lower and lower until the toes of my boots grind against the kitty litter poured out to soak up my piss and blood and pooling sweat, all of which threaten to taint the concrete slab with DNA evidence.

I get ceremoniously yanked back up to half-mast, inches at a time, jangling at the end of the chain each time whoever reaches the end of their arm's length. Each time, I bleed a little more so, and can concentrate only on the two steel hooks fished through the meat in my chest. Thankfully, that ache and agony exits stage left after he swings a thirty-inch-long steel breaker bar into my kidneys like a birthday boy with a sweet tooth gifted a piñata.

I piss blood before he finishes.

Fortunately, there are brand new boxes of bleach and ammonia at the ready, so I won't leave a mark on this world.

He leaves me for dead on the garage floor, atop the moistened wint-o-green Fresh Step.

Given my host's hard-on for Viking torture techniques, the tow-behind hydraulic log splitter I spot causes me a great deal of concern. As does the jump box—the power box—the whatever the fuck you call the thing that looks like a giant car battery strapped onto a furniture dolly with jumper cables coming off it.

My assailant wears the same shitty gas mask they gave us in boot camp, along with the chocolate chip desert camo-colored MOPP hood. Unfortunately, his eyes do not flood my mind with déjà vu. Of course, his Filthy Thirteen patch is inked into the flesh on his back. As if that will help identify him, should I live. His panhead bike belches exhaust into my open mouth every two to three seconds, causing me to cough and my eyes to well and overfloweth, making identification at a later date and time even more improbable.

"Have we met?" is all I can get out through the bubbling spit building in the back of my throat.

He kills the engine on the bike.

I'm next.

The tinkling sound of the cooling V-twin engine and exhaust pipes give way to the hum of a handheld butane torch. The stink of vinegar stings my nose rather than bleach or ammonia, which does not warm the cockles of my heart. The Filthy Thirteen cut their black tar heroin with instant coffee, so it'll be the coroner who names my killer—or at least the conduit. The cause of death on the certificate will read: accidental overdose. However, in the state of Oklahoma, karma dictates if you purposefully end another's life, the state will kill you in return. And though I hate to spend any time at all on the obvious, the room around me has the undeniable look of premeditation. So I let myself enjoy the moment, once the pain in my chest ebbs and turns to a flood of endorphins, oxytocin, dopamine, serotonin, and adrenaline which force me to forget my safe word.

"Mind telling me why you're smiling like an imbecile?" the dungeon master says.

"You'll get the needle." I try to laugh.

"You first," he says.

The needle the hooded executioner jams into the meat of my neck looks filled to the rim with Brim. It burns when it penetrates the skin and flesh and gristle running alongside my windpipe. But the burn goes away when the heroin hits my brain and gets turned into morphine—as God intended, leaving me with a smile similar to everyone Jack Napier knocked off after he started with the makeup.

I think back to how the cadre at the US Army's Survival, Evasion, Resistance, and Escape school hosted at Fort Rucker, Alabama, stripped me naked and decontaminated me with a cleansing shower of needling, freezing water from a fire hose before they tossed me into a three-foot-by-three-foot box made of half-inch steel. I did not get left alone with my thoughts in that tiny box. They piped in the soothing sounds of a screaming baby, on loop, the entire time, along with air conditioning set to a temp meant to keep butchered meat fresh.

Time stood still in that box.

Though I hear it's different when the child is your own.

However much longer later, the apparent spokesperson for the opposing forces asked me questions I couldn't answer, according to the Uniform Code of Military Justice and the Manual for Courts-Martial.

They were aware, yet unmoved.

Each time the proverbial beans failed to spill, an instructor—who looked a lot like the long-lost big brother of Harry Henderson and the giddy-up-oom-poppa-oom-poppa-mow-mow guy from the Oak Ridge Boys—slapped me with a hand afflicted with giantism, forcing me to pee some with each rising wave of agonizing pain.

I couldn't answer any further questions, thanks to his palm—damp with sweat from the humidity, courtesy of the summer sun baking the Gulf Coast states—making something of a suction cup around my ear each time he walloped the side of my buzzed bald head.

All I could hear was this test of the emergency broadcast system.

Then this one time, at pretend POW camp, super-sized Grizzly Addams encouraged me to take up extreme gargling as a professional sport and spent the next few hours doing his damnedest to convince me how no one official cared about what any enemies—foreign or domestic—did to me or demanded in exchange for it to end. No one other than myself could help me secure certain creature comforts, which continuing the man-in-the-box routine would not afford me.

I laughed. Then I told him, "You can't do anything my loved ones back home haven't already. Why do you think I joined the circus?"

After his spiel, voiced loud enough for my fellow pretend POWs to hear, they made like they'd ushered me into a hot shower and paraded a freshly laundered uniform to me before they sat me down in front of a grilled sirloin topped with farm-fresh chives, caramelized onions, a side of steamed carrots, a sizable dollop of buttery garlic mashed potatoes, an icy Guinness roiling in a frosty mug, and a still-steaming pan of not-my-mom's bread pudding in exchange for some juicy gossip concerning the activities of my unit.

I closed my eyes, closed my mouth, and lost twenty-seven pounds in twenty-one days. Had I accepted their offer, I could have slipped on that freshly laundered uniform and counted the seven days of the week on the belt loops of my Army-issued trousers, or kept track of the passing time with the beads on my dog tag chains until our rescuers arrived. Or ate that goddamn meal that had me salivating. Instead, they left me in that room long enough for me to watch flies claim the steak, sides, and dessert—long enough for the rest of the class to become convinced I cleaned my plate and even indulged in some intimate dinner conversation. Then they made like they were escorting me to my new sleeping arrangements far from the others, making sure to thank me for my cooperation along the way.

But I didn't speak, and back in the box I went.

45

Windchimes welcome me somewhere and get me stirring in time to hear someone say, "Hey, mister, you ever fart so good, you pee some, too?" through a sniff.

"The fuck is wrong with you? Can't you ever close your mouth for ten seconds? How you know he ain't still alive?" someone new says while a chill swallows my foot and slithers north of my ankle.

When the same happens to my other foot, I hear, "You ever do that, mister?" whispered into my ear. "'Cause you reek a little like both." But my dreams have never made much sense. So I curl into a tighter ball to warm myself and offer no fight whatsoever to Mister Sandman when he shows up to drag me down into Dante's ninth circle. Which I'll be so bold as to say stinks of methane and pools of stale beer teeming with life meant to indiscriminately digest the rotting remains of a half-eaten chicken strip basket and a Ho-Chunk Indian left for dead in a dumpster somewhere on the Creek Nation.

I'm sure they hoped I'd be a corpse by the time the trash truck dropped me off at the landfill, where I'd return to Mother Earth after getting crushed, compressed, and condensed alongside how many ever tons of garbage and God knows whatever else. Then I wake in a shifting sea of green and brown glass bottles, ebbing and flowing this way and that.

I breach the black plastic lid of the dumpster being hoisted into the air and tossed into the back of a trash truck seconds before I hear the hydraulics moan, as does everyone else within earshot. Which is why no one else hears my body slap the blacktop.

Beer bottles don't break clean the way a windshield does in a car crash, believe you me. Their glittery dust gets everywhere and leaves you looking like you spent a lust-filled evening in the company of Tinkerbell after Peter took off with Wendy hunting his shadow. Though, this doesn't come to my attention until after I do a double take in the floor-to-ceiling mirror in the men's room in the ass end of some dive bar that sells a shit ton of Tsingtao somewhere in the southeastern bowels of Tulsa.

Shortly after I catch sight of my glistening and glittering self in the mirror with those teensy flecks of green and brown glass dusted atop my moistened skin, some leather enthusiast comes around the corner from the row of urinals and says, "What can I do you for?" midway through zipping his barn door. "I thought this was a no shirt, no shoes, no service sort of spot," he adds while he closes the distance between us, looking me over once more and unapologetically adjusting himself like he's just found what was hidden on the other side of the glory hole.

I can't say what goes through my head in the moment, purely because I'm still not sure how I got here or where here is. And there are countless other questions that'll have to wait till later. For now, I let him stand nose to nose with me and breathe on me.

We're the same size.

He's just doughy.

I cut off whatever he has to say next by saying the one thing I can come up with at such a time. "I need your clothing, your boots, your motorcycle," and I trail a hand up and along the lapel of this leather jacket and let him interpret the gesture how he will.

That's to say, he didn't leave room for Jesus between us.

The AC does its best to stifle the smell of the sweltering bodies out on the dance floor, mixed with the eye-burning sting of the countless piss streams that failed to find their mark, and my dick into a stack of dimes. Meanwhile the teensy shards and granules of glass burrow deeper into the soles of my feet and gravity does what it can to ground me in the here and now.

"What?" he says.

Rather than repeat myself, I coldcock him upside the ear.

His knees bounce off the floor, followed by the rest of him. He screams at the ceramic tiles and crawls toward the stall doors. His flight or fight is fine-tuned and single-minded.

Nobody tries the door in the time it takes me to strip him of all but his socks and skivvies. He doesn't offer much in the way of resistance. Mostly, he feels sorry for himself. I let him cling to the base of a toilet bowl until it is time to give up his leather jacket and Flaming Lips T-shirt. I plant my knuckles atop the little protrusion at the back of his skull with a light jab. Anything resembling a right cross and he'd need a wheelchair, or six close friends. And I, a lawyer, to dodge the needle.

The shirt fits a bit snugly, and the pants bunch up where they ought not. The boots, though, are worn well enough to be comfy, though they nearly come to the knee, and the soles don't flex for shit. The heels stand too tall for the way I carry myself, so my toes slap the asbestos tile flooring with each step I take, until I get smart enough to drag my feet as if close to crapping my pants. Which doesn't make a damn bit of sense, as I'm leaving the men's room.

Not that I give a shit.

The pentagon-looking Plymouth ignition key I find in the front right-side jacket pocket of my new wardrobe guides me to a shimmering white Duster waiting in the back half of El Toro de Oro's parking lot the way a waiting war pony would, ready to whisk me away to safer pastures.

My last five Fentanyl tabs are waiting next to my toaster oven in the kitchen of my trailer. I don't need a locksmith or violence to get inside. Whoever grabbed me didn't bother to lock up when they left.

Something convinces me soaking in a tub of lavender-scented Epsom salt will be a phenomenal way to soften my skin enough to let the ground glass ease its way out.

I come back to earth waterlogged but still afloat, looking like a plucked bird with gooseflesh everywhere.

I refill the tub but cannot get warm, even with the hot on full blast.

I cannot stop pissing out my ass, either.

I puke a lot and nothing and often.

I feel my heart throb so hard my chest bobs.

I can't convince sleep to come my way.

I can't convince my eyes and nose to stop running, so I stop rubbing them raw and let them leak.

I can't eat either.

I can. I just cannot keep anything down.

I ache down to my bones.

I learn later it's called dope sick.

On the seventh day, I emerge from the tub, pounds and shades lighter.

46

"Kinky, you are a disgusting human being," Arlo says, punctuated by me leaning my back up against the door to the little bounty hunters' room in order to make certain it clicks all the way closed and will not crack open and fumigate the big boss's tiny office.

"It only thunders when it rains," I say.

"What kind of what is that?" Arlo says, half serious and half not wanting to be bested by a punchline coyly lying in wait.

"Ancient Indian proverb."

"I guess that's why I recognize it. Take a load off, Kinky," Arlo adds.

And I do.

"Do you feel as good as you look?" Arlo says. "You have a lost weekend? Could have used you around here."

"I ran out of my prescriptions," I say. "A couple days within each other. Felt like food poisoning."

"Pain meds?"

"I've had my face busted, my shoulder torn loose, and my ass beat like it's a job requirement," I say, and absently search my pockets for pill bottles.

"Pain is mostly inflammation," he adds.

I laugh at that. "Yeah, I'm puffy all over," I say, shifting in my seat, looking for a comfortable position. Small talk is hard to feign interest in when pain peeks its ugly head.

"Well, Kinky, when's the last time you got puffy?"

"Puffy?"

"Did you grow up on store-brand WIC bullshit boxed food, and commodities come the first of the month?"

"Yep," I say, still wondering.

"So we both got heart disease haunting our horizons. That's why we got college and rookie NFL players dropping dead on the fifty-yard line, clutching their chest like Elvis on the toilet. Growing up on garbage disguised as groceries and then putting all that stress on their hearts, hoping to crawl out of poverty ain't smart. I like to lower my blood pressure every chance I get. Folks got to remember where they came from. You'll be barrel-chested by forty by the look of you," Arlo says, and adds the Elvis lip thing to be an asshole.

"Aren't you just a ray of sunshine?"

"Sunshine I've got," he says and snaps his finger. "Kinky, since you cannot sit still, stand and lock the door."

By the time I turn back toward the desk, Arlo has headed into the bathroom. "Step into my office, Kinky," he says and leaves the door ajar.

Cautiously, I comply.

I find Arlo on the toilet with the top of the tank balanced on his knees. He points to the exhaust fan to explain the change of venue, and I scan the room. I see the litterbox, but I have not one time seen a cat.

I watch while Arlo produces a skinny pack of menthol cigarettes and searches between them like he has trust issues. Eventually, he finds what he's looking for and puts the tank topper back in place. "I've found so many stashes in there." Then he gives himself a police pat-down looking for a lighter.

He produces the joint from the pack and lights it, singeing the tip before putting it to his lips. He locks eyes with me, as if to say *like so,* before he inhales—twice—pinches it between his thumb and pointer and dangles it to his side. He whispers, "Y'inhale until you feel like you're about to cough, sit with it a second until your lungs stop fighting you, top it off with another hit, take it down deep, and leave it there." Then he exhales. "Once you get fidgety, let it out slowly, like a scuba diver. You don't want to get higher than your bubbles."

And I do.

And he does.

And I do.

Then I finally ask a question my inquiring mind has pondered since my first full day working for Arlo.

"Why is there a cardboard cutout of the Lone Ranger in the shitter? He doesn't match any of the other decor."

Arlo huffs, a half laugh. "Do you know why he wore a mask?"

"Why? Was he shy?" I say, and pass it back.

"No. Let me come at you from a different direction," Arlo says. "Do you know why the good guy wore a *black* mask?"

"When're you going to tell me who made it to the top of Arlo's most wanted list?" I say, hoping to end the bullshit session and discuss how I can fill my fridge.

He has a point to make. "The Lone Ranger wore a black mask on TV because blackface fell out of fashion by the time Hollywood tried to tell the tale of the real Lone Ranger, a Black man named Bass Reeves who came up from the Tejas territory to hunt down all the outlaws laying low in Indian Territory."

"Well, I'll be," I say. "I never cared about the goofy guy in the blue PJs. Jay Silverheels was my John Wayne."

"How many little boys would have been dressing up like him had they put Sidney Poitier in Silver's saddle?" Arlo says, and passes it back.

"Just little Black boys who want to be cowboys and good guys, I imagine."

"And the dollar stores wouldn't have sold one single black mask."

"Tell me how you really feel," I say.

Arlo exhales. “Hiram Lucas Williams. Goes by Luke,” he says, ignoring my smart-alecky mouth and answering my earlier question. “Failed to appear at a preliminary hearing while you took a week at the spa—”

“Ah, I—”

“Don’t care,” Arlo says, taking the roach back. “Next time, go to a beach. You look like a ghost. Luke’s a small business owner, so not a flight risk.”

“What’s he worth?”

“To you? Four months’ rent.”

“Hi-yo, Silver! Away!” I singsong.

“How ya feel?”

“Feel what?”

“Back to work?”

“Back to work,” I say.

At his desk, I crack the case file folder he hands me. “Huh. What—what’s the Santeria Smoke Shoppe?”

“It’s the headshop he owns. He sells pipes and papers, tobacco, dip, tarot cards, Black Jesus bullshit, cigarettes, dildos, powders, potions, and lotions to the Afro-Caribbean community. Tell him we need to talk. The judge, I hear, would like a word as well.”

“Tax fraud?” I set the file back down inside Arlo’s reach. “That’s white-collar shit, ain’t it?”

“Yeah, but the blue-collar redneck dumb shit tried to write his spot off as a church and got audited. Fake churches are frowned upon in the buckle of the Bible Belt,” Arlo says. “Especially if they check the *other* box.”

“Other?” I say, wondering which church became the default in the great state of Oklahoma other than Bacone Baptists.

Arlo laughs at that and says, “Yeah, it’s one of those holistic strip mall churches. You know what I’m talking about, right? Ever seen one for yourself?”

"Nah."

"Go have a look. You got the address. I'd hate to ruin the surprise," Arlo says and sends me out the door to grab another dum-dum who forgot to check the calendar after their morning shit, shower, and shave. Outside his front door, paying customers pace, hoping to have enough cash to spring a loved one out of the city zoo.

47

The gas gauge in the Duster I lifted off the leather fanatic points closer to full than my Mirada's, which is why I go with it for an in-town, failure-to-appear snatch-and-grab.

I let James Hetfield finish warbling his way through "Don't Tread on Me" before I pop the black album out of the tape deck and point the shimmering front bumper toward the Turner Turnpike. After I muscle my way through the local news, sports, weather, and evangelical offerings, I finally find something I can break the speed limit to. After which I nestle my ass into the crushed velour and pleather seat dyed a perfect shade of deep purple that'll conceal nearly every imaginable stain, from motor oil to a fatal amount of blood loss.

A hint of exhaust flutters into the cab courtesy of a tear in the boot on the shift stick, causing me to crack the windows. Minus the pinstriping and the hood, the outside looks painted mother-of-pearl. The hood, however, has a piss-poor airbrush rendering of Metallica's black coiled snake with SNAKE MAN written in their ripped-off lightning bolt font. The bolt-on bug deflector reads the same thing but backward and in big, bold, block black letters. Upon further examination, I don't feel all that bad about coldcocking him and leaving him in the men's room the way I did.

I doubt his dad beat his ass nearly enough.

The Santeria Smoke Shoppe sits on a frontage road running alongside Route 66, right before it turns into either tollway or a rural scenic byway kept litter-free by good Samaritans who never got told as children to play in traffic with any degree of seriousness.

I figure it for a ten-minute trip to the city jailhouse downtown.

The neighboring get-and-go gas station looks more welcoming to foot traffic from the adjacent shuttered elementary school turned low-income housing unit than to well-meaning tourists looking to get their kicks on the Mother Road. So witnesses are not something I expect to worry myself over. I park the Duster between the dumpster and the headshop's back door. After I kill the ignition and pop the trunk latch, I listen to the Duster's engine cool and clearcoat sizzle in the afternoon sun until a slender, gangly guy matching the description of one Hiram Lucas Williams, hauling a black trash bag in each hand, heads out the back door of the Santeria Smoke Shoppe and bounds toward the trash receptacle.

At that time, I exit the vehicle.

Shortly after entering the Santeria Smoke Shoppe, I toggle the power switch on the OPEN sign to the off position, spin the deadbolt, and pop a squat to make like I am contemplating becoming the proud owner of a green blown glass bong in the shape of an organ pipe cactus—all so I can watch him when he enters the back door and ambush him if need be.

This too is tradecraft.

Even crouched, I don't hide so well, so he says, "Can I help you?" before the door closes behind him.

"Yeah. I dig that bong. How much does that run? Couldn't see a tag or—" I say, but he cuts me off to correct me and inform me how, "Actually—technically—it's a water pipe. *Who-caw* is the term used everywhere but here in the good old US of A," he says, the over-annunciation almost sounding rehearsed.

"Oh, yessir, no wacky tabaccy for me," I say. "Just a conversation piece, ya know? Reminds me of a hotel I stayed at last night. Headed west to OKC now. Exploring 66."

So I can check his waistline for any suspicious bulges that might make me think *gun,* and as an act of good faith, I ask him to grab me a can of their top-shelf pipe tobacco, the way others will ask a shapely woman to grab something from the bottom shelf, so she'll bend at the waist and make her britches that much tighter. He's dressed in basketball shorts and a wifebeater with a short-sleeved flannel. I can plainly see I don't have to worry about having to return armed to detain and apprehend him.

When I say, "Are you Hiram?" I believe he hears me say, "You hiring?" asking for a job.

"Nah, sir, I am all staffed up."

"High-Rum?" I say again but break it down into its two syllables. Apparently in such a way that it sends him racing toward the mechanical room rather than the back door.

I give pursuit.

He reemerges with a shotgun in hand, but I'm waiting alongside the doorjamb opposite of the hinge.

You don't chase a snake into its burrow.

When he breaches the threshold of the doorway barrel-first, he gets greeted with a brachial stun from moi. He goes down hard on the tile, like Spock got 'em.

Perhaps, had I called him Luke, it wouldn't have flipped the stranger-danger switch in his brain. Regardless, inside the mechanical room, or what is labeled the mechanical room, I find a hall to the neighboring suite, which houses what I later learn is known as a botánica.

Botánicas sell candles every color of the rainbow and ones that will last for seven whole days, apparently. Along with ones labeled for a slew of patron saints. I see candles molded to look like women, too. Black, red, and brown only, sorry to report. Incenses and oils and beads and all that mumbo jumbo TV has taught us to expect, along with all eleven herbs and spices.

The quarter-sized grim reaper statue gives me pause. It has so many dollar bills stuck to it that it reminds me of a blushing bride following a prosperous dollar dance. Santa Muerte, according to the tags on all her lookalike take-home miniature models, holds a sickle with one hand, the world with the other, and rocks a hooded cloak. She even comes with a pet owl. Who knew the grim reaper was a Latina under that cloak? Everything else looks like it could be shelved in a cathedral supply store, minus any copies of the holy scripture.

A quick survey tells me it's the kind of place that caters to people who merely pray to make it through their day-to-day. I cannot count the times I've worshipped at that altar.

When you sucker-punch someone at the base of their neck, where their shoulder starts, you target a mass of nerves called the brachial plexus. Spock pulled this move, too, but he did so politely. What I did looks like a clothesline mixed with a right cross to the neck. When the spot gets hit with bona fide blunt force trauma, a sort of EMP gets sent throughout that entire side of the body. People lose vision on that same side.

Instant lights out, in other words.

The arm and leg on that same side go numb, too, so they meet the floor as dead weight, like they've been shot point-blank in the back of the skull.

When they do wake, they'll have a lot in common with a quadriplegic. The instructor who taught my hand-to-hand class at the military police academy at Fort Lost-in-the-Woods said, "It's like giving a sucker a stroke," so no one volunteered to let him show everybody how it worked when properly administered until I did—after he sweetened the pot by adding how the dummy who volunteered got to go home for the day. However, he neglected to tell us how the individual struck in the brachial plexus might piss their pants a little when they blacked out, too.

Hiram Lucas Williams does as well.

What comes next is boring: I check his pulse, handcuff and search him, lock the push bar on the front door to his place of business so his ware won't grow legs, and then carry the still-limp Hiram Luke Williams to the Duster while I sing, "She's got the whole world in her hands."

Once I get us back to the car, I crack the door, pop the trunk, and the handle comes free from the dash. The cable feels limp in my weak hand, and the handle won't snap back in for me. It's broke. I drop it on the floormat and resituate ol' limp Luke on my shoulder before I head for the back bumper. I take one last look around when I lift the lid all the way to toss all six feet and four inches of him into the trunk before anybody with an itchy trigger finger or a quarter to call Crime Stoppers can see me.

"I did not slam the trunk lid. It fell closed when I dropped him inside. There was no trunk key on the keyring. I tried the trunk latch a second after he started screaming. So, the circumstances around his demise are coincidental, not premeditated. No more premeditated than how I plan to eat breakfast in the morning," I say. For the record.

48

"So, to recap," the smug little prick from the state prosecutor's office says, "public nudity, criminal trespass to chattels, first-degree assault, grand theft auto, strong-arm robbery last weekend. Today: false imprisonment, kidnapping, manslaughter—maybe murder. Fingers crossed."

From his seat in the corner of the interrogation room, Arlo barks, "That's bullshit. Are you going to let my people go? Give him a badge, not a goddamn sentence—"

"Mister Bice, do you understand it is a privilege for you to be here during our interview with your employee?"

"I do," Arlo says.

"Shut it up, then, and chalk it up to a learning experience. Before you get a room of your own." He turns back to me. "Now, Mister Kincaid, do you understand working as a fugitive recovery agent in the state of Oklahoma without a license can become a felony charge of kidnapping without anybody in this building batting an eye?"

All I can do at that point is blink.

I can't come up with anything to say to sway my situation, so I stay quiet. God bless Miranda. Unfortunately, ignorance of the law does not excuse the breaking of the law unless you're sworn to uphold the law. Everyone else is on their own.

I drove with one former Hiram Lucas Williams, dead or damn close to dying, in the back of the car for however long it took me to find the nearest hospital.

DOA became the official prognosis after I convinced the cheesedick greeter working the ER's valet ramp that I did indeed have a patient needing immediate treatment inside my vehicle. An off-duty woman from some local pop-a-lock place issued from the ether and popped said trunk after hearing me holler from all the way inside the waiting room.

No one tried to bag him or wanted to waste any of their insanely expensive antivenom or even give the AED a shot with how shallow his pulse appeared. Not with the nature of his injuries still slithering where the jack and spare ought to have been, had I taken an automobile from any another other swinging dick at that bar. They could have at least intubated him. The only one with any brains was the orderly who dumped buckets of ice on the snakes so Luke could exit the vehicle and his body be brought wherever.

The cop at the hospital I turn myself in to says he'll need to call the real cops. The real cops play hot potato until the Oklahoma State Bureau of Investigation gets tagged and decides to play a different game with me.

"Since you failed to retrieve the deceased from the trunk, Mister Kincaid, and moved the body after the reported time of death, more charges'll get added, do you understand? All the pathologist needs to do is scooch the time of death a little to the left, and any grand jury member will agree with the recommended charges as presented," the shiny little dickhead from the state says. "The public defender can't even spell object. Kidnapping is a federal charge. We can hand you over to the federal prosecutor and be at Arnie's in plenty of time for tacos."

Then the wannabe Walker Texas Ranger from the OSBI says, "The Oklahoma Bail Enforcement and Licensing Act requires anyone acting as a bounty hunter to be trained and certified through the Oklahoma Council on Law Enforcement Education and Training.

Do you understand that, Moses?"

"Now, I do. Yes," I say. *Now it's Moses,* I think, and raise my wrists from my lap to my face to give my itchy eye a scratch—not yet ready to make eye contact—before I say, "What about reciprocity?"

"Asking for reciprocity right now is a whole lot like my asshole ex-wife asking for me to honor spousal privilege to suppress evidence, discovery, and testimony during our divorce hearing," the smug little prick says, and sits back in his folding chair, like he means to say he's done talking without doing so. "It's a little late for that. Oklahoma has a whole host of ways to bring your life to a sudden stop: lethal injection, electric chair, firing squad in case the first two don't snuff you out."

"What about the dude trafficking venomous snakes?" I say.

"What about him?" the trooper-turned-detective says. "He had a valid hunting license. And he hadn't left the state. Rattlesnake season closed, what, sometime last week or the week before last? Wasn't it? The fuck do I care about some goddamned snakes when I got the murderer right here in front of me?"

Manslaughterer, maybe, I thought. Though I figure it best to sit quietly and let him have his moment atop his high horse.

"I don't care, but since you're so worried, Mister Kincaid, the game warden's office got paged before you got booked. There's not one of us here who want to deal with that sort of shit," the trooper-turned-detective says.

"How many bite marks did you say?"

"They counted nineteen puncture wounds. Only sixteen of those are consistent with fang marks. The other three might be the real cause of death," says the shiny little prick from the state prosecutor's office.

I ignore the half-assed accusation. "What am I looking at? Timewise?" I say, leaning across the table and toward the prosecutor, trying to bring some relief to my back.

"More time than you got left on Earth," says the trooper-turned-detective. "Or an offer to hit the reset button. If you can manage to grasp the gravity of the shit pile you stepped into while trespassing through my beloved Oklahoma. Address me as is engraved into my badge," adds the special agent from the state investigation bureau.

"Are you going to investigate how I got into a dumpster, Special Agent?"

"Poor life choices," he says. "And you doubled down after you came to, didn't you? Case closed." And there goes my paddle.

"What do you want from me?"

"Stay as a guest of Oklahoma for a while—all-inclusive. Make some new friends, tell us all about it," says the special agent. "In a nutshell, snitches might get stitches. But they get a get-out-of-jail-free card, too," he says, in a voice as dry as his wife gets at the thought of his naked husk joining her in the shower.

The smug little prick from the state prosecutor's office nods. "Take the time to think things over this weekend in segregation. If the answer is no, the federal prosecutor's office will do everything it can to get you hard labor up in Leavenworth, making big rocks into small rocks until the food kills you or some skinhead takes a stab at it. Someone, please correct me if I am wrong, but isn't Mister Kincaid fresh enough out of the Army to still get jammed up with double jeopardy?" He shakes his head. "I bet there's an inmate or two who'd love you for a cellmate. Were you a fair guard when you worked there—disrespect any detainees?"

Extortion by any other name still stinks of pig shit.

"Mister Hiram Lucas Williams was headed to prison for a taste of his own medicine," says the special agent, so pleased with himself that a smile freezes his face and gets his eyes to twinkle.

"Tax fraud?" I say.

"The Bible says God breathed life into Adam, and along with it came free will."

"Hindsight is twenty-twenty all the way around, huh?" I say in a voice filled with a shit ton of regret. "Your forefathers believed in a separation of church and state, so what's that got to do with anything and me?"

"The Devil's Breath takes away free will," the special agent says. "Mister Williams sold a lot of bullshit folk remedies, but the scopolamine seeds are a bona fide pharmacological nightmare. Worse than ketamine. Worse than angel dust. Worse than rohypn—"

"What is it?"

"It's used to treat severe motion sickness and in hospitals to fight nausea in the recovery room—in *small* doses. The victim, or patient, won't know when it's been administered. It's to keep you calm as can be, feeling altogether average. Malleable. Compliant, complacent, conscious, but walking around without your memory chip."

"He was trafficking."

"Yup."

"So I killed the bad guy. You're very welcome."

"You killed the distributor for eastern Oklahoma," the special agent says back. "The subject of an ongoing investigation, but not the focus. The problem is, we think it's in the prisons."

"What's wrong with pliant convicts?"

"Everything," says someone from the DOC, who sat silently until then with arms folded so tightly I think of pipe tobacco.

The public pretender seated alongside me—who I'll call Shemp—seems too busy doing all he can to clean a smudge from the face of his watch to add anything to my plea deal arbitration meeting. So I chime in, saying, "I don't like this. I am getting fucked. And no one thought about lube."

"So what?" says the special agent from the state investigation bureau. "Put a bag on its head and do it for Old Glory. What'll it hurt to wear a uniform again for your Uncle Sam?"

"How long will I serve?" I say.

"Until you find it," the special agent says and makes a face I'll always wish I punched.

49

Seeing as how the place is populated by inquiring minds possessing nothing but time and a share in the booming black market, alongside broke motherfuckers working as COs with access to multiple national criminal search engines, it's best to go to prison as yourself. That's to say, I get sentenced in a public hearing at the county courthouse nuzzled in the Deco District of downtown Tulsa—alongside everyone else who'd broken laws too grandiose to be tried within city limits and in such close proximity to the innocent taxpaying townsfolk—where I plead no contest to several respectable felonies but get found guilty on all charges nevertheless.

No contest is the most Midwestern plea a man can make. Pleading no contest is like saying you are neither willing to confirm nor deny the actions of which you are accused, the same way a politician will say no comment as a way to brush off allegations from the watchdog media and let the court of public opinion decide the verdict.

No contest exists simply to save face when there's video footage of the accused doing a thing but no recollection of the act, time, and place, no matter how sweet the plea deal. Unfortunately, unlike the UCMJ's military necessity clause, there's no it-seemed-like-a-good-idea-at-the-time defense in anybody else's set of law books.

I face the consequences of my actions without any outwardly obvious malice toward the messenger of blind Lady Justice, dressed in the black silken robe, wielding the gavel as literal punctuation when pronouncing a sentence.

That's not to forget those who get incarcerated alongside me.

How many ever days later, I get herded onto a bluebird bus along with the rest of Santa's misfit toys. Thanks to the fleeing felon law and the vast array of both non-lethal and kill-you-dead weaponry on display for all to see, we all marry our asses to our seats and don't call attention to ourselves during our early morning field trip.

Somewhere south of Tulsa, sown fields the color of spent coffee grounds laid out like corduroys lie in wait to give a seizure to anyone foolish enough to stare. I divert my eyes while they strobe by my window on the way to *the* Oklahoma State Penitentiary, the only male-only maximum-security prison set in the northernmost edge of McAlester, Oklahoma—lovingly referred to as Big Mac. More infamously known as the home of the OSP Outlaw Rodeo, aka the Toughest Show on Dirt. Coincidently celebrating its fifty-fifth anniversary this Labor Day, a month or so after I will get assigned to a cell.

If I last that long.

Electric Avenue is the one exit in town that'll take you straight to the prison without needing to use your blinker or breaking any traffic laws.

Levity takes the same exit but hooks a right at the first light and follows the business route. Some rich bitch littered buffalos along the city streets, the same as before the land got clear-cut to make way for the Oklahoma State Penitentiary. Largely absent are the Choctaw people and their buffalo. The statues stand unblinking, turning to rust, as metal art does after enough neglect. Some have begun to take on the look of a live one, which inches me back to the one that loitered on a byway and brought Elise's life to a dead stop. I see that all again. Unfortunately, you can't close your eyes and turn your head when it's in your head.

More than my shoulder came loose the night Elise left this world.

Entering—or being ushered inside—the OSP's rotunda is an experience unlike any other. A fire-escape-looking catwalk encircles the inside of the domed ceiling where correctional officers pace or sit perched, armed, and itchy. They're anything but stealthy. It's almost as if they want their presence known.

Their dog-and-pony show reminds me of what the Army calls a psychological deterrent, a bullshit show of force meant to change a bad guy's mind. The same as airport security.

At my feet, two black guidelines on the floor dare me to step out of line, literally. Anytime anyone does, one of the gunmen circling above gets to work for a living. I'm assuming the red-and-white-checkboard tiled floor got installed to make the sudden presence of a pink mist or an arterial spray less unsightly.

Next to our heads, bullet holes pepper murals painted on the sheeting that came from the former inmate-run mattress factory. Someone painted a scene depicting Jesus Christ before the cross, George Washington at Valley Forge, along with one portraying the tragically outgunned Choctaw who once called this place home. The artist, I learn, is the Mad Artist of McAlester—officially known as the ousted German nobleman Conrad Maass. With his paintings displayed so proudly to greet newcomers, I'll be so bold as to say their arts and crafts programs is stellar. But the paintings are only there to cover the preponderance of bullets lodged in the rotunda walls before word spreads that the guards at Big Mac love their job. At thirty-three years old, Conrad Maass earned a sentence of lifelong hard labor for ending his wife's nagging with a shotgun. He did not want to go home to Germany, and he meant it. She got the message after he ground her into sausage meat to conceal the crime, but got caught when a customer found a fingernail in their schnitzel. Not much remains of his collection other than what's on display in the rotunda. The madness brought on by lead-based paints has put more artists in the ground than sadness.

Then there's the matter of the rat stuck in the cage in the center of it all, who controls every movement in and out of the Oklahoma State Penitentiary. He, too, is behind bars and an assortment of heavy-duty electronic magnets. And bulletproof glass. He can't even get tear-gassed in the event of a disarmed guard and an inmate getting to play with all the Gucci gear they wear on their web belts. I bet he doesn't even have to leave to relieve himself.

Everything between there and the cell I'll call home for however long is a nondescript maze, minus the cheese. OSP went to two per cell ever since the last riot in 1985, somewhere around a year or so after my roommate first wrongly visited the place despite Jesus knowing he never stole a single dime.

Forgive me for skipping the details of my quarantine.

"Cellie, tell me something: you Chinese? 'Cause you look like that puffed-up Chinese dude that beat Van Damme's ass at the end of *Bloodsport*—until he went all ninja master, or whatever, you know? You ever watched that one?" is the first thing my cellmate thought to say seconds after the magnet draws the door closed. Ronnie Leonard Carlisi is a nobody from Valdosta, Georgia, who got three to five years for armed robbery with two years already notched into his headboard. He snatches my papers to see if I got a plea deal for cooperation with arresting authorities or prosecutors. Or whether my crimes are sexually deviant. And lastly, to see which ethnicity box got checked by whoever did my paperwork on my behalf.

This part is a lot like when you bring your report card to Dad—if Dad decides to put a hit on you for bad marks, that is.

The boring part of the twenty-three-hour-long lockdown is that if you get killed, you get done in by your cellie, so the investigators need to keep sharp as a shiv made from a spork. Bury one and lock the other one down in a lower rung of hell. They'll get life or death.

Case closed.

"Yeah," I say, without letting on whether I am making mention of what continent my ancestors hailed from or if I am familiar with the catalog of work claimed by the Muscles from Brussels. "Bolo Yeung's the actor. The same guy who about beat Bruce Lee's little ass in *Enter the Dragon*."

"What's that you say?" He cocks his head the way a dog will, when its ears prick after hearing a sound its brain can't quite classify. "Oh, shit. I think you're right."

"I am. No reason to lie," I say and unfurl my sleep bundle on the bunk across from his. How far I've fallen from hospital corners and bouncing quarters off my tucked sheets.

I sit and look at Ronnie eye to eye, which gets him to break the ice a bit more. "So, you yellow then?"

"My name's Moses Kincaid," I say and offer him my right hand.

"Yeah, alrighty," Ronnie says and shakes my hand with half-assed conviction. "Fucking dotted up already, too, I see. Ain't your first rodeo, looks like to me," which gets his old ass to scoot forward so he can have a closer look at my artwork. Then, without a hint of comedy or hurry in his voice, this motherfucker says, "How do I know you didn't get adopted by some nice white church folks or an Oklahoma oilman who likes to diddle little Asian boys and raise them how he likes?"

"How about I already talked to the prison shrink, and it never came up. But I wasn't born until after you pulled out of Vietnam," I say.

"Only time anyone ever successfully got me to pull out," he says, as dryly as the damp air inside the underground, windowless Unit H permits.

Unit H houses death row inmates too, along with the yellow door that takes folks on a one-way trip to the execution chamber and the long-since-retired electric chair, nicknamed "Old Sparky" by not-so-creative correctional officers. It claimed eighty-two souls in the span of ninety-nine years. So a special sort of silence hangs in the air between breaths and words spoken inside the place.

Placing the defunct electric chair in the prison for posterity feels a lot like walling a woman up inside a new building because each one needs a ghost.

"How big of a chance do you think there stands I might be your deddy?" Ronnie adds, doing his darndest to hide the smile in his eyes.

"Motherfucker, I'm Indian. Winnebago. Ho-Chunk," I say and point toward the ceiling, meaning to say I came from north of here. But he hasn't a clue what I mean—his face tells me so—so I say, as plainly as possible, "I am not Vietnamese or whatever you're thinking."

"As long as you aren't contagious, I could not give one shit concerning what you are or are not at the present moment," he says. Deflates his chest and brandishes a complete set of dental implants before laughing to himself—at himself.

Someone has to, I suppose.

I put my back to the wall and cast my best thousand-yard stare out our door's window, wondering whether I've finally found where the wild goose goes.

Ronnie's laugh turns to a cough, which forces him to clear his throat. Then he says, "As long as you're not some godforsaken gook," and makes the sign of the cross.

I don't blink. I don't let my face flinch or my mouth move. Nor do I take the time to turn in Ronnie's direction. We got locked together in a lo-fi sound booth, so he has no doubt I heard the thing he said. And he continues.

"You're staring out the window like your life depends on knowing what's on the other side. Do you want to know what your future holds?" I scan our cell for a crystal ball, but he goes on. "Your headstone will be a gray patio block-looking thing made in the masonry shop. Someone will stamp your name and birth date onto a blank license plate that'll get bolted to that block. If the warden has orders to send you on a stainless-steel ride, he'll make you dig your own grave beforehand. Unless you try to run. Then a detail of men will do it. Nothing else is for certain here."

"Personalized license plates?"

"Yeah," he says, and hands my papers back to me. "I see your charges on this sheet, but what did they convince the courts you did?"

I don't bullshit him.

"You're about as wrong as two boys fucking. Kid, you got a lion in your den," Ronnie says. "But y'ain't no diaper sniper or son of a bitching snitch, so you won't end up on a bad news list from the jump."

I deflate, relieved he doesn't want to take me for a walk on the wild side. "Boot camp was the last time I heard that one about two boys playing hide the wiener," I say, and let myself laugh a little.

"Probably where I picked it up. Y'ain't got to worry about me wanting to get romantic," Ronnie says. "Where'd you serve?"

"Army. Six years. I was a POG," I say, and scrunch up the corner of my mouth and let my eyes wander back outside our cell door.

He catches my boredom with my own lack of war stories and offers no further questions. He understands. Being a veteran himself, one with not one story about Vietnam he feels like sharing with the world, let alone some cellie on day one. He respects my candor.

"I did my time in Desert Storm and Haiti, too," I say.

"Moses…do you mind me calling you Moses, Moses? Or are you still stuck in that last-name-only buck sergeant bullshit?"

"Moe," I say. "Call me Moe, if you would, please."

No one suffers from an identity crisis in prison. Whatever you are, you are, and no one will let you be anything but. Ronnie proved a chatty fellow, but that happens when you are left alone for too long a stretch.

Ronnie—Raiford is what I ought to call him, with that accent—catches me staring out the window once again and says, "If you put on the gorilla suit, you got to wear it every day." Something tugs on my nostril hairs and gets my eyes to well up, too. I snap my head to see where Raiford wandered off to and find him popping a squat.

"Are you talking—doling out advice—while taking a shit?" I say, stupefied.

"No," Raiford says, followed by another grunt and a splash. "I'm feeding the warden. We all have to do our part."

"Gorilla suit?"

"Yup," Raiford says and puts his hands out to his side and folds himself into a ball to flex every muscle he can from the neck down, the way Doctor Banner does after his eyes go white and his flesh turns green—followed by another heavy-sounding splash.

"Do you want to watch me while I wipe my brown eye, too?" Ronnie says, waving a white flag of toilet paper in the air between us.

Chow is an eraser and choke sandwich hand-delivered through the bean slot by whatever boss works today. I forget the name Raiford said.

They give no jelly with the peanut butter because it can get turned into pruno.

Pruno happens after jelly ferments for three days' time, if added to a leftover fruit cup along with a bit of the yeast generously sprinkled atop a dobie dinner roll by the brownies and trustees in the kitchen. Assuming you pay the piper beforehand.

I'll be the first to admit it's a good thing the Army got me primed and ready for prolonged exposure to another human in tight quarters. The place feels comfy. What some might call déjà vu. What the initiated call institutionalized.

Instead of keeping the conversation afloat while he wipes his ass, I regard the ceiling, interlace my fingers behind my head, cross my ankles, uncross them, cross them the other way, and wait for

Raiford's stench to rise toward the return air vent and for him to flush before I take in another full breath through my nose.

50

"*On the door for rec—two-minute warning,*" rings out from the PA speakers.

I pause or freeze or stay sitting statue, depending on whoever's vantage point.

"It's in your best interest to take full advantage of this time to distance yourself from this cell and comingle with others such as yourself," Raiford says. "I get rec. I am going to rec, so it'll be just you in here. In theory."

"I'm all right on my own," I say. "But some sun on my face, fresh air, always sound good."

"That's good," Raiford says, moseying his way toward the door. "Your face wouldn't bode so well with you sitting in here all by your lonesome. Take a nap, and you're fucked. Well, fucked in a roundabout way, not the way you're thinking."

"I'll bite," I say. "You put the bait on the hook and cast your line into the water. Please set the hook."

"We got this fellow in here for two lifespans, okay? Two."

"Well, my great-great-grandchildren can breathe a sigh of relief," I say.

"Yeah, mine, too, huh? I don't think he's going to hold up his end of the bargain. But he's screwy," Raiford says. "Remember that."

"Are you saying there's an abnormal individual incarcerated in here with us?"

"Yeah, but forget about normal. Normal doesn't exist in here. Definitely not out in the Big Mac rec yards, but not outside the outside fences either."

"What are you saying?"

"Some guys are into different kinks. That's all. It's not weird—for them. Some folks need it missionary, ten toes up, ten toes down, two balls bouncing round and round as the blessed baby Jesus intended it to be between a man and a woman, with the only light in the room the glinting off their gold wedding bands."

"You don't say. How's that related to cold cuts?" I say.

"Lunchmeat likes it rough."

"S-u-r-prise," I say in a singsong whisper.

"Yeah, okay. Look, Moe. I don't know what in the name of the fuck Lunchmeat's folks did to him, but don't ever let on to him that you might like smoking cigarettes."

"But is that not worth its weight in platinum in terms of prison bartering? Cigarettes, I mean," I say. "Cigarettes are the ultimate ice breaker. Are you saying he trades cigarettes for sex? He prostitutes himself for nicotine?"

"You need to learn how the fuck to whisper is what you need to know," Raiford says, while shifting weight from one leg to the other and back again.

"I'm listening."

"Cigarettes after sex is a consolation prize when talking about Lunchmeat," Raiford says and smiles in a way I don't like. "You snooze, you lose. That's part of it for him."

"That's what now?"

"You got to be asleep for him to get off," Raiford says.

"Sounds like the best part of waking up," I say "You mean like he's got himself a Sleeping Beauty fetish?"

"Nah, kid," Raiford says, shifting his volume down into a lower gear, nearly grinding against reverse. "He gets off on giving pleasure.

Picture this, okay—"

"Nah," I say this time. "I got zombies and stampeding camels unafraid of gunfire and other shit you don't want ever to know already lodged in my brain."

Raiford stares at me like I missed history class when it came to nightmares of Vietnam. "The hell if I'm not going to tell you. Information—intelligence—is a currency for the incarcerated, too, kid—to be bartered when your inquiring mind needs to know something from outside your social circle. See what I am saying? Nodding is fine. You're going to pay me back for this handy bit of information."

"For why?"

"You can let me know when the Indians got on their kicks," he says and looks down at the skippies on my feet and then to the kicks on the concrete shelf above my bed. "That day, I might let Lunchmeat have his way with me come our time to roam the rec yard."

"What the fuck are you talking about?" I say to Raiford.

"Lunchmeat is a cocksucker, you hear? He'll suck your pecker to completion without complaint."

"Okay. Thoughtful and thorough," I say. "Sounds like his cellie won the lotto."

"Shit, that's cause you ain't listening to the thing I am trying to say to you," Raiford says. "Besides, the warden doesn't allow him no cellie. Sending him to seg won't break the habit, either."

"What's the big deal? I'm good and lubed up already. Tell me if you mean to. Your mind ain't straying, is it, old-timer?"

"Are you going to get quiet long enough to let me finish with what it is I am trying to tell you?" Raiford says to me.

So I do.

"He doesn't like to hit the exercise yard. He's not socially equipped, for one thing. It gets quiet after everyone shuffles outside. Lunchmeat takes walks, but he don't bother going outside. He just walks around the house. He keeps his mouth shut and takes in the sounds of the silence. Of course, convicts can't close their own cell doors if they don't feel like engaging in outdoor exercise. Some folks just stay put and play cards or read. God help you if you choose that time to punch the clown.

"If some shut-eye is on the menu, you best not snore any louder than his boots fall. The element of surprise is his foreplay."

"So you're saying this isn't a preordained tryst?"

"That's one thing it is most certainly not," Raiford says. "I call him a predator, but his eyes are set so far apart he looks like a brim. He's got the peripheral vision of a fish, I'm telling you. He could tell if a chess piece got moved in someone else's cell without turning his head.

"When he finds whoever will become the object of his affections, he'll do a right or left face crisper than any member of the Corps' Silent Drill team could ever dream before he goes Samsonite gorilla on their coconut. He's not beyond body shots, either. Understand—he's not trying to soften someone up enough so they can't fight off rape. He's a known vampire, but drawing blood is not good enough. He beats them bloody because he does not want anybody looking at him when he's slobbing a knob.

"Ashamed, I guess. Can't blame him now, can you?

"Have you ever tried to maintain an erection while getting your ass beat by some mongo motherfucker? Or keeping it up afterward? No, I'd say that's near impossible. He has to knock a feller clean out cold," Raiford finishes. Telling on himself some more is how I take it.

"How's he for pillow talk?"

"Guards say he is nonverbal."

"Bless his heart," I say. "I was gonna stick around for med call and ask the doc for a nicotine patch for a pick-me-up, but I don't dare now."

"You better get on that door for rec then, huh?"

And I do.

Raiford stands and starts for the door too. Monkey see, monkey do is the best way to achieve longevity in any institution. Once you boil down the transferability of the training the Army gives every single solitary soldier—how to do more with less, how to secure a building regardless of who's already inside, how to fire a weapon proficiently and destroy the intended target, etc.—you're ready for either prison or homelessness or the local police force in whatever neck of the woods is hiring. Only option A comes with free food, shelter, medical, and mental health care on par with any other government-led program.

Raiford got sent on enough raids in the Vietnam policing action to handle a locally roasted coffee and smoked meats specialty shop called the Perk-N-Jerk following the morning rush, all by his lonesome and without the aid of anything resembling a squad. He made sure to say how there are cameras nowadays when telling me the story of how he got here this time.

Being the new guy, I go first through the door. Hurry up and wait reenters my life.

"Lunchmeat, let's go! Rec! Time to toss your cell," a guard belts out behind me. I can't tell who or how far off, courtesy of the acoustics created by concrete, raw steel, and zoo-grade glass.

"Anybody going to miss you back home?" Raiford says once he too steps out onto the walkway.

I can see ears perk around me after Raiford asks me about home, so I say, "Oh, yeah. I'm the chief meteorologist for my people, don'tcha know?" which makes those eavesdropping on our conversation pay closer attention and then tune out entirely. At least that was the plan on my end. I think my accent gave me away.

51

Outside, Raiford carries on about Lunchmeat. He's a man who reportedly can't feel pain. Or is too shy to show it around strangers. Liberally applied pepper spray gets him to blink, lick his lips, and break the bones of whoever tried to hurt him. COs who've tried pain compliance through the use of pressure points get the ligaments and tendons torn on their fingers and thumbs before he pulls them from their sockets and snaps the bones inside.

I would have loved to see the tango with the taser for myself. They got him good, I hear. One barb buried itself in his right shoulder, and the other found a home in whichever muscle is the teardrop-shaped one atop the kneecap.

In theory, when the trigger on a taser is pulled, electricity surges to each barb before it jumps back to the other barb—as alternating current does—forcefully flexing every muscle in between, paralyzing the individual long enough for the LEOs to restrain the individual safely, and painfully enough for the suspect to submit.

In theory.

After brandishing the taser for the entirety of the cell extraction, to make certain Lunchmeat knew it was on the menu, as trained, the CO yelled, "Taser, taser, taser," three times at the top of his lungs before they pulled the trigger—so their friends and coworkers could skedaddle. They made sure they got it all on camera too.

By the book.

When the trigger squeezed and the barbs shot across the cell to where he stood, nothing happened. The snapping clack, clack, clack sound is heard on the film, but it looks like a sound effect.

Most men who can stomach the voltage will rip the barbs from their flesh and bleed for a little while when they fight the taser and taserer. The CO who shot you can still bum-rush you and zap you with the taser itself. Then there's no loss of horsepower. Then you give up or lose control. Except Lunchmeat left the barbs in and leapt at the extraction team so he could bear-hug the CO and teach him things Louie the Lightning Bug did not.

What a CO is to do in said scenario isn't listed anywhere in the use of force manual or the manufacturer's handbook. The CO took every last one of those ten thousand volts, and regretted every time he poked the bear—instantaneously.

Lunchmeat didn't stop until the CO's heart did.

I buy Raiford's story about Lunchmeat at face value, despite how it sounds like it drips with bullshit, thanks to an uncle I have back home. I remember when I was in high school, how he had to hotwire his garbage cans to keep the bears from dumping them and spreading the trash around the neighborhood the way a wolf will with the entrails of a kill. My uncle told his brother-in-law what he'd done, how he wired up his trash cans, but his brother-in-law didn't think it'd work since there was only one electrician in the family, and it was not him. To save face, my uncle took hold of one of the trash cans and stood there unaffected until his brother-in-law came over to laugh in his face.

My uncle said to his brother-in-law, "You're right. I was wrong. I am man enough to admit that at least," and offered him a heartfelt handshake. That's when his brother-in-law's boots about melted to the blacktop driveway. That's to say, both my uncle and Lunchmeat proved well-grounded individuals.

Raiford goes on about how every known compliance technique,

both current and no longer deemed constitutional, prove a waste of time, work hours, and the inventory at the prison's disposal whenever Lunchmeat needs to move elsewhere for whatever reason.

Seeing as how meals get dropped at our doors three times a day by a dedicated room service staff, showers only happened three times a week, and rec's only an hour a day, any movement might seem minuscule, but a welcome break from the monotony, nevertheless.

Yet some people don't like change, or others touching their few sacred belongings, let alone taking their eyes off their things, to the point they become as predictably violent as Old Faithful. Folks don't get that way after they get here. They bring that wherever they go. It follows the way thunder does lightning. Lunchmeat became his official alias because the guards guessed his IQ matched that of the processed foodstuffs. Coupled with how he proved equally ticklish.

"Why's he here?"

"Fucking A," Raiford says and shrugs. "Shitty lawyer, most likely, right?"

"Why is he *here?*" I say again. "He's not a damn supervillain. He needs trained staff."

"Yeah, but they like to mix the perverts and dum-dums in with the rest of the model citizens and save the state some cash," Raiford says.

That answers that.

My new uniform of blues and skippies glow brighter than anyone else I see circling the yard. It's the same uniform as a sailor, minus the cute hat. I figure they'll get dingy before too awfully long, anyhow, and my new car smell will fade shortly thereafter. Five days out of the week, we get afforded the opportunity to stretch our legs and walk the track like the road dogs or sift through the iron pile to broaden our physiques or sit and soak up some vitamin D on the bleachers with the lame ducks who are too afraid to turn their back on the crowd of cliques. That's where the june bugs gather too,

Raiford says. They're the walking dead in the sense they've given up everything and live life in service to someone else or the entire group. They're serviceable, used to barter with or as scapegoats, or for carnal pleasure.

With three scheduled showers a week, purposefully sweating seems ill-advised, though there's no limit to what a person can become accustomed to if given enough time. That's to say, if everyone stinks, nobody stinks.

I keep moving clockwise around the yard until I spy cowboys training for the coming rodeo in a far-off corner. I am not sure why, but learning the Oklahoma State Penitentiary houses dozens of former members of both the Professional Rodeo Cowboy Association and the Professional Bull Riders League comes as something of a surprise to me. Of course, a whole slew of amateur wannabes eager to try their hand in the time-tested traditions of man versus beast without working their way up from mutton busting clamor for Coach to let them play too.

Rodeo in the real world gets cowpokes from every walk of life to compete for cash prizes and some of the most ornate trophy buckles made by some of the most sought-after gold and silversmiths working today. Bragging rights and a few dollars not amounting to anything worth mentioning is all that is at stake in the Oklahoma State Penitentiary's Outlaw Rodeo, unless you try your hand at Money the Hard Way. Only then can you come out a hundred dollars richer—unless you piss off the wrong guard, then you'll have to wait an entire year before you can hope to brag about how you bested a rank bronc or bull for an entire eight seconds of your life sentence.

Unfortunately, the prison does not provide the same amenities as a dive bar that's gotten overly attached to the cowboy, country, and western theme. Instead, someone straddles a steel barrel draped with cowhide and holds on for dear life with one hand to a braided rope looped around the belly of the beast. Meanwhile, four other dudes try to jerk that one man off onto the wrestling mats below.

Once there was an actual hydraulic bull, I am told, which broke. They didn't want it to get stripped down for parts, so it went away. *They* being the guards who have to do the paperwork when any inmate-manufactured weapon comes in direct contact with another inmate's insides.

52

The special agent explained to me that "falling asleep beneath the borrachero tree"—the source of scopolamine—had grown to be an issue of concern around the Big Mac rec yards. But I got sent to go and look for the existence of and source of the Devil's Breath with the same set of commands as any other drug-sniffing dog.

So I let my intuition off its leash.

Scopolamine's nightshades, when in bloom, look like an angel's trumpet. Though the tea made from those ground petals got named after the most adversarial of all angels. It can be made into an ointment or a poultice, as well as a tincture. Medicinally speaking, it's used to stave off asthma attacks and kill pain by blacking a person out of consciousness, as well as to stave off post-op nausea when the opioid pain meds wear off. Though scopolamine is more commonly considered a cause of elevated heart rate, spasms, confusion, dry mouth, diarrhea, robbing, raping, and murdering—once whoever it is gets done with you.

That's to say it causes all the above, along with making a person's pupils widen until they look possessed. It can cause paralysis of the muscles in your eyes so all you can see are shapes and colors and hallucinations. Paralysis can strike your insides, too. If enough is administered, you can't breathe or digest. Meaning, it turns you off the way your grandma at the gynecologist getting treated for genital warts ought to. One guy cut out his tongue and severed his penis after drinking one cup o' tea, so it's best to sip slowly.

Ingest it, purposefully or otherwise, and it's *Howdy Doody* time for you.

Spooks all over the globe are guilty of using it for a sort of truth serum, seeing as how it makes a man more forthcoming. But it causes a guy to see and hear shit no one else can, too. So when someone hollers out, "Did you guys see the size of that chicken?" during their interrogation, intelligence is the last thing they're gathering.

The seeds are the size and color of a piece of pea gravel or sunflower seed, so they can get stuffed almost anywhere and walked inside the prison by either visitors or staff or trustees. They grow inside a little coconut-looking thing called the cacao sabanero and get ground into a powder, bleached, and alkalized, like when coca and ether get married.

A bump the size of someone's pinky fingernail is guaranteed cardiac failure and a backstage pass for a meet-and-greet with Saint Peter himself. A gram will kill ten men, but a light dusting will make the genie pop out, and whoever rubbed your lamp gets endless wishes.

Simply being in the room with scopolamine makes you obedient, pliable, programmable. Witnesses will say you seem of sound mind and body while the scopolamine has you under hypnosis. Luckily, you won't remember a thing, *if* you're not made to overdose once they're done pulling your strings.

Who's pulling what strings?

Inquiring minds want to know.

After the spiel from the OSBI, I got left in an observation cell for the weekend. Not a seg cell, like how he threatened. Then came the dog and pony show before the judge at the Tulsa County courthouse, adoringly called the Denver courthouse because of the avenue's name. Dinner that first night in seg came without ceremony: chicken pot pie, a half-pint of vitamin D milk, sugarless—not sugar-free—

Kool-Aid, and a pudding cup. Vanilla, if memory serves.

When I wave my napkin to wipe my mouth after that mouthwatering meal, salt from that packet you get sometimes—or powdered coffee creamer—goes everywhere. I sneeze so hard my brain hurts at the stem. After, I blink and blink, and everything gets slathered with that same mustard-yellow light that shines down right before a tornado comes to town. Then it hits me: that's how easy it is to get someone with the shit.

Now, I'm got.

It's not just a Big Mac problem.

Tulsa's been got, too.

53

A siren cries, causing the whole rec yard to do an about-face. "Head back to the house!" someone bent at the waist hollers into the ear of an old-timer.

As soon as I turn back toward Unit H, I feel claustrophobic. I haven't made any friends yet, and I'll need to meet a lot of different folks if I care to learn who's trafficking.

When I move through the corralled crowd, I roll my shoulders, careful not to bump into anyone accidentally. I keep my eyes peeled for Eric Delvin Drumgoole Senior, Charles Denver McDaniel, Filthy Thirteen tattoos. I'm hunting for someone with a similar complexion and bone structure as me, hoping I don't mistake a Mexican or Asian for an Indian.

Here's where all Indians not looking alike becomes a real bitch.

"Do you know where I can catch a whiff of the Devil's Breath," I say to the dark-complected, definitely-not-Ojibwe dipshit with the dream catcher tattooed onto the top of his right hand with a feather trailing toward his thumbnail.

"Sulfur, you say? You like sniffing farts?" he says back through a lazy drawl, sounding like he's just woken up. He sounds like any other Okie, too, so there is little to no chance he is Anishinaabe and only co-opted the dream catcher and knows as much about being Indian as me. After that, it feels like the right time to make my introduction.

"Biggest guy in the yard, right?"

"Goddamn close there, big swole. Ain't yah? Looks like you, FBI?" Mr. Dreamcatcher says.

I about shit my pants when he says that loud enough for anyone with zipped lips to hear. I laugh and say, "How's that now?" hoping they aren't my last words.

The crowd gets thicker around me right then, I swear. Breath warms my neck from two different directions. But then he clarifies, "You, FBI, aye. You're a *fucking*—BIG—Indian."

Breathing comes a bit easier once I work out his meaning. I might pass a little gas, too, once my asshole comes unclenched. But he hasn't said anything to my first inquiry, so I, too, clarify and say, "Drop the biggest guy in the yard, right?"

"Man—hush," someone else says, loud enough for me to hear even if I weren't paranoid and eavesdropping.

Then I spy the guilty party, Montana. Montana is the nickname of a guard best described as a baldheaded version of the big bastard wrestling fans know as the Great Khali. Montana because he's Mexican and the size of a mountain, and anyone who's watched enough Sesame Street can fill in the rest for themselves. Then I remember there's also a bundle of nerves everyone is born with that sits nestled atop the meat of the midthigh. Striking it with even a glancing blow will force a fellow to greet the pavement, whether they're expecting it or it comes unprovoked. It's something cops are taught to use when escorting someone who gets a bit too froggy. By simply popping them with the inside of your knee on the outside of their thigh, you can send them tumbling down to the dirt for a time-out.

But I hit the meat of Montana's left thigh with the most explosive sucker punch I've ever managed. The big bastard's brain doesn't even have time to tell his arms to brace for impact. He just folds. His face slaps the concrete hard enough for his teeth to leave their outline on the insides of his cheeks.

“The fuck did you say to me?” I scream, and nail him on the left side of his face, hoping I hit him hard enough to make it match his right. Then an alarm trills so loud I swear I can hear my perforated eardrum flutter.

Pavlov would be proud to see how every inmate lies down and makes like the Vitruvian man.

I try to follow suit but get fumbled by a dogpile of COs.

54

I'll spare everyone the finger-pointing with respect to who did what to poor old me in the interest of properly restraining me for my and everyone else's safety, as they say. I will say, however, that no one asks me a damn thing until a lieutenant joins the little task force formed to learn what wild hair went up my ass.

"Public nudity, criminal trespass to chattels, first-degree assault, grand theft auto, strong-arm robbery, false imprisonment, kidnapping, manslaughter, and now giving Officer Felix Montoya dentures. Our insurance doesn't cover dental implants," says the lieutenant in the polo shirt. "And he is in dire need, from what I have heard. I'll check in on him after the medics get him cleaned up."

Montana was an asshole. The lieutenant sounds more annoyed than upset with me. I heard another guard say he'd grown sick of him always walking around thinking he's right about everything that comes out of his mouth because he's just that much bigger than anyone else, the same way a big rig takes to the early morning city streets after driving all night as the king of the barren interstate. The other guards secured and escorted me to seg as soon as humanly possible, leaving Montana in a clump with his ass in the air and his face on the floor smeared with blood, drool, and whatever else everyone else tracked in on the bottoms of their boots and skippies.

"You're already a guest of Oklahoma's only supermax facility for the next twenty-five years, and on the first day after you join the general population, you do this? There's no worse place to send you. Do you get that? Except to leave you here for life," says the lieutenant, sounding baffled.

Atop the fact that consequences do not concern me at present—seeing as how I am on a mission from the All High when it comes to investigations in the great state of Oklahoma—some folks don't understand how hard it is to come by respect when those you are courting get to see you only one hour a day, including weekends and holidays. What you did yesterday doesn't matter when short-term memories plague the schools of fish so sick of being bottom-feeders.

"You'll stay in the seg housing unit for the next one hundred and eighty days. That's six months, if math ain't your strongest subject," says the lieutenant.

Six months seems excessive. It turns out it is, in fact, the maximum they can coop one up all by their lonesome.

The lieutenant goes on before I can open my mouth and object. "Nope. We don't need your input. You're not built for it, so I'll let you know, in basketball, this is called a slam dunk," he says, sounding like he'd given up a promising career as an auctioneer to come work within these hallowed walls. "We have video from three different cameras. You stalked and ambushed that man, from what everyone can see. Aggravated assault is the charge. How do you plead at this time?"

I plead the fifth.

I knew that not one member of that man's clique carried a shank, shiv, or any sort of formerly innocuous object an industry insider might call an inmate-made weapon. And I figured I could make it back to my cell on my first day escorted by them rather than wading a sea of actual violent criminals. Some me-time sounded good, too. Atop that, I wanted a guided tour of the facility.

And they gave me one.

"Medical will come to see you next," the lieutenant says. He stands and pushes the little red squared button to get buzzed out.

His lemmings follow.

Medical takes their time showing. They take my vitals, strip me, search for any injuries they think might bruise as time progresses, and document everything with film and triplicate paperwork before they remove my restraints and leave me bare-assed for every minute of the allowable hour before my seg clothing and bedding finally arrive—dusty, might I add.

My seg cell looks a lot like the cell I shared with Raiford in Unit H, except half the size and twice as cramped. No one should ever have to shit so close to where they eat, pray, and lay their head. Humans are the only animals made to do so by their keepers.

Shortly after lights out, that line about trading a walk-on part in a war for a lead role in a cage makes a lot of sense.

This, too, is a training I've already been subjected to—tenfold—by my dear old Uncle Sam. Having no clocks and windows is not only a trick used by the casinos to make time seem endless. Corporate cubical farms, nightclubs, Chuck E. Cheese's, and big-box department stores of every imaginable flavor all operate on this credo. Time deprivation works in a way that gets the mind and body to stop trusting each other. If you are not allowed to watch the sun float and fall, lots of shit loses context.

"Hey," I hear someone whisper. "Moe," Elise's voice says. "What did you go and get yourself into this time, Juggernaut?"

I let a smile come over me.

"How long have you been watching me?" I ask the darkness. I hear Elise's laugh, the one I miss. The one she'd let go after she called me a nerd or a dork or dummy with the warmest smile I've ever known.

The forehead kiss that followed before doesn't.

At least I've only lost my mind halfway.

"You're on the wrong side of the bars," Elise says, so crisply and rapt that I cannot stop myself from looking for her silhouette in the dark. "How'd you get so turned around?"

Coming to my senses seems a lost cause, so I say, "You left me, Elise. I lost my navigator."

"Sheesh. The pills, though, Moe."

"They're—were prescribed. From when the buffalo took you from me."

"Yeah, by a guy who makes a nice living getting sick people to feel less so," she says, the words heavy enough to convince me she has her head on my shoulder. "I don't like to see you sick. Steer clear of doctors for a time, huh?"

"I'm done with them now." I sit up straight.

"Look at what it took, though," she says from somewhere off in the darkness. "Took my dad too."

I'd hide my face, but she's in my head.

"You went all disco on that buffalo, Moe," she says. "Like it'd back up the car and bring me back too. He didn't need to suffer more."

"I did."

"If you think living is suffering," she says back to me, "try dying."

Guilt-ridden, I go quiet. "Where've you been?" is all I can think to ask her about the hereafter.

"Around," she says, so close I swear I feel the mattress shift from her taking a seat next to me. Except my bedroll isn't much more than a beefed-up yoga mat, and beneath that sits how many ever feet of concrete supported by steel beams with pig iron rebar reinforcement, so maybe it's just my imagination. "Thanks for making sure I got home to my family so they could send me off," she says. "It meant everything to them."

"Of course," I say. Not knowing what else to say, or whether she even needs me to talk, or whether my mouth is even moving.

"Tulsa turned you into something different, Moe," Elise says, sounding distant again. "I almost didn't recognize you. Never thought to look for you here."

"I'm working."

"They tell you that? You're bait," she says. "It's the same as when the company commanders and platoon sergeants stuck my uncles out front to walk point in Vietnam, because Indians are born with extra senses fine-tuned for hunting and tracking—"

"I never met them," I say.

"That's because they weren't special and got killed like everybody else. You ain't either, Moe," Elise tells me. "How're you getting out of this?"

"The investigation is ongoing," I say. Then I fixate on what sounds like condensation dripping off the p-trap beneath my sink, or the footfalls of someone with nowhere to go and everywhere to be, the distant clicking from the stiff soles on a pair of Corframs that doppler down the hall so slowly the right footfall wouldn't recognize the echo of the left.

"You know the problem with playing roulette with your life for collateral?" I hear Elise say, which gets me to lift my head to search for her in the dark again. "All those numbers on the roulette wheel equal 666 for good reason, babe," Elise says. "The Devil's house is never a good one to bet against. The Devil's Breath will blow any house down."

She knows. I've been put back in a uniform and done as told without question.

Sometimes, if it's sour enough, you can smell disappointment.

Right when the cold finally gets to me, I swear I can see the light glint off the sweat formed on her forehead and all the curves that come together to form her smile.

"Do me a favor and sleep tight, Moe. The circus is coming to town," she says. "How about you sit this one out?"

55

The grand marshal follows on the heels of the countless broncs, bulls, and steers that've come to town to help the toughest show on dirt get underway. High school marching bands, 4-H students, feel-good philanthropic fraternities, feed stores, Boy Scout troops, Shriners, the electric co-op, leaders from every sizeable local house of worship, and, of course, the principal sponsors all float down Main Street on the way to the fourteen-thousand-seat rodeo stands built inside the prison walls back in 1940. Cops galore, too, because who doesn't love kicking a dead horse? Off-duty guards pulling time and a half wear their dress uniforms, including all the bells and whistles, shoulder cords, and chest candy to exude pride and professionalism.

The parade boasts and celebrates everything but the cowboys competing in this weekend-long Labor Day event. Said cowboys are otherwise preoccupied, indisposed for longer than a koala likes to snooze each day. Spectator sports are funny that way. There's always some sleight of hand that the crowd is meant to miss.

If any inmates had any visitors who had to drive from any sort of distance and planned to book a room in a nearby hotel, they'd have to keep moving until they got well outside of the county. Anytime a town doubles its population courtesy of a circus coming to town, to borrow Elise's words, the locals get stuffed so far down the wanted list they're all but considered missing persons. There is not one single business in this town that's not back in the black after the rodeo.

Sidewalk sales spring up, along with street dances and church art, crafts, and bake sales, whose proceeds go to someplace that makes anyone inquiring feel all warm and fuzzy.

Though, there are those opposed.

A few folks show up with signs expressing concerns about the exploitation and welfare of the incarcerated cowpokes. Not just the cowboys. There are women, too, the sweethearts of the prison rodeo, bussed in from a sister facility north of here where Merle Haggard's dad once called home, where unless they wish to carry their sentence to full term, they work at a call center every other day of the week—breaking into people's homes, disturbing their dinner, chewing up the minutes on their call plans, and earning a shorter sentence while doing it.

PETA's president sent a letter to the governor urging him to buck tradition, abolish the rodeo, and put it out to pasture. They told the governor how prison is no place to encourage violence and likened bull riding to the violent act of cow-milking. A spokesperson replied the governor would not entertain their request and interrupt a proud Oklahoma tradition.

People like this cling to anything. Nothing's traditional until it outlives the first generation. And I've got a grandma born before the great state of Oklahoma.

Every rank bull I'd ever seen tolerate a rider for the few fleeting seconds they do weighed more than a Chevy Luv truck. Bulls bred for the rodeo circuits move with a purpose the same as any fully realized tornado. But the bulls they've brought in for us look more like steers. They're not rough stock, that's for sure. Livestock, maybe, which are not bred to be rode for shits and giggles and belt buckles.

Alvin Dingman, a twenty-seven-year-old former Elmore, Oklahoma, peace officer, draws the first bareback bronc ride of the night. Alvin pled guilty to a laundry list of charges with varying degrees of stickiness. The big door prize got awarded for assault with a deadly weapon while operating a motorized vehicle.

Road rage is something you hear about a whole lot in the news out in LA, where the traffic turns to molasses, and pulling a gun on another motorist often turns to a sort of stalemate until the heat and exhaust and exhaustion get to them and of one of them jerks a trigger, making their Monday afternoon commute that much more of a bitch.

Minus the media coverage, it's the same for that claustrophobic stretch in OKC where I-35 meets I-40 meets I-44 meets US Route 66, on which everyone and their grandmothers are headed home from work, tearing down the interstate at five miles an hour. It's closed track racing in slow motion, which only dials up the drama.

"People park so close on the interstate you can't even use your mirrors," Alvin told the judge. "Instead, they go where they want, and fuck fellow motorists or anyone else on the road," he adds, flirting with contempt.

That kind of thinking gets under the skin of some men more than others.

Small-town cops like to drive their police cruisers when they have business in the big city so they can drive like asshole tourists and not worry about the traffic. The downside to this is that anyone on the road will slow at least somewhat when they see a cop car in their rearview mirror, delaying an officer even further in his duties, as he explained to the jury.

Traffic crept and leaped along the textured concrete merge maze. An accordion could never crush and aerate as fast as the roiling commuters swarming between Dingman and his destination. Had he turned on his lights, his camera would have come on too. There'd be no explaining his actions, considering he was merely headed home after testifying. So he sat and stewed like the other commuting professionals. Then that thing happened, where the natives get restless and take the time to read the stickers on the cop car struggling to maneuver through traffic the same as everyone else, and they realize the small-town peace officer idling in interstate traffic is about as pertinent as a mall cop at the airport. And who wouldn't want to cut off a cop car with impunity in the middle of such mundane madness.

"Lunged aggressively" is how Dingman described an approaching sedan, which drew his attention and concern, seeing as protecting and serving the public at large was his sworn charge and backup nowhere in sight. Make and model proved difficult to discern, seeing as how the heat rose from the roadway like a mirage grows out of the ground in the desert once the sand is seared by the sun.

"The driver seemed enraged," Dingman said. The car's horn blared every few seconds, and the driver did all they could to wedge themselves between two marked lanes of traffic, including resting their front bumper against the rear bumpers of two other vehicles before aggressively accelerating the vehicle enough to nudge others out of their way, the way Biblical Moses did on the shore of the Red Sea. He did all he could to dial in a local police channel on his cruiser's CB radio. Then he yelped his siren twice to announce his presence to the approaching vehicle, which witnesses saw rubbing along the length of yet another vehicle that failed to yield to her, bringing her within a vehicle's length of Officer Dingman.

At that time, his cruiser got struck and shook. The vehicle that hit him overcorrected and swung the nose of their car toward the shoulder, allowing the sedan to lunge forward again, bringing it alongside Officer Dingman's police vehicle. The driver then laid on her horn the way a distressed soldier will when doing their best to send out an SOS.

Officer Dingman testified he had no way of knowing her intent. He felt she had the opportunity and capability to do grievous bodily harm to the public. So when she brandished a black metal object in her hand, he felt compelled to return fire.

He shot four times, center mass, into the area of the vehicle's B-pillar, striking a child secured in a booster seat, directly behind the driver, who was suffering from diabetic shock. After the round burst through and exited the child's thigh, it came to a screeching halt after shredding the heart, liver, and lungs of said little girl's mocha-colored cockapoo.

At that time, the driver dropped her daughter's blood glucose monitor and shifted her screams from desperate to blood-curdling.

The defense tried to deem the tragedy circumstantial, since the child was near death already when her mother approached the patrol vehicle for help. They got it all bargained down to assault with a deadly weapon and an accompanying sentence that'll see Alvin Dingman free before he's eligible for Social Security.

Every head of roughstock sold to the prison rodeo should've instead gone to the slaughterhouse, and at a quarter of the price. It's a lot of work to clean so little muscle from so much bone. Broncs get sold as bucking horses. Ideally, saddled or bareback. Their breeding tells them to buck, hop, rock this way, that, and the other, pop into the air and twist, and put on a show. If I wanted to come back as a pampered pet, I wouldn't ask to be some rich bitch's purse dog. Rodeo rough stock is where it's at. PBR or PRCA-sanctioned events only. Premium grains, premium stalls, central heat and air, premium heifers, and when that's not at the ready, there's always some farmhand ready to jack me off to jumpstart the coming generation. But roughstock comes with a bill the warden is not willing to foot for his spectacle.

What these rodeo officials call a bronc fits the description of a colt. Colts aren't meant to bear any more weight than their own. So when the deposed two-hundred-plus-pound Dingman settles onto the colt's back, cinches down on the rosined rope, flexes every muscle he can recruit, and lets go of a head nod to the guy controlling the gate, all hell breaks loose.

A bucking horse is what the audience is primed and lubed for, but what they get is a rocking horse. The horse's haunches launch Alvin Dingman's face forward into its wither, which sends his bottom teeth through his lower lip and blood into the air. After a flurry of kicks and a blind spin, the horse's knees buckle and send Dingman to the dirt floor of the arena.

The crowd then watches while the horse gets dragged back into the corral by some overzealous wranglers. There isn't enough time for the crowd to realize its shin bone snapped under the shifting weight, and a forklift is needed to move the animal somewhere where it can bleed out backstage. Luckily, the alarm clamors and the crowd jeers regardless.

The judges give the ride a three out of five.

Each housing unit—save seg—gets tasked with sending ten inmates to try their hand at breaking a supposed bronc or bull or roping a steer. A byproduct of me putting Montana in the hospital and myself in seg is I get to avoid becoming a rodeo clown and stick to the detective work. So call me confused when my cell door springs open and a cowboy costume spills inside, along with an order to get dressed.

56

"Your cash is low. Your commissary too. You got an old lady to rectify that, or do you need to earn some money?" a backlit guard says, and slaps the cowboy hat atop my head so hard it knocks loose whatever dust settled into the felt since this time last year when the convicts got made to dress up like cowboys. Or maybe it's dried dung from the floor of the rodeo arena.

There's a hint of that in the air, too.

I shake my head at the first question and say, "How's that?" doing all I can to hold back a sneeze while blinking away the dust doing its best to settle on my eyeballs. Any movement of my hands above the waistline can be called an act of aggression, just like when I was a soldier in the presence of an officer, so they stay put.

Same shit; different pile.

"Money the Hard Way," he says. "You want to do that?"

"I do," I say, surprising even myself.

"Yeah, like fast-acting Tinactin, ain't it?"

"Excuse me?"

"No, your trespasses are forgiven," the guard says, sounding foolish with a mouth full of gibberish. "You know about cows, then?"

"I do," I say and follow him out of the cell. "You can hunt them with an apple and a hammer."

He laughs at my joke. "Bulldogging looks a little different here. Spectators call them rodeo clowns, but we can't have you smearing makeup on your face with the next shower two days out."

"No?"

"No, it's unsanitary," he says. And I agree. "What we do is stick a hundred-dollar bill in an envelope and let some volunteer bulldoggers like yourself try your best to snatch it and take it back to the house. You're going to best the bull and come out richer for it."

"Too easy, boss," I say and stick my hands behind my back so he can cuff them for our long walk.

~

Huddled amongst the dusty clay and cow manure, they tell us to space out, and they'll let the bull go. Money the Hard Way will continue until one of us gets the envelope or we've all had enough, they tell us. If it comes to that, they'll send someone to rope it and bring it back. We won't have to worry about the bull charging us, since we're the ones charging the bull. So, in that way, it will be more like a game of keep-away. And we all get ready to snatch the bragging rights.

That's when we get let out of the corral.

Instead we scatter like billiard balls after the break.

The roaring crowd and blinding stadium lights add to the bull's bombastic nature. It snorts and lunges at us. A hoofed animal of any size hurts when they kick, no matter how glancing the blow. That fact is nearly enough to make a guy forget about the horns.

The bull's figured out that we are all after it now, so it kicks and turns toward any sound with that gyro-twist-spin thing everyone in the audience wants to see it do.

I let go a nervous laugh when I see the first idiot nearly take a headbutt from the bull.

Someone else takes a half-hearted kick.

Another dude runs at him so damn fast he trips and slides

beneath the bull and gets stepped on, twice.

Stamped the second time.

I feel I should say here how convict cowboys don't get goalie helmets, mouth guards, or flak vests like they do in the pro circuit. They don't even let those riding have spurs.

Cows aren't apex predators like human beings, so their eyes aren't in the front of their face. Instead, they stick out the sides of their heads, like goldfish, looking for meat eaters trying to flank them while they graze. That's why they move in herds. That's why they spin this way and that when alone amidst others they figure mean them ill will.

It's anxiety.

I remember watching Crocodile Dundee when he came at the water buffalo from straight on. His skinny ass turned sideways and crept up to the animal and laid hands on it, tickling that massive bundle of nerves that runs down the snout of every animal—people included. He mystified the animal and made it submit, confused.

I am not Crocodile Dundee.

When the thing turns its head and sees how close I've come, it widens its stance, lowers its head, and dares me to come closer. The envelope keeps getting in its eyes, so it keeps tossing its head side to side to side, spinning left and right. And up, once it sees I've leaped close enough to reach out and touch it.

And I do.

I jab like Bruce Lee taught with fingers spread. Once I feel fur and twine touch my fingertips, I make a fist.

The bull answers my jab with an uppercut.

My hearing is gone. There's blood in my mouth. And both nostrils. I can't get air. But I stand and brandish the envelope for all to see, and the stadium follows suit.

When I turn to my left to show those behind me, either the guards or God kills the stadium lights.

~

Tubed oxygen tickles my nose hairs and makes the lungs tingle a terrible sort of way. And a terrible sort of familiar sets in. Sometimes eyes won't open when told. Sometimes everything hurts so much so you can't move your arms. Sometimes you can get so drugged you can't move. Sometimes you don't know how drugged you are until you stand. Sometimes you don't get to see or feel the leather restraints that bind each convict taken outside of the prison walls for medical treatment once the correctional facility's infirmary has reached max capacity. Sometimes you're so miserable you can't even feel the C-spine collar they put on you in your concussed state. All of which convinces me I'm paralyzed.

A flash of green light greets me seconds before I feel my chest explode in what I'll call excruciating agony. The kind of agony that makes you pass out from pure self-preservation. When that wanes, I see someone dressed in white, veiled in blinding light with their hands centered on my chest. I figure former friends or patrons of Hiram Lucas Williams found me in the infirmary and are exacting whatever flavor of revenge they practiced on me. Santeria, Voudon, Hoodoo, who knows?

I feel myself floating, falling. I look around and realize I'm in an ambulance nailing potholes and riding up on curbs, driving erratically, which does little to ease the patient. I'd also call the green used on the inside of the ambulance anything but calming.

The fog lifts a little when the medic hovering over me, leaning on me with all her weight, continues to rub her knuckles into my sternum, which I figure she figures for the quickest way to my heart. The EMT stops the sternum rub and speaks to me at long last. "Moses, can you give me a thumbs up?" But I cannot. I don't have the strength. My hand feels like someone has deboned the damned thing. "Moses," she says. "How about this hand?" and reaches across my body and slaps my left wrist.

That one I can. Lefty loosey; righty tighty.

"Moses," she says over the siren. "Can you tell me your last name?"

"Kincaid," to my ears, sounds like a series of small clicks coming from the back of the throat. Not to mention how moving my tongue makes me gag like maybe I'll choke on it. So gagging becomes my family name.

What she hears is the patient is unresponsive.

"Moses?" she says. "Can you move your mouth to talk? That's a pain I want you to push past if you can. I want to hear what's going on. Got a few easy questions for you."

It turns out it's difficult to communicate that you can't physically speak due to mechanical failure. The EMT sticks her pointer finger into the palm of my hand and says, "Squeeze my finger if you can. How about it, Moses?"

Sticking my thumb straight out did not prove as much of a problem as does coiling my fingers into a fist. So liquid Tylenol gets added to my IV drip.

57

"Normally, when someone is out for three days in a row, it's called a coma. But you don't ever stop talking. Even when you're knocked out harder than a blown fuse," the OSBI special agent says to me once my eyes open.

"Hi."

"Howdy, Mister Kincaid. Your tox screen came back yesterday. You did good. Pissed off the right people."

"Excuse me?" I say, trying to raise my voice.

"Your Indian name could be Canary-in-the-Coal-Mine. You're a lucky-ass tweety bird. UC pay is $500 a day. Lucky fuck. You did ninety-three days in in-processing alone. Real detectives don't make that starting out their first year. You're off the clock after the docs discharge you. Whoever has the pleasure of driving you home will have the check."

"What?" I say, twisting my hips in the bed beneath me, trying to loosen my lower back.

"You found it, Columbo."

"What?" I repeat, cracking the corner of my lip this time, which trickles blood onto my teeth and tongue.

"They found recreational levels of scopolamine in your system," he says. "That's called probable cause in this business, Moses. We got what we need. If I were you—but luckily, the world ain't that fucking cruel—I'd take off until next year."

My hands roam the bed, searching blindly for the call button.

"Oh, yeah," he says. "How's that liquid Tylenol treating you after you went toe to toe with the moo-cow? I should have liked to have seen that, you smart-mouthed son of a bitch."

"Where am I?" I say, looking out the window behind him.

"As far from Big Mac as we could get you. Clinton. IHS is treating your boo-boos. All the staff here knows is that we found you in need of medical help—trespassing, as you fuckers love to do—and I told them I saw the CIB in your wallet, so I brought you here. Let them sort it out. And now, being that it was us who found you, it is us they called when you started to stir—as promised."

"But my babysitter?" I say and point toward the door.

"No such animal," he says. "That's what you get watching too many cop shows. Without your wallet on you, your chart would have read *John Doe*."

"They don't restrain inmates here?" I raise my hand again and marvel at the lack of shackles on my wrists.

"If anybody knows how to bullshit emergency room triage staff, it's LEOs. Have some pudding."

"Don't want any."

"Come on, don't be bullheaded. There's always room for pudding."

I look to the right of my hospital bed and see the TV tray. A pudding cup sits alongside a plate of sliced bananas and a yellow folder. I dump the latter into my lap.

"That's a care package from the Council on Law Enforcement Education Training, aka CLEET, for services rendered. Your boss, Arlo Bice, leveraged that for you. Hope you don't mind us using your booking photo."

"A state commission?"

"Not on your fucking life, you simple sonofabitch," he laughs.

While flipping through, a laminated piece of paper the size of a credit card slides between my leg and the hose for my catheter. I again buzz for a nurse and reach to see what prize fell from inside the cereal box.

My ugly-ass mugshot stares up at me, along with the words ARMED PRIVATE INVESTIGATOR MOSES AMOS KINCAID, plus a license number and expiration date too small for me to read. What I can read, I read aloud. Then I say, "Not fugitive recovery agent, or bail enforcement agent, or surety—whatever it's called down here?"

"Yeah, that bull knocked you into the middle of next week, didn't he? There's no fucking way that'll ever happen, after the shit you pulled. What bondsman would work with you, anyway? Not Arlo. And he went to bat for you."

"That's feast or famine, ain't it?"

"Tell me what job ain't."

"How the hell, with my record?"

"I haven't the foggiest what you're jabbering about. Your jacket is cleaner than a church floor, Mister Kincaid. So keep your goddamn voice down, why don't you? Here's hoping you don't get yourself killed on your first case."

I make a show of pushing the nurse's call button again. Then I stab my pudding cup with the straw from my apple juice box and suck, never once breaking eye contact with him while he stands and marches to the oversized door that leads to the hallway and nurses' station and who knows what else.

I hear him say, "You can come in now."

The duty nurse, I guess, whose name I try to glean from the whiteboard along the far wall to no avail, follows him back into the room. He doesn't retake his seat. Instead, he stands beneath the muted TV and folds his arms like a gym coach assigned to lunch duty, again.

"Sir, I am sorry, I heard the buzzer, but the detective said he didn't want to be disturbed, and—are you ready for some ice chips?"

She hoists a Styrofoam pitcher onto my TV tray.

"Pain," I say through sort of a hushed yawn.

"How much?" she says. "One to ten, ten being the worst—"

"He's been asking what's wrong with him, how bad he's broken up. Asking what I thought the doctor would give him for pain. You should call the doctor first. It sounds like pill-seeking behavior to me, Nurse."

"I am the doctor," she says. "And that'll be enough from you, Detective. We still don't know what caused this. The films are still being developed," she adds and then turns her attention back to me.

"Cow tipping," I say, trying to chill everyone out.

"Jesus fucking Christ," the special agent says.

"While that seems unlikely, Mister Kincaid, it does match your condition when you arrived."

"Your smell too," says the special agent.

"That's enough," the doctor tells him. "However he got here, he doesn't deserve any of your badgering."

Funny how badgering's the default setting for anybody gifted a badge, I think, and laugh to myself. And cough. I may have solved one of the great mysteries of modern English.

"I was nearly about to leave anyhow," he says.

"I'll walk you out," I say, as loud as I can manage over the blood pressure machine, letting out a melodramatic sigh.

"You stay put," the doctor says.

"A cigarette would help," I say.

"I'll put in for some pain relief for you for the next time pharmacy comes around. And ah—as far as the cigarette, someone will bring you a wheelchair."

After the orderly exits, the detective and I both nod and stare at each other until I say the obvious. "You smoke? I must have left mine in my other pair of work pants."

"You smoke?" the special agent says. "Didn't take you for a

smoker," he adds, and fishes one from an inside pocket.

"I like to have one after getting fucked rougher than I was ready for."

"That's fair," he says, taking hold of the wheelchair from the orderly who brings it in. "Hop up. Nothing wrong with your legs. Wheelchairs are a must to lower liability costs," he adds, and rolls the wheelchair into the bed hard enough for it to right itself.

Prick.

I follow the chair with my eyes and see a cigarette of his land on my lap.

"Thanks," I say.

"How about you get the lead out. I'll push you downstairs." He smiles a Cheshire grin. "*Take* you down the elevator, I mean. Freudian slip, sorry. Don't get your dress in a ruffle. I got to get headed back to Tulsa. Civil rights don't violate themselves like they used to do in the good old days, Mister Kincaid."

"Yeah, thanks," I say, and hoist my ass into the wheelchair.

Of course, they put the Indian Health Services buildings out back of a chintzy casino shared by the Cheyenne and Arapaho. Worse yet is to see that off the backside of the hospital's upper parking lot waits the Clinton Indian cemetery, giving the whole place the feel of Hotel California.

The special agent left me with a single Camel Light cigarette and a matchbook from Big Jim's Boobie Bungalow & BBQ—home to exotic dancing for gentlemen, with free drinks every Tuesday and Wednesday from six to eight p.m. in Elkton, TN.

Call my interest piqued.

Obviously, he visited as part of a family vacation.

Or a cop conference.

Outside the hospital, grackles hop around, aerating the trash cans and sorting through what falls to the ground while I burn through a stale piece of shit cigarette that should have tasted better than anything—given my last few days, weeks.

Months.

Fuck.

The grackle's bluish-greenish-purplish and black feathers shine beautifully from what I can see. A pretty bird is a pretty bird, no matter its role.

A scrunched-up ball of tinfoil has every one of their attentions. Mine included. Shiny shit does that to simplified minds. I figure it for a sandwich half or something that came off the taco truck that a nurse had to toss after getting beeped back inside the hospital.

My stomach pits and protests over its unoccupied state as soon as the thought strikes me. Shooing starving birds away isn't all that hard after casting the first stone in a dick-measuring contest with a rank bull. But sustenance is not what I find wrapped in the crumpled aluminum foil.

A controlled substance seems the safe bet.

The short glass tube for a pipe is full of resin, gummed up and blackened from end to end. I suspect the blackish, caramel candy-looking stuff sticking to the tinfoil soothes aches and pains better than the liquid Tylenol. But the matches the special agent left me don't do shit. So I find myself in an unfortunate position until the second person I ask for a light comes along.

He hands me a rechargeable palm-sized butane blowtorch instead of a lighter. I offer him ten bucks, because "That's all I got."

Had it been a bingo BIC, I'd have offered only my thanks.

Most folks coming and going from the hospital have a whole lot on their minds, but almost always take pity on someone dressed in a robe, wristband, and gown. God only knows how much time they've got. They might be about to meet God, so why not act as Christlike as you can in the moment?

He tells me to keep it.

And I do.

Fucking Clinton, Oklahoma. That's where this life has brought me. Bubba Clinton from over yonder couldn't be a better poster boy for the country hitting rock bottom. *It can't get any worse,* I think. So I click the pedal on the lighter and bake the black tar from beneath the aluminum foil until it smokes.

TV tells me to stick the resin-caked glass dick between my lips and chase the dragon.

My face feels warm and flushed.

It comes on so fast.

My arms fall to my lap.

The heroin wastes no time turning to morphine once it hits my brain, where my pain receptors live, and they've nothing to say.

Are you there, God? It's me, Moses.

What did that little piece of paper say? ARMED PRIVATE INVESTIGATOR. Imagine that shit. Me, a detective? Helping dames in distress with nowhere else to turn. Living fat off retainer fees. Helping wives bend over their husbands in divorce court. Tracking down guys on the lam, cracking cases cops can't. Locking up crooks and throwing away the key. Maybe I'll get a frosted glass door for my office with little hand-painted letters. Hire a seductive secretary. Buy a fedora?

Fuck that.

Five percent of prisoners ought not be. The rest rot and get better at bad. But what if I take appeals cases, instead, and pore over old police files, become the technicality talked about on the nightly news?

A feeling comes over me like I have a mouth full of Canada Dry. Sparkling water. Or Pop Rocks. Bubbles consume the roof of my mouth, along with my tongue. The bubbles get so bad my lips part on their own, the way they will right before you vomit something you don't remember eating. But I feel nothing splash onto my lap.

Still, I look.

I see what I'll call an easy three hundred black baby spiders wriggling out of both ends of the gummed-up, blackened glass pipe I hold in my hand. Momma has already started her way up my sleeve.

I hope that's in my head.

How I hope.

Then they make their way onto my eyelashes, and the Lord starts to play with the lights.

ACKNOWLEDGMENTS

I'd like to thank everyone who read and applauded this novel in its previous life as *Sangre Road* and *Money the Hard Way*, in their limited runs. Those two novellas got started my first summer in Oklahoma (2019) while I waited for my PhD program to begin, which I ultimately opted out of. It is now my fifth year here, and I get to teach an old dog new tricks thanks to the fine folks at Dzanc Books. *Coydog* began as a series of short stories: a self-assigned writing exercise over the summer. A weak muscle I needed to strengthen.

But I soon remembered I am a novelist.

I'd purposefully rented the house farthest south in the tiny town where I found myself living. My nearest neighbors were a junkyard next to the sign mentioned on page one of chapter one. I was in my forties and wanted to live as far as possible from the school and the 25,000 undergrads who attended. Though, in summer, the city turns into a ghost town, which is the best time to learn the lay of the land.

The few folks I did spot seemed proverbially sore thumbs, out of place. But the place—Oklahoma—is something else entirely.

The first draft came quickly over the summer months. I rose at five and wrote until my daughter woke around ten. After I brought her home for her school year, and I opted out of mine, I set out to explore Oklahoma. I saw swamps, salt plains, prairies, sand dunes, desert, mountains, and the Milky Way clearer than I ever have above the Black Mesa. Buffalo, wild boar, feral dogs, and alligators surprised me in my travels. The highways were littered with former coyotes, armadillos, and oil boomtowns. To clarify, Oklahoma is not the South. Oklahoma is the westernmost reaches of the Ozarks, the northern reaches of swamps associated with Cajun Country, the southern most of the Midwest plains, and the southwest mashed together atop Indian Country.

Pop and ranch dressing are served in restaurants.

It's just Oklahoma. And Oklahoma just is.

When COVID made the entire state a ghost town, I sought to make pilgrimages to Oklahoma's literary legends' homes, etc., but came up wanting. Sure, there's a nice Dick Tracy mural and marker in the hometown of his creator, Chester Gould. The town museum even has an exhibit for him. But when I went west to Anadarko, Oklahoma, in Caddo County, there was nearly no mention of America's Dimestore Dostoevsky. His books were on display next to mine at the local library, on the Oklahoma Authors island. But that was it. Nothing on the welcome sign. No plaque outside his birthplace, which would have sat atop the Caddo County jail, since he was born at home and his father was the sheriff.

Jim Thompson is the author against which other noir novelists are measured.

His books are the ones I used as palate cleansers between canonized required reading in college and grad school. Stanley Kubrick and Stephen King sing Jim's praises. But not the locals. Which was not cool. Anadarko, Oklahoma, hosts the Southern Plains Indian Museum, Anadarko Philomathic Pioneer Museum, Indian City USA, National Hall of Fame for Famous American Indians, and the Delaware Tribe Museum, but not even a little bookstore with a window display for Jim.

Since Jim's books embody Greek tragedies, I set out to write my ode.

First, understand that Oklahoma itself is a story of the grotesque.

People like to pretend the characters in Jim's books are caricatures, simple archetypes. But every archetype has an origin story far more interesting than any influencer on the Gram. I learned the grandchildren of the minor characters who drove the plot in Jim's books were alive and well in the local news. Two gay castrating cannibals come to mind. Then there's the guy who got stopped with a trunk full of snakes, along with cases of whiskey, handguns, and plutonium. That's not to forget the endless folks who shoot each other with crossbows to keep things interesting. But the article I read, concerning the drug and prostitution sting at the strip club on a night they hosted dwarf wrestling, really got me to see what a magical place Oklahoma is today.

Moses Kincaid's name is a mix and match of two people listed on an Oklahoma Civil War memorial, which I found comical since the math didn't add up—Oklahoma wasn't a place at the time, and I felt they should have sat that one out.

Then I dug.

I read some more. I traveled some more. I read about Oklahoma legends like Jake McNiece and Bass Reeves.

Then I wrote some more.

Thanks for reading.

Let's do it again some time.

ABOUT THE AUTHOR

David Tromblay served in both the United States Army and Navy before he earned an MFA in Creative Writing from the Institute of American Indian Art in Santa Fe, New Mexico. His memoir *As You Were* was named one of the Best Nonfiction Books of 2021 by Kirkus Reviews. He now lives in rural eastern Oklahoma with giant dogs and tiny goats.